The Vitruvian Mask

BJ Sikes

Copyright © 2023 BJ Sikes

All rights reserved. This book is a work of fiction. Names, characters, businesses, organizations, places, events and incidents either are the product of the authors' imaginations or are used fictitiously. Any resemblance to actual persons, living or dead, events, or locales is entirely coincidental.

Printed in the United States of America.

ISBN 9780997437577

Cover design by BJ Sikes and CV Sikes

For Dover

In retrospect it seems I've lost
I could have won, but at what cost?
Is it too late now to be brave?
When there's no love left I can save.

—Unwoman, "Casualties"

One

Adelaide rested her hands on the cold metal chest of her creation, her skin pale against the gleaming brass. The Automated Dauphin lay upon the worktable before her, inert, needing her to secure its future life, and that of France itself. The mechanical engineers she had fled with were of no help. Adelaide could hear the three of them now, toiling away in their own workrooms in the farmhouse. Later, no doubt, they would supply her with more of their concern 'for her condition' or, in the case of Dr. Gregoire, his derision. Then, their obligatory male behavior dispensed with, they would resume their argument over how best to restart the Weather Machines. As if the new regime would not immediately destroy any of the devices found to be operational.

The ache again filled Adelaide, the familiar, urgent craving for that which she had been raised to desire in the Science Academy. All else faded, as meaningless as her compatriots and their endless tinkering. Even the child in Adelaide's womb could not inspire her to action beyond her immediate needs. None of it mattered, because none of it could make France whole again. Only the Automated Dauphin could deliver that promise, and only Adelaide could make it function. And so she went to work, to restore France. Her France. Not this untidy, chaotic mess the new king had created. She unscrewed the chest plate, looking for the source of the Dauphin's most recent malfunction.

Her back ached, tired with the weight of her huge belly. She paused to rub it and took a deep breath. The child in her womb, an unintended consequence of a rash decision, didn't stir. He only seemed to move at night when Adelaide tried to rest. With her eyes, she admired her mechanical child on the scarred wooden table then caressed his cold metal face. The profile, sculpted to look like the old king, would be enough to have her executed for treason. "Why won't you speak to me anymore? Was that cursed orb the only method you could use to communicate?"

Months ago, before her belly had grown so big, before the ruins of a farmhouse had become her refuge, a strange man had convinced her that he had a device, an orb that would function as a brain for her automaton. Installing it had been a disaster. The Automated Dauphin under the control of the orb had spouted false prophecies, not the words of wisdom she had hoped for. Adelaide had disconnected the orb and tossed it into the Seine, thinking her troubles over. But her creation, so briefly alive, had ceased entirely to speak.

The only response to her question was the hum from its servometers. At least his movement functions were still operational, although she would need to recharge his electric batteries soon. And she had nowhere to do that on this forlorn little farm in Picardy, miles from the bustle of Paris. The farmhouse itself was barely habitable, without running water or even gaslight, let alone electricity.

Adelaide exhaled a weary breath and continued opening up the chest plate. She squinted into the interior of the automaton's chest cavity, looking for loose wires, and jerked away with a gasp. Deep in the workings, a bundle of rags served as a bed for squirming baby mice. A rodent had made a nest inside her creation. Adelaide growled under her breath, then gently lifted the intruders and their messy bed out of the automaton.

What damage have those little creatures done? How many wires will I have to replace now?

The adult mice squeaked and leaped out of her hands to the floor, scampering into a hole in the ramshackle wall. Adelaide followed with the nest of their tiny, squirming, pink babies. Huffing, she lowered herself to one knee and placed the bundle on the floor near the hole. The parent mice could take care of the rest. She moaned and heaved herself back to her feet, leaning heavily on the splintered wooden wall. It creaked under her weight.

Adelaide grabbed a dripping tallow candle and held it above the automaton, trying to get better light to see the damage. The molten tallow dribbled onto the table and Adelaide held her hand to catch the drips from touching the metal figure. The gleam of polished metal tubes in the chest cavity was duller than it should have been, but she couldn't see any damaged wiring. She traced a delicate finger along the primary nerve-wire bundle to the processor. And there it was.

She groaned. The wires were chewed right at the connection point. Couldn't the mice have gnawed anywhere else? It would take hours to repair what they had destroyed. Adelaide opened her small chest of machine parts, the only pieces of her former life that she had time to scrounge before her escape from Paris. The soldiers had been so close to discovering her hiding place in the Montmartre garret full of the wires, tubes, servos, and batteries she had hoped would be useful in finally making her automaton fully functional.

But she had not had time to complete her work in the garret. The Naturalist revolution brought a swift and sudden end to her former life, as the new king's soldiers searched Paris for any Scientists, and especially those closely connected to the former regime. Adelaide had watched in horror from the secluded safety of her garret as people tore Watcher Spheres from the eaves of public buildings and trampled them to the ground. Monsieur Noyer, one of the Scientists in hiding with her at the farmhouse told of escaping a mob tearing apart a Weather Machine. Adelaide knew that none of the Weather Machines remained working in this region. They had endured too many daytime rain storms, complete with dripping ceilings and now moldering window frames, for them to still be functioning.

A knock on the door frame startled her back to the present. It was Monsieur Noyer, a shy smile creasing his pasty face.

"Madame, you've been back here for hours. Surely you could take a break for some tea? We are debating on the appropriate settings for the Weather Machine in this climate. We thought perhaps you might have something to add to the discussion."

Adelaide sighed to herself. She had no interest in the other Scientists' discussions but they persisted in interrupting her, trying to draw her into their own work. "I am right in the middle of a crucial repair. I'm afraid I must decline."

Monsieur Noyer shook his head and departed back to their shabby sitting room. She and the three other Scientists had been in hiding now for six months. They were among the few, she knew, to escape the great purge, the Naturalists' first act after seizing power. The day after the revolt, Paris newspapers had declared all Scientists to be enemies of the state. One particularly disturbing headline announced that the villainous Scientist President and his entire cabinet had been executed for crimes against Naturalism. Adelaide knew she would have likely met a similar fate if the Police Secrète had discovered her in the garret. She had not been part of the Royal Household for some months before the Revolution, but she had once been the scientist-doctor who cared for the Augmented monarchs and nobles at Versailles. The new king, it seemed, detested Science. He would not look kindly upon Adelaide if he knew of her existence.

So now here she was, hiding in this miserable farmhouse in the middle of an equally miserable region where it seemed to drizzle rain constantly. Even during the day. Despite knowing the Weather Machines were destroyed, she was still surprised to see daytime rain. The damp seeped into her clothing and turned her hair into an even frizzier mess than normal. She tried in vain to smooth it down, then gave it up as impossible and returned to her work, reconnecting wires from the Dauphin's processor down to the actuator. She scrabbled her fingers in the tin of tiny brass connectors, feeling the bottom of the tin as she plucked out the piece she required.

"Almost empty," Adelaide said to the Dauphin, placing a hand on his brow. "I need more than I was able to bring with me. I have no idea where to begin looking."

She bit her lip. Without her Academy of Science connections, the artisans who made the intricate metal pieces she relied on were lost to her.

I wonder what they're doing now? I'm sure the Naturalists have no need of artisans who create useful metal pieces for electronic work like this.

She sagged against the table and gazed out of the grimy window. The rain sluiced down the glass, weaving muddy rivulets and obscuring the view of the dilapidated courtyard. The lack of a view was no real loss. No flowers bloomed out there for Adelaide to enjoy, just thick, sticky mud and decaying hay bales. A sharp pang of longing for the beauty of the gardens of Versailles struck her.

I can't remember the last time I smelled a rose in bloom. I thought the countryside would be full of flowers and greenery but it's just barley fields and mud. And destroyed Weather Machines.

The baby kicked at her and she winced.
"Be still, child. Why must you kick me so ferociously?"
She straightened her posture. The baby must have been squashed by her leaning forward against the table. Adelaide shook her head at her own negligence. It was so easy to forget that she carried a tiny person inside her, one that responded to her actions, especially now, as her pregnancy advanced. She rubbed at her back again and a wave of exhaustion broke across her.

I need to rest. I can barely stand here to work.

It was still early in the day, but Adelaide was in desperate need of a nap. She covered the automaton with a torn sheet, patting it as she pulled the cover over its face.
"Farewell, my prince. I will return and work more on you when I have rested. Don't worry, my child, we'll soon have you working again and we will have wonderful conversations like we did before, in Paris."
She turned to the door and halted. Dr. Gregoire stood in the doorway, his dark eyebrows raised, his mouth pursed. He had previously been a Weather Machine engineer and

coming to Picardy had been his idea. It was quiet here, too distant from Paris for the Police Secrète to notice them. They'd be safe here, he had said. It just happened to be close to one of the Weather Machines that Gregoire had installed and was now trying to repair.

"Madame Coumain? I understand a meal will be ready soon. No doubt you have smelled the bread Zilda is preparing?"

Adelaide noticed the scent of baking bread. She had been smelling it for some time, but had ignored the meaning in her distracted state. Zilda, their one servant here, was preparing the evening meal. It was much later than she had thought.

"Thank you, Dr. Gregoire. I was just finishing here and will join you all in the dining room after I freshen up."

"Of course," he said, half turning as if to leave. But then he asked, "Were you speaking to your machine? Or perhaps to the unborn child?" Malice dripped from his tongue. She knew he despised her for her pregnancy. They all did, despite the concern expressed by Messrs. Abelard and Noyer.

"I often talk to the Automated Dauphin," she replied, matching Gregoire's haughty manner. She may have been near the end of her tether, but she would not pander to his sense of propriety. Gregoire, it seemed, was prepared to fence with her as well. He took a step into the room.

"And what does your talk accomplish?" he spat.

"It's part of his learning protocol. He must know how to receive input as spoken words, in order for him to fully function."

Gregoire sneered. "You refer to the machine as 'he'? Doesn't that seem a bit ... odd? It's just a machine, not a person, Madame."

Adelaide stiffened. She tilted her head back and stared down her nose, emulating the nobles she'd worked for at Versailles. "I refer to the Automated Dauphin as 'he' because he closely resembles the man he is based on, the late King Louis X. Once he is fully functional and is responding to his subjects, they will refer to him as 'he' not 'it'. We wouldn't want them to think of the Automated Dauphin as anything less than a person."

Gregoire snickered, the sound incongruous coming from an elderly man in a frock coat. "Less than a person? It's a machine, Madame, as I said. Thinking anything more of it is folly. This project of yours is a waste of time and resources. Our lamented Presidente did not approve of it, I had heard. Was it not the cause of your dismissal from the Court?"

Adelaide clenched and unclenched her fists, grasping at her skirts. Her face burned, and her eyes stung with unshed tears. She didn't respond to his taunts, taking time to draw a slow breath. She raised her chin again. "The Automated Dauphin will help restore France to us. He will show the people the right way to be ruled, the fair way. He will hear all of their voices, not just the crooked advisors who flock to the king. He will give the people of France a voice. He will rule France fairly, justly. And he won't forget how powerful Science has made the French. We Scientists, we will rise again, Dr. Gregoire. We won't have to hide in backwater farms in fear of our lives. We will be respected again."

Gregoire shook his head. "Madame, your folly blinds you to reality. The people don't need a voice, they need bread. They are starving already without my Weather Machines. The barley and wheat are rotting out there in this incessant rain. When I repair the closest Weather Machine and the rains here return to their nightly pattern, the local people will be grateful once more for Science. Then word will spread to the next region, and the next, until enough people have been satisfied that Science can provide for their needs. Food in their bellies, Madame. That's what they care about, not your lofty ideas of pure democracy."

He spun on his heel and marched away. Adelaide wiped her sweating hands on her grease-smeared apron.

Weather Machines! That man has no vision. What's to stop the king's men from destroying his precious machines again?

She approached the metal figure, prone on the table. He looked so noble lying there, that Bourbon nose jutting towards the ceiling. She tugged the cover over his face and left her workroom. She needed a nap more than ever. Now that Gregoire had openly expressed his disdain for the Automated Dauphin, Adelaide would have to enlist either M. Abelard or M. Noyer to assist her. Neither option was particularly pleasing to consider, but, perhaps one of them still had connections with metal workers and could acquire the needed parts.

ಙ Φ ೞ

The smell of cabbage and boiled chicken drifted from the farmhouse kitchen into the poky dining room, fighting with the odor of men's sweat and tobacco smoke. Adelaide sat at the table with her fellow Scientists, but she could barely breathe, let alone eat. She shifted on the hard wooden chair, trying to get comfortable. It creaked under her weight.

I'm an elephant. How much heavier am I going to get before this baby is born?

She cast a glance around the table, hoping no-one had noticed the creaking seat. Gregoire and the others were deep in conversation about pulleys and tensile strength, taking no notice of her at all. Adelaide suppressed a yawn. Their discussion reminded her too much of the boring civil engineering classes she'd endured at the Academy. She wondered about her fellow roboticists. Were they all dead or imprisoned? These mechanical engineers seemed to be the only Scientists remaining free after the great purge. Perhaps the new king's loathing for technology had been aimed at the Scientists who had kept his great, great aunt and uncle alive for nearly a century. Or perhaps Dr Gregoire and his fellows were all too provincial to reach the notice of King Henri.

Zilda, shuffled into the room with a tureen of stew. The smell of cabbage intensified and Adelaide swallowed down bile. She needed to eat for the baby's sake, even if the food looked and smelled repulsive.

Monsieur Abelard didn't seem to mind the sulfurous stench rising off the dish. His plump red face shone in the watery lamplight. "Ah, Zilda, you are feeding us at last! I hope you made enough; I'm utterly famished." He smacked his lips and inhaled deeply, his eyes closed.

Zilda glowered at him from under her eyebrows, but didn't respond. She heaved the tureen onto the table and went back to the kitchen. She returned with a breadboard laden with fresh country bread and butter. Adelaide reached for the bread knife but Zilda was already slicing the loaf. The servant handed Adelaide a generous wedge, a smile creasing her wan face. "Some bread for you, Madame.

Still hot from the oven. You'll be sure to use plenty of my fresh butter. Good for your babe."

Adelaide accepted the bread with a murmur of thanks and obediently slathered butter onto her piece. Zilda's solicitous manner baffled her. She barely knew her, but the old woman treated Adelaide like a granddaughter. Adelaide only vaguely remembered her own grandmothers, but they too had baked sturdy country bread.

Zilda served the chicken and cabbage stew, heavy on the cabbage. Adelaide had never liked cabbage. The men ate heartily with no word of thanks to Zilda. She didn't slice bread for them and left the dining room with another admonishment to Adelaide to eat more. She poked at her stew with a spoon. Chicken fat congealed on the surface of the broth. Adelaide shuddered and laid her spoon back on the wooden table. Zilda would scold her for not eating enough, just as her own grandmothers had done. Adelaide chewed on Zilda's bread, careful not to bite down too hard. The flour Zilda acquired was poor quality and, despite sieving, full of tough grains and small rocks even after baking.

"Madame Coumain, you're not eating your supper. Are you not feeling well?"

Adelaide looked up into the eyes of M. Abelard. His red face, painted with mock solicitation, glistened in the candlelight and she suppressed a shudder. "I'm feeling quite well. Thank you for your concern, Monsieur."

He slurped a spoonful of stew and wagged his spoon at her. "You must keep up your strength, Madame. Your child will be born soon, I am guessing? And you will need a great deal of energy for the birth. Have you decided where the birth will be?"

The young Monsieur Noyer choked on his food. He gaped at Adelaide, his thin face flushing. "Oh no, Madame, not here, to be sure? All of that fuss and mess."

Adelaide shook her head. "I haven't really given it much thought. I'm not sure what one does in these circumstances." Leave? And give up her work? The thought appalled her. But what would she do with the baby? And where would she give birth? She had avoided the decision for too long.

Dr. Gregoire cleared his throat. "It's not for me to say, of course, but I believe . . . desperate mothers in Paris send their infants to the countryside for fostering. Keeps them out of the filth of the city. Healthier for young children, I'd say. We're already in the country but I'm sure you could find someone willing to take the babe in this abysmal province. For a price, no doubt. These people of Picardy would do anything for a little money."

Adelaide widened her eyes at him. Send her baby away? Was that truly the way of things? And how would these Scientists who had pledged to remain bachelors for Science know? "Can this be true, Dr. Gregoire? Mothers send their children to live with strangers?"

He shrugged his response. "Haven't actually experienced this myself, being sworn to celibacy, Madame." He stared pointedly at her swollen stomach. "As were you. You've never told us who the father of your child is. Or was it an immaculate conception?" He gave her a stern look. "Or more likely one of those decadent courtiers at Versailles. I've heard tales of the goings on there before our new king arrived."

Adelaide flushed and tears filled her eyes. She gulped back the salty tears and dropped her gaze to the table.

Monsieur Abelard reached a pudgy, moist hand to pat hers. "Now, now, Dr. Gregoire, be kind. Can you not see that Madame Coumain is overwrought? A typical state for a woman in her condition."

Adelaide pulled her hand from under his. Why was he always trying to touch her? She suppressed a shudder.

Dr. Gregoire muttered under his breath and stroked his whiskers. "I apologize, Madame. Of course it is not my business who fathered your child. But the question remains. Will you be leaving our humble shelter when the child is born?"

Adelaide clenched her spoon, watching her swollen fingers blanch. "I have nowhere else to go, Monsieur. I haven't heard from my family since they sent me to the Academy twenty-five years ago."

"And the father of your child?"

"Gone. He fled France last year, I was told."

Dr. Gregoire leaned back in his chair and looked down his nose at her. "You are in a desperate situation, I think."

Adelaide looked around the table at the men, hoping for sympathy or a solution. Monsieur Abelard's hand crept back to grip hers. "My dear Adelaide, after your child is born, perhaps you should discontinue the work on the automaton and assist us in our work repairing the Weather Machines? The one nearby appears to be almost intact. With four of us at work on it, we might be able to start it up again soon. No more of this cursed daytime rain. What a glorious thought, eh?"

She pulled her hand back and glared at him. "Monsieur, I am a roboticist, not a mechanical engineer. I simply don't have the brute force to work on a Weather Machine. And my own project is too important to set aside. I'll just have to rewire some of the connections to make up for the lack of parts."

Dr. Gregoire shook his head. "You are too persistent in regards to this automaton of yours, Madame. Why will you not see reason? Even if you managed to make it function as you intend, how will you bring it to the people without the king or his soldiers stopping you?"

Adelaide waved her hand at him. "I need to get him functioning first. Can't you see how crucial it is and why I need your help?"

Dr. Gregoire sighed and spoke, his cadence slow, as if explaining something to a young child. "Madame Coumain. I'm sorry, but none of us believe that this idea of yours is realistic. All of your persuasive speech is for naught. We are not going to distract ourselves from our own project for this useless obsession of yours. Am I correct, gentlemen?"

The other two Scientists murmured their agreement, neither meeting her eyes, though she did not miss that M. Noyer paused before adding his voice.

Dr. Gregoire steepled his fingers and regarded her over them. "I have a proposal for you. I will pay for the child to be fostered, Madame, in exchange for your assistance repairing the Weather Machines. You can't keep the babe here, after all. Perhaps Zilda can help find a foster mother for you nearby."

Adelaide let out a breath of exasperation. "Monsieur, I have told you already I cannot assist you with the heavy work of repairing your Weather Machines. And I must ask again how you hope to keep it functioning when the first soldier to see it will call for a cannon. They will be destroyed again, faster than you can repair any of them."

Monsieur Noyer leaned on one elbow to look down the table at her. "Madame Coumain, if I may, some of the work on the Weather Machines does not require much strength at all. In fact, it can be quite delicate work, to make the necessary connections between the motors and receptors."

"Yes, of course," M. Abelard added. "And the temperature monitors as well. They can be extremely sensitive and require a fine hand to adjust."

Adelaide noted his own hand approaching hers, like a snake from across the table. She placed her hands in her lap, out of his reach.

Dr. Gregoire sat at the head of the table, regarding her over his steepled fingers, eyebrows raised in question. Adelaide met his gaze, trying to read his brown eyes for sincerity. Would he pay for fostering, or was this merely some trick of his, designed to humiliate her?

"You will pay for a family to take the child?" she asked him, rubbing her hands across her belly.

"I will, Madame. You have my solemn word. And you will lend your capable hands to our work. That is our agreement, yes?"

Adelaide nodded. "Yes, we are in agreement. And thank you, Monsieur. I will repay you when I can."

"No need," Dr. Gregoire said, waving a hand. "Your help on the Weather Machines will be my compensation. As M. Noyer has noted, some of the work can require a more delicate touch. And it won't be terribly burdensome, I assure you. Most of your day can be spent at your leisure."

Adelaide let out a breath she hadn't realized she'd been holding. She would have time to continue her work on the Dauphin after all. And without the burden of a child to raise . . .

"In that case, might any of you know where I could locate the finer parts required for robotics work? If I am to be idle at all, I would prefer to spend that time working on my automaton. I merely need to replenish my supply of connectors and actuators—"

M. Noyer cleared his throat. "Parts for an automaton? I'm sorry, Madame, but the robotics labs at the Academy were destroyed. And no one would dare to manufacture such things now."

The robotics labs were gone? The news sent a pang of despair through her. Adelaide had spent long blissful hours as a student in those labs, before Piorry had decided to take her under his wing. Piorry. Her gut twisted at the thought of her ex-mentor and his betrayal. He'd almost murdered her to take credit for her most famous invention, the Archimedean Heart. She hoped he was still rotting in the Bastille where he'd been imprisoned.

Hot, choking tears closed Adelaide's throat and she swallowed hard. Insufferable, these easy tears that threatened her dignity. Pregnancy took so much of her self-control away from her. She dragged herself to her feet using the table to support her weight. Dr. Gregoire rose to his feet, as did the other men.

"An early night for you, Madame?" M. Abelard asked.

Adelaide suppressed the shiver that ran through her at his words. Not trusting herself to speak, she nodded at the men and left the room. She passed through the dimly lit kitchen, not seeing Zilda until she spoke.

"Madame, are you well?"

The servant sat near the kitchen hearth, knitting. Adelaide sniffed back her tears and wiped her wet cheeks.

"Did those men upset you?" Zilda scrambled to her feet, holding out her arms. "You poor dear, why don't you let me make you a nice cup of chamomile tea?"

Adelaide backed away towards the hallway, aching to be alone in her room. "No, no tea, thank you, Zilda. I'm tired. I just need to rest. Good night."

Zilda dropped her arms back to her side. "Go to bed, there's a good girl. You need rest. You work too hard. Good night."

Two

Henri had never liked being on the water. The miserable excuse for a boat he now suffered on was no exception. It rolled and bucked, crashing through the waves of La Manche, that dratted English Channel. He would be lucky to keep his lunch, assuming he survived the trip at all. The water, the sky, even the air all around were rendered in shades of clammy grey. Henri peered into the gloom but saw no sign of the coastline. If France were still there, she was too far for Henri to discern through the abysmal weather.

He drew the collar of his wool coat closer to his ears, but still the wind still managed to insinuate itself, chilling his neck, and crawling down his spine. How long had they been traveling on this cursed boat? The captain had said it would only take three hours, and yet it felt like days had passed since he had last had soil beneath his feet.

I suppose I should be glad I'm not inside puking like Isabelle. Poor thing looked as grey as those clouds.

He peered again into the gloom. France was close, it must be. A surge of pure joy filled him at the thought of being home. His exile had been less than a year, but he had chafed at the English ways every day he had been in Great Britain. How he had longed for France. Even after wedding Isabelle, and being feted by the Naturalist supporters of the French king in exile. Now that the duc de Bordeaux had been crowned King of France and the Scientists swept from power, Naturalism reigned again and Henri could go home. As long as the Police Secrète didn't keep prison records from the previous regime. But his imprisonment had been unfair. He had always been loyal to the duc de Bordeaux. Now that King Henri V reigned, new laws were in place. Hopefully the authorities would no longer consider Henri a fugitive from the law.

His half-brother John strolled onto the deck towards him. His brown hair was swept around his head by the wind, but the disarray was typical for him. Henri smiled at the sight, wondering again how John could be so much paler. Their shared African grandmother's looks didn't show in John's features. Henri raised a hand in a wave. "Good afternoon! You're not feeling as pathetic as Isabelle?"

John shrugged. "I suppose not. The waves seem to be less violent. Are we close to land?" He squinted across Henri's shoulder towards the bow of the ship.

Henri let out an exasperated breath. "Who can tell in this mist? It's almost as if we never left the island of fog and smoke they call England. But we'll be home soon." He grinned at John. "Are you pleased to be returning? Had enough of the English?"

John drew his eyebrows together, looking like an anxious pup. He always worried more than he should. "Are you sure it's safe to return, Henri? We were wanted men ten months ago. What if we're arrested when we arrive in Calais?"

"John, you don't need to be concerned. Our good King Henri is in power now. He will support us, as we supported him in exile. I'm sure our records have been expunged in the regime change. I have heard talk of mobs destroying buildings and burning anything to do with the old robotic monarchs."

John shuddered. "And executing Scientists and nobles who were loyal to the old King and Queen. What if someone remembers that I painted the Queen and her court? What if someone remembers Marie-Ange?"

"Hush, not so loud. They'll only remember if you blab that sort of thing in public. You're just an artist, not a court official. You were making a living, not declaring your loyalty. If you're smart, that's what you'll say if anyone asks."

John's face was dark with concern. He bit his lip and stared out to sea. "I regret Marie-Ange. I miss her still. If I hadn't agreed to help the revolutionaries, she'd still be alive."

Henri snorted. "And married to that lizard she was affianced to. She was a noblewoman, lost to you at birth. Alive or dead, she would always be lost to you."

John didn't respond. He swallowed visibly, his Adam's apple jerking in his throat. He nodded with a jerky movement. "What if nothing has changed?"

"John, stop worrying. We've discussed this at length. We've both read the newspapers. All those articles extolling the new Naturalism laws. And we've corresponded with Arthur. Remember how he said that Paris is free of those hideous Watcher Spheres and Augmented policemen? And the rains have returned. We won't suffer under bright skies day after day."

John quirked an eyebrow. "I thought you were tired of rain?"

"I'm tired of drizzling English rain," Henri said, looking at the grey skies, "not honest French rain."

"I didn't really notice much difference. There was always plenty of drizzling rain in Paris. So no more Augmented people? What about the nobility? You've had more correspondence from Arthur than I. Did he say if anyone at Court was in exile?"

Henri eyed his brother. "Anyone? Or your lovely duchess?"

John started, as if stung, but quickly waved away the comment. "She was just a client, nothing more."

Henri continued, "Arthur didn't say who had been exiled. He doesn't have any contact with Court, remember? His students come to him at Gleyre's old studio. So we don't know if your duchess is still at court."

John's cheeks flushed. "She was not my duchess. She was kind to me and Marie-Ange. And she is also a noblewoman, and a married one, remember?"

"Married to an absent husband."

"We've had this conversation, Henri. He may have returned to Court to serve King Henri. Unless all the courtiers were dismissed and sent to their estates. Did Arthur's correspondence say anything about that?"

Henri leaned on the railing of the ship and looked towards France. Was that coastline ahead? "No, there was no mention of nobility, Augmented or otherwise. The king outlawed Science, including all Augmentations, and the Weather Machines as well. He executed a few of the top Scientists, but they weren't all named in the article."

His voice changed, alerting John to something hidden. "Scientists were executed? Do you suppose the Royal Scientist-Doctor was among them?"

Henri's response was a nonchalant lift of one shoulder. He stared at the approaching coast.

"Henri? Her name was Coumain, right? The one you seduced?"

Henri's flare of anger startled both him and John. "Enough! I don't want to discuss her. She's probably dead. And Isabelle knows nothing of it, nor do I want her to."

John opened and closed his mouth then thankfully kept it shut. He turned to survey the view of Calais, its black and white lighthouse rising high above the harbor.

Henri touched his shoulder. "I apologize, brother. My brief affair with Adelaide Coumain was regrettable. I was weak and don't want that to be known further than between you and I. But look, we're almost home! Soon we'll enjoy real French food. Butter ... bread. And no restrictions on brandy anymore. I won't have to beg that weasel of a wine merchant to sneak me bottles. I can't wait. We'll head straight back to Paris. I'm sure Arthur can put us up until we find flats."

John smiled, charmed as always by Henri's exuberance. "If only my house hadn't been burned. I'll miss that studio. The light was magnificent."

"We'll find you something even better. I'm sure we'll have clients clamoring for our paintings, throwing obscenely high fees at us. After all, I did paint the king before he was crowned. And that lovely painting of the children in the garden you did last summer—you would've received prizes if we'd been in France."

John leaned on the railing, looking towards the approaching coast. "I hope so. I have some money set aside from my English commissions to get set up, but I'll need clients quickly. And you? Did the court in exile ever pay you for the paintings you did of the king?"

Henri flapped a hand. "Not yet, but now we're back in France, I'm certain they will send me my fee. I'll simply present myself to Court and wait for the commissions and fees to flood in."

"Hah, that would be nice. I wonder, is Court still at Versailles? Do trains still travel between there and Paris, or are trains also banned?" He bit off his words, bitterness apparent.

Henri twisted his mouth in chagrin. "John, you don't sound entirely convinced in the valor of the Naturalist cause. I'm sure they still have trains to Versailles. We don't want to return to barbarism, after all."

The ship drew closer to shore and the brothers paused to watch their approach. A small tugboat bobbed through the waves until he reached their prow. Sailors on both vessels tossed lines and tied the tug to the larger ship. As they were led into the harbor, Isabelle staggered to Henri's side, still looking peaky. He wrapped his arm around her slim waist and drew her close to him. "There you are, darling. We're almost home." He pushed her curls back and kissed her damp forehead.

"Thank heavens. That crossing was much too rough for me. I wish the King hadn't banned dirigibles flying into France. If only there was some sort of tunnel under the sea so we could avoid traveling by ship."

Henri chuckled. "A tunnel? Foolish girl. What an absurd idea. But we won't need to leave France again."

With a thump, the ship docked against the quay and dockworkers hastily tied it to the bulwarks. The rain grew heavier, spitting cold spears of water as the passengers huddled into their cloaks on the deck of the ship. The captain approached the trio, a concerned look on his face. "I received word from the tug boat that the local officials wish to speak to you, Monsieur Desjardins."

John stepped closer to Henri and took his arm, chin tilted in defiance. "And what about me?"

The captain shook his head. "No, monsieur, they only asked for Monsieur Desjardins. This way, sir."

John and Henri exchanged glances and John nodded. "I see. They may not have asked for us, but Madame Desjardins and I will accompany my brother."

They walked down the wooden gangplank together, Henri in front with the captain. A quartet of policemen stood on the dock waiting. One of them moved forward and scanned the group. "Henri Desjardins?"

Henri signaled with his hand, fighting the surge of panic. This was not how he had pictured his homecoming. "I am Henri Desjardins. You wish to speak to me?"

"This way." The policeman stopped, looking at John and Isabelle. "Who are these people? I was only ordered to bring you."

"This is my wife and my brother. They will accompany me. Anything you need to ask me can be answered in front of them."

The officer sniffed. "This is irregular. My commander will have to decide what to do about these two. Come along."

They walked through the cobbled, bustling streets of Calais, drawing stares from passersby. Henri glared in return, his head held high. Isabelle clung to his arm. Henri glanced back at John, who looked stern and forbidding. Henri recognized that expression. He wore it when trying to hide his fear. Henri tried to reassure him with a smile but his face was too stiff for more than a grimace.

He tripped on a loose cobblestone and Isabelle steadied him. She threw him a worried glance. He knew she was thinking along the same lines as him. What was going on? The Naturalists were in charge, so why was he being brought in for questioning? That was certainly what was happening. Were leftovers from the old regime still here in Calais? Impossible, not with the new king so recently returned through this port, triumphant after the old monarchs had died. Or been shut down. Whatever it was that had sent those two relics to the grave, Henri did not care. They were gone, forgotten, and so should his offenses.

The gates of the old citadel loomed in front of them, the stone walls of the fortress worn but still impressive. Grim-faced guards stood at either side of the portcullis. Henri surveyed the building. It was a prison, just as the Bastille was. His stomach turned, nausea filling him. No revolutionaries would come to his rescue this time. They were the ones in power now. And they were taking him into custody.

Henri cast one look behind him as he was led into the fortress. He wished he'd had Isabelle and John stay outside. At least that way someone would know he was in Calais.

Another policeman approached them in the courtyard of the citadel. He and the officer exchanged some quiet words, then Henri was led to a door in the inner wall. The policemen ushered John and Isabelle in a different direction. Henri opened his mouth to object but the new officer hushed him with a sharp gesture and a fierce glower. Henri gulped. His hands were damp with sweat. The bright, comfortable office surprised him as he was taken inside. A uniformed woman stood up from behind the desk and smiled. "Ah, Monsieur Desjardins, welcome to Calais. Thank you so much for coming to speak with me. I am Commander Thibault. That will be all, Lieutenant. Please, Monsieur Desjardins, be seated."

Henri sagged into the offered chair, trembling. "Commander. How may I assist you?" So he wasn't to be imprisoned? The commander looked friendly. Henri tried his charming smile, hoping his trembling wouldn't be apparent.

"I have a few questions for you, monsieur. You left France last November? Before His Majesty took the throne? And why did you leave France at that time, monsieur?"

Henri gulped. He had prepared this speech but the words stuck in his throat. "Clients, commander. I have clients in England. And married, I married, so we went on a honeymoon in Scotland. Ah, the king, that is the new king, I mean King Henri, His Majesty. I painted him while he was er, still in exile. I'm a painter, you see."

"Yes, I am aware of your profession, monsieur." Her tone took on a sharp edge. "You left France of your own accord? You were not forced to leave? You were not fleeing persecution?"

Henri felt his face grow warm. Would he have to outright lie if he didn't want to go back to prison. No, he didn't want to lie. "Persecution? For what crime? The crime of being loyal to the Naturalist cause and our king?"

Commander Thibault smiled, her face feral. "You admit that you did flee the country?"

"I went to England to support our king. What crime do you suppose I committed?"

"You tell me, Monsieur Desjardins. Were you charged with a crime or did you leave the country first?"

She doesn't know anything. The records of my arrest and incarceration must have been destroyed in the revolution.

Henri stood, the chair scraping on the floor behind him. "This has been a lovely chat, Commander Thibault, but I really must go. I'm hoping to be in Paris this evening."

"Sit down, Desjardins. I don't know what kind of lawlessness you expected when you returned to France but we still prosecute criminals. I can't let you back into France until I am assured that you are not a danger to the peace. Do you understand how things are done now? There is no more free bread. We do not have the surplus grain anymore without the infernal machines controlling weather. How do you expect to support yourself and your wife? Have you established connections here in France?"

Henri crossed his arms, looking down at the commander. "I am an artist, not an outlaw. I have friends in Paris who are waiting for me. They will help me establish my life here again. Once my client list grows, I will have no trouble supporting my wife and myself."

The commander stood and leaned forward, arms braced on the table. "How can I be sure of this? Do you have letters from these friends?"

"I do have letters but they are all in my luggage. Which is sitting unattended on the dock still. If my belongings have disappeared during this farce, I will be most annoyed, commander."

She waved away his concern. "Your luggage is in our strongroom. I am waiting for the results of the search."

"You're having my luggage searched? Without my permission?"

She shrugged. A knock on the door echoed in the room. "That will be the report of the search. Enter."

A policewoman entered holding a bundle of papers. "Commander, we found no contraband in the luggage we brought in from the dock. Here is correspondence with French return addresses."

The commander took the letters with a smile at her subordinate. She flicked through the papers, scanning pages. "This ... Arthur? He is the friend in Paris who will help you establish yourself? What was his position regarding our glorious revolution? He is also an artist, I gather? Is he loyal to our cause?"

Henri furrowed his brow. Arthur didn't share his thoughts readily. He could be a staunch Naturalist but he was an American. "We don't discuss it. We talk about art."

Commander Thibault sniffed. "You have friends who could secretly be in opposition to His Majesty's new policies?"

"What? No! This is ridiculous. He's an American. I don't care what his beliefs are. What is the point of all this?"

"You seem upset by my questions. Are you hiding something, Monsieur Desjardins?"

Henri squirmed, retaking his seat in hopes that solid wood beneath his backside might help him remain firm in his protestations. His head throbbed from fatigue and hunger. He rubbed his temple and glowered at the commander. "Apart from my need for luncheon, I am hiding nothing. Can we finish here? I just want to get back to Paris. My home. The city where I lived for all but one of my 38 years." Would she believe him? Did he sound more confident and blameless than he felt?

The commander returned his glare then blew out an exasperated breath. "I will send my report onto the Paris police station. If you cause any trouble there, or show that you are anything less than a loyal subject, you'll be arrested immediately. Do I make myself clear, monsieur?"

Henri lurched to his feet. "Abundantly. Good day to you, commander. May I have my letters?" He reached out a hand.

She shook her head. "No, I think not. I'll retain them for further analysis."

"And our travel documents for Paris?"

The commander waved him away, already reading from a sheaf of documents on her desk. "Talk to the clerk on your way out."

Henri suppressed a growl of disgust. He half-bowed then turned and strode out of the office. What had happened to France? What about the Naturalist ideals espoused by the new regime? These police were even worse than the old Police Secrète. What else had changed for the worse?

Three

Adelaide dragged herself up the stairs to her chilly bedroom. A draft from the leaky window moaned its way inside. She moved slowly across the dim room to her wash basin. She poured tepid water from a pitcher and began her nightly ritual before bed. She had barely enough energy to wash the scent of Zilda's cabbage soup from her face and hands, and changing into her rough linen nightgown was an ordeal all its own. Finally able to sit on her bed, Adelaide patted the huge dome of her belly. "At least we've figured out what to do about you, little one. You'll be safe and cared for by someone who knows something about children. That will be better for you. And for me."

She maneuvered herself into her lumpy bed, drawing the meager covers up as high as she could. Gregoire's offer to pay for fostering the child had been generous, and she would follow through with her agreement to help him in return. But he could not seriously hope to repair the nearest machine and have it remain operational. The Weather Machines all sat exposed in the fields. They were too vulnerable, even in this remote region. The new regime's opposition to Science was ferocious in its measure.

They destroyed my laboratory at Versailles. All of my work, my tools.

Did Gregoire have some scheme to protect his Weather Machines from sabotage? The project held no interest for her, but at least it would be work. And in the evening hours, after yet another bowl of Zilda's cabbage soup and stony bread, Adelaide would be free to work on the Automated Dauphin.

She found her hands moving on their own to caress her swollen belly once more. Adelaide breathed a sigh. Her infant would be cared for, and raised by those who knew better how to manage such a task. And it was not as if Adelaide would be completely absent from the child's life. She would make sure the foster mother was nearby, so she could visit. A stray thought of her own mother intruded. They hadn't seen each other in years, not since eight-year-old Adelaide left home to attend the Science Academy. Adelaide wondered if she should write to her parents, perhaps tell them about the child.

No, even if she could remember their direction after all this time, they wouldn't want an illegitimate grandchild anymore than they had wanted her. Adelaide had no friends, no family, nowhere to turn for help. She shifted, trying to find a comfortable position under the weight of the child. This had to be the right decision. She repeated that thought as she drifted into sleep, rubbing a tired hand across her wet cheeks.

Four

The Automated Dauphin's face was a lifeless, dull grey, reflecting the rainy afternoon outdoors. Adelaide leaned forward against the automaton once more, trying to rest her aching back and swollen ankles as she fought against her fatigue and continued her work in rewiring the machine. Her fingers moved clumsily in the chest cavity. Each knuckle felt twice as thick as it should be, and stung with the ache of overuse. She struggled to reach the connections behind the machine's main actuator, and scraped her fingers against a rough metal flange. Adelaide pulled her hand out slowly. Her knuckles were smeared with blood.

"Damn, damn, damn. Now I'll need a bandage. Oh, why won't one of those pigheaded men help me with this?"

She waddled out of the workroom, holding her bloodied hand to her mouth. She thought she bled more freely with the pregnancy. Her medical school training hadn't covered obstetrics in any real detail so she wasn't sure if it was normal or even if she was imagining it. "Zilda? Where are you? I need a bandage."

Zilda popped her head out of the sitting room, her hair bundled into a cloth. Was that a dusting rag in her hand? Was she actually dusting this hovel? "Did you call me? Oh, madame, you're bleeding all over the floor. What has happened? Is the baby coming?"

"Oh, I'm sorry," Adelaide said with a start, taking a step back and looking to the floor. Droplets of blood marked her passage. "I didn't realize—I cut my hand. Have you got something I can use to bandage it?"

The servant came closer and examined Adelaide's hand. "Yes, of course. It is not so bad. Nothing that would require prayers to fix, but it never hurts to plead one's case," she added, tilting her face upward as if appealing to the ceiling itself for help. Coming back to herself, she regarded Adelaide anew. "Let's get that wrapped up."

Zilda drew Adelaide into the kitchen and bustled about, mumbling to herself, making more prayers perhaps. Adelaide fought the urge to scoff at the simple woman.

As if praying had any power.

Zilda rummaged around in a drawer and pulled out a rag, then tore it into strips. Adelaide pressed two fingers against the cut and watched the servant woman work.

What a lot of fuss for a little blood. I can't imagine what she'd be like in a surgical theater.

She let Zilda wrap her hand and images of the Augmentation surgeries she'd performed flickered across her mind. Would she ever be able to help people with her surgical skills again? She exhaled a sigh. Not until the child was born.

And not with the current regime.

Finally, Zilda was finished. She clasped her hands over the bandage and closed her eyes, muttering more prayers. Adelaide waited patiently, then thanked Zilda for her care, withdrawing her hands from the woman's grasp. The servant nodded and went about her duties, and Adelaide returned to her workroom in the back of the farmhouse. She slumped into a chair, but only allowed herself a moment's rest before struggling to her feet, and shuffling to her worktable. She was determined to keep working on the Automated Dauphin. She pored over her notes on the Automated Dauphin. He had once functioned beautifully, but not since she disconnected that strange orb. Adelaide frowned at her own marginalia. She must have missed something crucial when she rewired his control center to allow the orb to be inserted in the first place.

Loud muffled voices called her back to the present. The men had returned from their daily sojourn to the wrecked Weather Machine nearby. They insisted that it would be just a matter of time before it was functioning again. Adelaide had grown accustomed to their daily grumblings and was prepared to ignore this one as well. But the voices sounded louder than usual, and the note of fear in them set Adelaide's heart racing. What was going on out there? She heaved herself to her feet and lumbered towards the door, but she paused before exiting.

The men were shouting at each other now, filling the poky hallway with their clamor. Some of the voices were not familiar. Adelaide risked a look beyond her room and found herself staring at a soldier's back. He was marching forward, with Dr. Gregoire ahead of him. The soldier had his hands clamped around Dr. Gregoire's arms.

"You're a scientist, all dressed in that black garb like they do. You and your friends here. We saw you messing with that machine out in the field, trying to get it to work again. And that's illegal, working on machines. So you're coming with us, monsieur Scientist. You're under arrest."

Gregoire's hair flared wildly out around his head, his hat tumbled forgotten to the floor. "Unhand me, you brute. This is preposterous. We are trying to help you people. Don't you realize that? Your barley is rotting out there in the unregulated rain. What will you feed your families with?"

The soldier forced Gregoire to the front door. Adelaide peered out, catching sight of the other two Scientists already in custody outside. An entire platoon of soldiers filled the muddy farmyard, their serious faces grim in the drizzling rain, rifles at the ready.

Why would they think it would take twenty men to arrest four Scientists? Are they afraid of us?

They hadn't spotted her yet. Perhaps she could escape through the kitchen. But what about the Automated Dauphin? Would the soldiers search the farmhouse? Adelaide stood at the end of the hallway, indecisive. Should she leave through the kitchen or try to hide her life's work from these men? Men who would no doubt destroy it upon sight.

She had dithered too long. A soldier spotted her and cried out, "Halt, madame!" He marched towards her, seeming too young to be in uniform. "I'm afraid I'll have to ask you to step outside, madame." He took in her bulky form, clad in rough brown wool, the pregnant belly declaring itself. "Your husband is being taken into custody, madame, and this property confiscated in the King's name. You must leave here."

"Husband? I'm not married to that man."

The soldier snickered. "Oh, his little morsel, are you? How did you find yourself in the company of fugitives? Bad luck, I suppose. And now with a babe on the way? I'm sorry, Madame, for your trouble, but you can't stay here."

He gently grasped her arm and led her out of the farmhouse. The other Scientists were shackled now, their heads bowed with misery. None of them looked in her direction. Would they turn her in? She looked away and saw a group of the soldiers lighting torches. There were still several hours of daylight. They didn't need the torches for light. Which meant they were intending to set a fire. The soldiers spread out around the house.

Adelaide gasped. "What are you doing? You can't mean to set fire to the house?"

The young soldier still held her arm. He spoke to her as if she was simple. "These men have forbidden devices inside the house. They could be dangerous. We will burn down the house and destroy the machines. Then it will be safe. Don't worry, Madame. We're taking the bad men away."

Adelaide's stomach turned with fear. How was she going to get the automaton out of the house? "My cat! I need to get my cat out of the house!" She yanked her arm away from the soldier and grabbing handfuls of her skirts, headed towards the front door as quickly as she could.

"Stop! The house has already caught fire. See the roof? I'm sure the cat got out; the windows are all open." The soldier had her in his grip again. She struggled to get free but he held her firmly. The flames licked along the eaves then jumped inside an upper window, catching the curtain on fire. It ignited with a whoosh. More of the roof was on fire now and flames flickered in the downstairs windows. The heat burned Adelaide's skin and she backed away, never letting her gaze drop from the inferno. A coldness filled her despite the heat. Her life's work, her dream for France, was burning inside that building.

Zilda dashed across the farmyard to Adelaide, smiling her relief. "Madame, you're safe! I was afraid you were still inside."

Adelaide turned to the servant in a daze. She'd forgotten all about Zilda. How did she know to leave the building?

Adelaide hadn't seen a soldier lead her out. Had Zilda betrayed them to the soldiers? Adelaide scowled, her eyes burning as brightly as the farmhouse.

Zilda's smile drooped. She took a step backwards. "M-madame? What is it? Are you well?"

"As well as I can be while my only refuge burns behind us. How do you suppose this happened, Zilda? Why have the soldiers come to this farm in particular?"

Zilda dropped her gaze to the dirt. "I suppose the provincial government found out that these men are Scientists. So of course, they sent soldiers to arrest them. We must all follow His Majesty's orders, Madame, even here in this abysmal province." Her words, parroting Dr. Gregoire's in a mocking tone, told Adelaide all she needed to know. She had reported them out of spite, but why was Adelaide spared? Was it the child she bore? Zilda had been more than solicitous of her once her pregnancy became apparent.

A loud crack startled them as the support beams collapsed, followed the crash of the upper floors falling to the blaze startled them. The group backed further from the burning house as it crumbled in on itself. As if the collapse was a signal, the soldier released Adelaide and bowed to her. "We must take our prisoners away now. Goodbye, mesdames."

The wind shifted and smoke drifted into Adelaide's face. She coughed, her eyes stinging and watering. Zilda bowed silently to Adelaide and disappeared as quickly as she had come, following the soldiers as they marched their prisoners away. Adelaide watched in silence. Monsieur Noyer stole a glance at her as the men passed but there were no words of farewell spoken by any of them. The young soldier raised an eyebrow at her, seeming to expect some protest, some womanly expression of grief and loss for her lover's arrest. Adelaide leveled a gaze at him, daring him to make more idiotic remarks. He passed by and marched out of the farmyard. The tromp of boots faded into the distance, leaving Adelaide with nothing but the warmth and crackling of the fire for company.

Five

Henri turned up his collar against the frigid wind blowing rain into his face. Grey clouds loomed over the Citadel of Calais and the streets were dark and slick. He looked down at Isabelle, shivering under his arm. She still looked worried, her mouth drawn in. He kissed the top of her head.

"Don't fret, ma chère. All is well. We're home. The carriage will be here soon and, in a few days, we'll be back in Paris!"

She glanced up at him from under her dark lashes and a smile flitted across her mouth for a moment. "I'm cold and tired, that's all." She snuggled closer to him, head bent.

"At least we're not still on the water." John teased his sister-in-law. He didn't seem to mind the cold as much as she did. She snorted in response.

Henri glowered over his shoulder at the hulking Citadel. "Or in that godforsaken prison. I still can't believe they detained me. Who are these people? The king will hear of this. I have always been loyal to him and this is how his police treat me? I thought all that nonsense was over. And keeping my letters? Ridiculous."

Isabelle placed her gloved hand over his and squeezed. "I'm sure it was just a misunderstanding" She echoed his words. "All will be well once we're home in Paris. Provincial people are always slow to adapt to change."

Henri sighed. "Not the homecoming I was expecting but you're right, she was just a provincial police chief." He looked down the cobbled street and spotted a tawdry carriage rocking toward them. "At last. Let's hope that vehicle is sturdier than it looks. Where did you find that wreck?"

John shrugged. "It was our only choice. All the others were spoken for. With the train to Paris not running, carriages are in demand."

Henri squashed his feeling of foreboding. They wouldn't be in Paris this evening as he had hoped. Calais was too far from the capitol to make travel by rail profitable perhaps. After all, he had arrived here by carriage last year when he was fleeing to England.

The carriage driver pulled up his horse and nodded down at them. "You can put your luggage up on top if you like but it'll get wet. Like to be a storm this afternoon."

The three exchanged looks. Henri shrugged. "Inside then?"

The carriage would be crowded with their trunks and bags but it was better than having waterlogged belongings when they arrived in Paris. John and Isabelle nodded their assent. Henri handed her into the carriage then he and John loaded the luggage inside. Once they had all settled themselves amongst the trunks, with bags on their laps, the carriage lurched away. The interior of the vehicle was shabby and reeked of garlic.

Henri grinned and gestured to the worn, dirty cushions. "Not exactly luxury but it'll get us home! Just a few more days now before we're in Paris."

Isabelle almost immediately grew pale as they rocked along the rough pavement. "Perhaps we could open a window? I'm feeling a little queasy."

John looked out. "It's pouring out there. We'll be soaked if we open the window."

"Perhaps just a crack? I'll sit next to it."

Henri opened the window. The wind whistled through the crack. Isabelle scooted closer, climbing to sit on a trunk. She pressed her face against the glass and breathed deeply. The temperature inside the carriage dropped and they all shivered.

"It's freezing in here, Isabelle." John huddled into his overcoat but his nose was red with the cold. "Must we really have the window open?"

Isabelle glowered at him. "Yes, we must. Unless you wish me to be sick on your lap?"

John scowled back, his arms crossed. "Your delicate stomach is a damned inconvenience."

Isabelle inhaled a sharp breath. "I don't do it on purpose, you know. I can't help that my stomach has been so upset." Tears glimmered in her eyes.

Henri held his hands up to quell the argument. It was going to be a long five days to Paris if they were going to be at odds. "Please, let's not bicker. We're all tired and uncomfortable. Let's try to be calm and enjoy the views of the countryside." At that, the carriage lurched and slowed to a crawl, shuddering with every forward movement.

John leaned against the window and squinted out. "What's going on out there?"

Isabelle lowered the window and stuck her head out. Wind and rain blustered around the carriage. "Looks like the road is washed out. Driver's taking us up on the verge." She closed the window. "Gracious but it's stormy out there. Tree branches everywhere. And the clouds ahead are positively black."

Their progress was slow as the carriage shuddered and rocked along the ruined road. They passed fields flattened by wind and rain. The carriage sped up a little when they entered a small village.

Isabelle leaned forward. "I wonder if we could stop briefly? I need to use the facilities. If there are any here." She frowned, looking at the darkened buildings. John rapped on the ceiling of the carriage and the driver stopped.

He appeared at the door, water dripping off his hat. "There's naught here to stop for, sir. Village is empty. We'll be changing horses in another hour or so."

Isabelle stood and stepped into the doorway. "I can't wait that long. I need to relieve myself. There must be somewhere open."

The driver shook his head. "Everyone left a while back."

She jumped down. "We'll see. I'm sure I can find somewhere. I'll be back in a bit." She bent into the wind and approached the nearest house.

Henri followed her with a sigh. "Please wait a moment. I will accompany my wife." His feet crunched on gravel and broken glass. Isabelle slipped into the open doorway of a stone cottage. The window glass was gone and torn curtains flapped in the openings. Henri glanced around. Other cottages slumped against the side of the road. Burn marks scored the walls of the house next door. He shivered at the desolation and followed Isabelle. Henri poked his head into the doorway of the cottage Isabelle had entered.

"Isabelle? Where are you? Be careful." Henri shook his head. Since when did he act like a nursemaid? These abandoned buildings must be affecting his nerves. The wind buffeted him, knocking him against the door jamb. He rubbed his shoulder and stepped into the house, blinking in the dim interior. Broken furniture littered the floor and writing smeared the walls. He moved closer, trying to make out the words. Something about the king? Long live the king? And something else he couldn't make out. Henri stepped back. Who had done this? What had happened here? He stumbled out of the cottage, disturbed by the destruction. He crossed his arms and leaned against the cottage wall, examining the neighboring houses. They had all been abandoned. Isabelle touched his shoulder and he jumped.

"Henri, it's just me. What's wrong? I'm here, see? Everything's fine, nothing happened to me in there."

Henri cast a look at her and nodded. He took her arm and led her back to the carriage. John and the carriage driver stood there waiting, sharing a flask of what Henri suspected was John's good whiskey. Wordlessly Henri put his hand out for the flask and took several swallows, the liquor burning its way down his throat. He helped Isabelle into the carriage and climbed in after her. "Let's get out of here."

John followed, slamming the door behind him and the carriage rattled along the road, quickly leaving the abandoned village behind. Henri sat without speaking, staring out the window. John and Isabelle watched him, worry creasing their faces.

After many long moments, John finally broke the silence. "What did you see in that cottage that troubled you, brother?"

Henri rubbed his forehead and sighed. "Besides the destruction of someone's home? It seems that violence reached even small hamlets during what was meant to be a peaceful transition. And there was writing on the wall. I don't understand. Long live the king. Why would someone feel the need to scrawl that on someone's home?"

John leaned an elbow against the carriage wall, gazing out at the passing countryside. "Certainly seems overzealous. I wonder what happened to all the villagers?" His mouth turned down in a frown.

The carriage's speed slowed again. Isabelle sat forward and pointed out the window. "There's a roadblock ahead."

Henri craned over her. "Really? Has the road washed out here too?" He sat back against the dusty cushions. The carriage came to a gradual halt. A barricade crossed the road and soldiers in a guard box on the verge watched them approach. Henri's breath caught. What was going on? He glanced at John, pale and quiet. The driver spoke to the soldiers but Henri couldn't make out his words. His heart sped up, thudding uncomfortably in his chest. Isabelle squeezed his hand and he started.

"It'll be alright, Henri. We've done nothing wrong. Just returning home, remember?" Her eyes were dark and her hand trembled.

He nodded and forced a smile. "Of course."

The door opened and the wind slammed it against the outside of the carriage. A soldier, ruddy and far too young to be in uniform, scrutinized them. His voice squeaked. "Your papers, please, messieurs and madame."

Henri pulled out the travel documents the Calais police had given them. He hadn't had a chance to see what they said and his heart sank, remembering the commander's hostility, He handed the papers over to the soldier with a half-smile. The young man didn't return his smile. He took their papers and returned to the guardhouse. They waited in the chilly carriage, not speaking. Finally the young soldier returned, accompanied by a jowly older soldier. His sharp eyes took in the three of them and he held up the packet of travel papers.

"Says here that you are all residents of Paris but I don't see anything from the Préfet de Police. Just your passport from Calais. Where's the rest of your papers?"

John stuttered. "Did you need our international passports too? We've been in England for the past year."

The older soldier shook his head. "No, not those ones, you already gave them to us. We need your internal passports from Paris."

Henri trembled. They didn't have passports to leave Paris since they'd been escaping the authorities last year. He took a breath to steady himself. "Officer, I'm afraid we gave our internal passports to the officials at Calais when we passed through on our way to England last year. Were we meant to keep them?"

The soldier scowled and looked at his partner. They stepped aside and conversed in low tones. Henri strained to hear them but the wind howled around them. The younger soldier shook the papers at the older man who shrugged.

Henri slapped his hands on his thighs and he growled. "This is absurd, they can't keep us here." He rose to his feet but John took hold of his arm, restraining him.

"Brother, calm yourself. Please. Let's not provoke them."

John and Isabelle looked concerned and more than a little frightened. This was not what Henri had promised when he had campaigned for their return to France. He submitted to his brother's gentle tug and sank into his seat. He smiled at them, his face stiff. "It'll be fine. I'm sure it's just a formality. We'll be on our way soon."

The soldiers returned to the carriage. They both wore dark looks.

Henri swallowed, trying to keep his tone level. "Is there a problem? Are we permitted to continue our journey?"

The older soldier handed back the packet of papers, scowling. "Not sure about that Paris passport but since you're on the way home from foreign places, I suppose that's alright. On your way then." He slammed the carriage door and stepped away, waving them through. The barricade creaked open slowly and the carriage rolled through. Henri let out a breath he hadn't realized he'd been holding.

Isabelle shivered. "How many more checkpoints will there be, you suppose?"

Henri squeezed her hand with both of his own. "There's no need to worry, ma chère. I'm sure it will be fine. See how easily we got through this one?" He grinned at them both, his irritation slipping from him. John shrugged and looked out the window.

Six

The smoldering remains of the farmhouse were still too hot to comfortably approach, even hours after the conflagration. But Adelaide had to see, to know the destruction with her eyes, and so she trudged over the sodden earth, heavy with the weight of her unborn child, nestled safe within her swollen belly. Misty rain obscured the ruined house from her view. Water droplets decorated her hair. Circling the farmhouse to the back, where her workroom once stood, Adelaide recognized the window that had once let in meager light, but still enough to illuminate the metallic chassis of the Automated Dauphin.

She edged closer, holding her skirts away from the smoldering embers and blackened wood as she squinted into the gloom. Maybe the fire had not burned hot enough to damage the automaton? Maybe he'd escaped by himself, triggered by the self-preservation protocols she had so carefully programmed? The hours and days she had spent designing and then constructing him. All that time, all those exercises and tests. Surely it had not been for nothing.

Sparks flew into the sky, and a gout of flame leapt up inside the room. Adelaide glimpsed shining metal. The fire roared anew in the misted night air, giving Adelaide a clear view of her life's work, now nothing more than a ruin. The once noble profile of the Automated Dauphin was blurred, vague, melted by heat. Smoke blackened his metal skin. He lay in a pile of burned wood and rubble, arms spread as if to embrace the falling ceiling that had crushed him. Adelaide couldn't see his legs, buried under part of the fallen roof.

She could neither breathe nor tear herself away from the destruction. Her feet moved of their own accord, as if to carry her to him, but the weight in her belly held her back. She could not move past the collapsed wall. Stepping back, Adelaide tripped on a fallen timber and spun, landing hard on one knee. Fighting back nausea, she pushed against the ground, and lifted herself on shaking legs. One hand found purchase on charred wood, and Adelaide forced herself to turn around, to see the automaton as he now was and always would be. Gone.

This can't be real, she thought, and then, speaking to the blurry mess of metal, Adelaide said," "You were my creation. You were supposed to be my future. Now—." A giggle escaped her, half sob. Another. She tried to stifle her laugh, holding a hand to her mouth as the laugh became a cry of sorrow.

"My beautiful boy. You're all melted, like a pewter plate left carelessly on a stove. Three years of work, and that is all l have to show for it. A melted plate."

Again the laughter rose in her throat. This time, she let it come.

"You're gone. It's not funny. But l have to laugh. It's all ... too ridiculous."

Adelaide chortled, unable to control herself, her breath ragged. She wrapped her arms around herself, squeezing, trying to stop the giggles until wetness blanketed her cheeks. Her hysterical laughter turned to sobs and she stared at the ruined automaton through a veil of tears. She raised her hands to cover her face, not able to look anymore. A wave of nausea and exhaustion hit her and she trembled.

With one last look at the melted brass figure that had been her Automated Dauphin, Adelaide turned and walked to the front of the farmhouse. Parts of the structure still burned. The soldiers had been exacting about their work. Nothing remained whole, not even the stables.

Gloomy clouds welcoming the setting sun, drawing it down. It would be a cold night, not one for sleeping rough. Where was she to go? Adelaide wiped her face, wishing for a clean handkerchief or some warm water. Being clean had always felt comforting and she could dearly use some comfort. With a deep sigh, Adelaide trudged towards the farm gate. Zilda stood there, her sharp eyes glinting. "Madame, where are you going?"

Adelaide halted. Why was this traitor still here? "That is none of your concern."

Zilda simpered and tried to lay a hand on Adelaide's arm, but Adelaide shook her off. "My dear, you need to rest so that your babe can be healthy. Why don't you come to my cottage? I will feed you nourishing, healthy meals and you can sleep all day if you want. I will take care of you and your precious child."

Adelaide gaped. Why was she so interested in the baby? They barely knew each other. Gregoire had hired Zilda when they arrived in Picardy five months ago and yet the woman was acting as if Adelaide was her long-lost daughter. Adelaide shook her head. "I can't stay here. I need to return to Paris."

She had acquaintances in Montmartre who might be able to help her. Other Scientists in hiding right under the nose of the king. And there were real hospitals in Paris. She loathed the idea of giving birth in some dirty country hovel, attended only by an ignorant peasant. She had no idea what her future would hold but she didn't want to die in childbirth. The hospitals in Paris were staffed by doctors trained at the Academy of Science who would deliver her baby safely.

Zilda tugged at her sleeve. "Paris? Why would you want to return to that filthy city when you could stay here with me? The air here is wholesome, unlike that awful, smoky place. I have plenty of food to share. My cousin brings me fresh milk from his dairy. Stay with me and I can help with your baby once she's born. You can be my daughter. Let me be your baby's grandmère."

Adelaide shook her head and pulled her sleeve out of Zilda's grip. "I'm not staying here. Goodbye, Zilda."

Adelaide's heavy steps took her past Zilda and onto the wide dirt road that led to the nearest village. It would be a long walk, and for a moment Adelaide almost heeded Zilda's calls to stay. With a shake of her head, she forced herself onwards. Hopefully she could beg a ride from a farmer taking his goods to the market at Les Halles.

Seven

Adelaide reclined on a giant bag of sugar beets, wincing as her womb clenched again. Each time the contractions were tighter and more painful. When she had climbed onto the farmer's cart, with his help, she expected a bumpy but uneventful ride to Paris. Hours of constant jolting over rough roads must have shaken something loose inside her, specifically, her baby. The farmer hadn't looked over his shoulder all morning. He sat slumped, endlessly whistling the same off-tune song.

In the space between contractions, Adelaide breathed and cast her gaze across the landscape, wondering how much longer it would be until they arrived in Paris. She wasn't familiar with this region, its flat grain fields seeming to undulate on into infinity.

I really don't want to give birth in the back of this cart. The farmer said four hours to Paris. But that was ages ago. The sun was barely up when we left Beauvais, and now it's overhead. Shouldn't we be getting close? At least it isn't raining.

That last though gave Adelaide reason to smile, almost enjoying the warm sun on her face. In response, another contraction gripped her and she moaned. They were getting stronger and more frequent. The farmer must have heard her moans through his whistling. He looked at her over his shoulder, mouth twisted in dismay. "Madame, are ya well? You've gone all pale. Is it the babe? Ya look close to your time, as I did say when I said as I'd take ya to Paris."

Adelaide bit her lip. She couldn't catch her breath to speak. Finally, the pain eased. "How much longer, monsieur? It appears that the jostling may have encouraged the baby to make his appearance."

He turned forward to survey the land, then called back to her, "Looks like St. Denis up ahead. I'm guessing we'll be to Les Halles in less than an hour."

Adelaide relaxed a fraction. An hour. She could make it to a hospital. First births were slow, she'd heard from Zilda. She had time. The baby wouldn't be born in a cart after all. Zilda. She hadn't thought much of her on the long ride but now memory niggled at her.

Should I have stayed and let Zilda take care of me? She was so insistent about caring for me, always concerned about the baby. What did she really want? A replacement for her daughter? Or maybe she just wanted a baby?

Another pain tore through her belly and a rush of water poured from her, soaking her petticoats. Adelaide clamped down her jaw to stop a scream from erupting from her. She had no idea what was happening. She'd never been around childbearing women and hadn't seen a birth. Was this normal or was something terribly wrong?

"Monsieur? Do you suppose you can drop me off at a hospital once we reach Paris? I'm afraid this child wants to be born rather soon."

In response, the farmer hunched up his shoulders and touched his whip to his horse's flanks. The horse picked up her pace, from a slow saunter to a fast walk. This added to the jostling and jolting Adelaide was forced to endure, but the increased pace was an improvement to be sure. Hopefully it would be fast enough.

Soon the suburbs of Paris surrounded them, small houses surrounded by gardens that got closer together as they moved into the city itself. The farmer navigated his cart carefully through the streets as they grew more crowded and winding. The narrow buildings towered on either side but Adelaide panted through the cramps in her belly, not paying much attention to her surroundings. Curious people peered at her as the cart passed but all their stares and whispers were inconsequential to the drama in Adelaide's body.

It was mid afternoon when they clattered over the bridge to the Île de la Cité. Adelaide recognized the building. It was the Hôtel-Dieu, one of the teaching hospitals she had served in when training as a roboticist, aiding the surgeons with Augmentations. A small smile tugged at her mouth.

It's almost like coming home.

The Hôtel Dieu seemed like an appropriate place to birth her child. The farmer helped her down out of the cart. Her legs wobbled, but she stayed on her feet.

"Here ya are, madame. Best of luck to ya and your babe." He tugged at his cap then climbed back into his cart and drove away.

Adelaide lifted a hand to wave, but the farmer seemed to have already forgotten her. She faced the five stone steps up to the door of the hospital. To Adelaide in her condition, they were daunting. She took a deep breath, then scaled them one by one, pausing to breathe after each. By the time she reached the last step, the porter had spotted her and came dashing out to help. He looked her up and down and paused. His mouth twisted in disgust. Adelaide looked down at her filthy dress.

I must look a fright, covered in straw and soot, and who knows what my hair looks like.

"I'm sorry, Madame, we can't help you. All our charity beds are full. Go back home and have your baby there." The porter turned and entered the building, leaving Adelaide standing on the top step.

Eight

Finally back in Paris, Henri headed to his grandmother's flat. He dodged the knot of people surrounding the man sharpening knives and stepped off the pavement and into a puddle. He winced and shook his wet foot. At least he hadn't stepped in the pile of horse manure next to the puddle. Henri continued along the Rue des Abbesses to his grandmère's flat. His feet ached after the long walk from Gleyre's house. He hadn't been able to find a horse-driven taxi and the steam omnibuses were gone, banned by the new Naturalist laws. Hopefully the old horse-driven omnibuses would soon return to Paris's streets. The familiar calls of the street vendors brought a smile to his face. He'd missed the din of Paris. He'd missed Grandmère even more and his spirits rose as he grew nearer.

The burgundy painted facade of Edouard's wine shop came into view and Henri grinned. Almost there. He'd stop at the boulangerie across the street and get Grandmère a fresh baguette. He sauntered around a buxom snail vendor and exchanged a flirtatious smile with her, then reached the door of the old bakery. The doorbell tinkled as he pushed open the door.

"Bonjour, mademoiselle!" he called to the girl slumped behind the counter, one hand propping up her head, the other covering a yawn.

She blinked at him like a grumpy cat roused from a nap, "Bonjour, monsieur."

Henri moved towards the counter. "I'd like a baguette, if you please." Henri's mouth watered in anticipation of the fresh bread he was about to purchase.

The girl scowled, her dark heavy eyebrows drawn together. "We're out."

Henri scanned the empty baskets behind her. "No bread at all?"

She waved a languid hand at the tray of croissants on the counter in front of her. "We've got a few croissants but all the bread's gone."

Henri shrugged. It was after lunch, too late in the day for fresh bread perhaps. Sadly, Grandmère wasn't fond of croissants. "Ah well, perhaps another time." He ambled back out of the shop. Flowers. He'd buy her a bouquet of flowers. She adored flowers, the brighter the better. They would have to be hothouse flowers this time of year, so expensive, but she was worth it. Henri whistled as he made his way down the street then stopped abruptly in front of the boarded-up florist. Closed-down. How long had it been closed? Since the King's rise to power? He was sure it had been open last year before he'd left. He hated to go to Grandmère empty handed after being gone for so long. He cast his gaze down the road. Edouard's wine shop was open. Perhaps a nice bottle of wine would do. He stepped into the dark, fragrant interior and inhaled. What a gorgeous scent. The English had nothing to compare with a Parisian wine shop.

The man behind the counter cleared his throat. "How can I be of assistance, m'sieur?"

Henri squinted in his direction. Could it be Edouard himself? He had certainly filled out in the past year. "Edouard! Mon ami! It is I, Henri, Henri Desjardins."

"Henri Desjardins? It's been an age since I've seen you about. Your grandmère pines for you, you know. Where have you been hiding all this time?"

Henri waved a hand, squelching his unease. "Ah, I have been abroad, in England and Scotland. Wedding trip. Isabelle and I finally married so I took her abroad."

Edouard guffawed, hands on his round belly. "Vraiment? You, married? And how did you afford such a lengthy voyage? You never had two sous to rub together. Why, you used to coax bottles out of me all the time."

Henri studied the bottles on a nearby rack, avoiding Edouard's eyes. He turned a bottle to more closely read the label and cleared his throat. "I painted the king and his court when they were in England. And you know my brother John. He has many English clients so he went along."

"You took your brother on your wedding trip? I'm sure your bride was none too pleased about that."

Henri winced. Why had he mentioned John? The trip hadn't started as a wedding trip after all but he wasn't about to tell Edouard he had been fleeing the old monarch's Secret Police. Henri picked up the bottle he'd been toying with and brought it to the counter. "Isabelle likes John. And he didn't journey with us the entire time. Have no fear, I gave her a proper honeymoon." He winked at Edouard who cleared his throat and crossed himself. That was new. The old Edouard never showed any outward sign of piety. "And how are you faring these days, old friend. You look well."

Edouard patted his belly and sighed, a sound of contentment rather than worry. "Doing well, doing well. Especially now that my gout has been cured. I went to the nuns at the Hotel Dieu Hôpital and they took care of me. Rendons grâce à dieu. Their prayers are powerful."

"Nuns? At the hospital? What did the doctor say about their cure?"

Edouard snorted and pursed his lips. "No doctors. They were all sent away during the purifications. Too enamored of science, I've heard. The King decreed that there was to be no more of that technological filth. Now we have the nuns and they pray for us to be healed."

Henri nodded. He didn't miss the noise and stink of the steam engines or the looming Watcher Spheres on every corner but no doctors? That seemed a little extreme. Ah but he was a healthy man so perhaps a nun's prayer was all he'd need. "Glad to see you're looking so well. I'd better get up to Grandmère. She's already going to be annoyed with me after being away so long. If she hears me chatting down here with you, she'll be furious." He paid for the wine and made his farewells to Edouard. He wasn't sure why Edouard gave him such an odd look as he left. It was as if the wine seller was trying to assess his story for flaws.

He sprinted up the steep stairs next to the wine shop. His grandmother had lived two floors above the wine shop since his grandfather's death many years ago. Henri was sure she'd be home. The climb up and down proved hard on her joints these days so she didn't go out much. Perhaps he'd run into one of his cousins bringing her food. He reached the top floor without meeting anyone. Dust floated in the air and he sneezed. No one was sweeping up here. Grandmère must be slowing down. Henri stepped up to the faded wooden door and rapped. "Grandmère? It is Henri!" He paused, listening for the shuffle of her footsteps. The cold penetrated his wool coat as he waited. "Grandmère?" Where was she? He frowned and knocked again. Henri pressed his ear against the door and heard movement inside. The door creaked open and his grandmother appeared in the doorway, squinting up at him. She was swathed in multiple shawls and what looked like more than one dress.

"Henri, it really is you. I thought you must be dead, not to visit or even write to me for ten months." She grimaced and crossed her arms over her thick layers of clothing.

Henri dropped his head. "I'm sorry, Grandmère. My life was ... complicated. I had to leave France."

She tapped his chest with her wizened little hand. "Excuses. You could have sent a letter. I can read, you know."

He nodded, still looking at the floor. "I know. I worried that it would've been dangerous for you to be corresponding with me."

She snorted and drew him inside then shut the door. "Trouble with the law? That's not like you, my boy."

Henri shook his head. "It wasn't what you think. I fell into the company of people who were working to bring our king to power. Before the old king and queen died. Things went wrong and John and I had to leave the country. Now that King Henri is on the throne, it's safe for me to be home again."

She harrumphed. "The police is no better now, even with those cursed Watcher Spheres gone. Harassing people on the street when they beg for food. And no free bread! I'm not sure I much like your new king, Henri."

Henri stepped closed and placed his arm around her shoulders. "I'm sorry life is harder for you now, Grandmère. I had hoped France would be much more pleasant without all that technology. But you shouldn't speak out against the king. I don't want you to get into trouble like I did and have to flee. I don't think you'd like England much. Too cold."

She laughed and gestured to her bulky clothing. "France isn't exactly balmy, my boy. Maybe I should go to Senegal. I'm sure I have cousins who would take me in."

"But I would miss your cooking too much if you left, Grandmère." He gave her a sly smile. She whacked his chest. "My food is all you care about? Too bad for you, you won't be getting my Thieboudienne today. I haven't been able to get hold of fresh fish for months. It's too expensive. Your cousin brings me what she can but every day, prices go up."

Fish was too expensive? How could that be? What else was she having to do without? Wood for her stove, it seemed. Her flat was freezing.

"Is that why you're not using your wood stove? It's too cold for you to go without heat. You'll get sick."

She sniffed, disdain writ across her features, and shrugged. "If I get cold, I just go down to Edouard's apartment. I'm fine."

Henri grimaced. She would never admit that she was in need. His grandmother was too proud for that. Not that he had any money to spare even if she would accept it. He pulled the bottle of wine out of his coat pocket. "This'll keep you warm." He winked at her.

She guffawed and reached for the bottle. "That it will. What did you bring me? Ohh, a nice Burgundy. Good choice, my boy. Will you sit and have a glass with me?"

"Of course, Grandmère. I would be delighted."

They sat on her lumpy sofa and drank wine together, laughing about Henri's childhood escapades.

Nine

Adelaide stood on the steps of the Hôtel-Dieu, clutching her cramping belly. She swayed on her feet as the smell of smoke and sweat wove around her. She held back a groan and narrowed her eyes at the closed door. No. She hadn't come all this way from Picardy to have her baby in a flea-ridden bed in an inn, or worse, in some alleyway. Adelaide needed a civilized Parisian hospital, and she would not be turned away now. She took a hesitant step towards the door, then a more determined one, and another. Bracing herself on the frame with one hand, she hammered the door with a fist. The porter peered at her through the peephole.

"Go away, woman! I've told you—"

"Monsieur, please! My house has burned to the ground, so I can't go home. And my confinement has come."

Her cultured accent must have reassured him that she wasn't a mere vagabond looking for charity, despite that being closer to the truth than Adelaide cared to admit. The porter opened the door and approached, then held out an arm for her to take. His face was now a mask of concern, though whether for her or himself, she could not say.

"Madame, I apologize. Please come inside. I'll fetch one of the sisters to aid you."

He led Adelaide inside and helped her settle onto a carved wooden bench. He then rang a bell then stood waiting for response. Adelaide rubbed her belly, wishing she could lie down. She had never been so exhausted.

A woman clad in flowing grey robes and headdress appeared in a doorway and approached them, a frown creasing her face.

Is that a nun? I didn't think we had any nuns in France. So much has changed with this new king. What is she doing here?

The porter gestured towards Adelaide. "Nurse Emard, this lady is in need of assistance."

Nurse? This nun is a nurse? What happened to the nurses trained by the Academy?

Adelaide hoisted herself to her feet. The Emard woman regarded her, pursed lips telegraphing her disapproval. "Are you looking for your husband, Madame? Or are you injured?"

A contraction gripped Adelaide and she winced, gripping her belly. "No. Not injured. Baby coming."

The porter spoke up. "Madame says that her house has burned, and . . ."

Nurse Emard turned a quelling look on the porter, then beckoned to Adelaide. "This way, Madame. Can you walk or should I summon orderlies?"

As answer, Adelaide tottered forward. Her damp petticoats clung to her legs. Her hair fell across her face, the smell of smoke choking her. Perhaps a hot bath would be recommended by this stern nun. Adelaide was so desperate to be clean.

She followed Nurse Emard through the marble hallways of the hospital, struggling to keep up with the nun's brisk pace. She looked longingly at the wooden benches lining the corridor, wanting nothing more than to sit down. They passed more of the nun-nurses, walking in pairs and conversing in hushed tones. The hospital was enormous, Adelaide recalled.

It seemed as if they'd traversed the entire length of the building when at last, they reached a ward lined on either side with at least twenty beds. Tall windows illuminated the women occupying the beds, from young girls to elderly ladies. With a doctor's eye, Adelaide scanned the patients, spotting bandages on some, the signs of fever in others. It appeared to be a general women's ward, not a maternity ward.

The nun, Nurse Emard, called across the room to a grey-haired woman clad in a simple linen gown, who was bent to the work of scrubbing the floor. "Madame Azoulay, it appears we will require your skills."

The woman glanced up and her eyes widened when she caught sight of Adelaide.

She climbed to her feet, wiping her hands on her apron. She walked to Adelaide and held out her hand to shake. "Madame, I am Lucie Azoulay. I am the midwife here. It is not often that the Sisters require my assistance." Her clasp was strong and warm, surprising considering her advanced age. She smiled into Adelaide's eyes. "How long have you been feeling pains? Is this your first child?"

Adelaide tried to smiled in return but her face was tight with strain. The contractions were almost continuous. "All day. Yes. My first."

Lucie placed a gentle arm around Adelaide's shoulders. "Let's find you a bed. Perhaps there's a quieter room available, Sister? These events are better when there are not quite so many witnesses. We wouldn't want to disturb your other patients."

Nurse Emard sniffed. "You'll have to speak to the ward sister. I have say only over my own ward, to which I must now return." She spun on her heel and tromped out.

Lucie shrugged. "Nurse Emard is always such a delight. Come along, dear. I'm sure the ward nurse will be able to find us a private spot."

Adelaide nodded, too weary to speak. She followed Lucie to the nurses' station in the center of the ward. When would this pain be over? Her lower back cramped and she stopped to rub at it. The half-corset she still wore didn't allow for real relief.

Lucie watched her and clicked her tongue. "Still wearing a corset? I don't understand that practice at all. Come, we need to get you out of these clothes. What happened to you? Your clothing is full of smoke."

"A fire. My house . . . it was burned."

Lucie's expression of sympathy brought Adelaide to tears. No-one else had seemed to care. Adelaide sniffed and rubbed at her nose with a dirty cuff.

I hate being so pathetic. When will these easy tears dry up?

The ward nurse appeared and had a quick conversation with Lucie. They led Adelaide to a small anteroom with a bed and a basin. It looked like the night staff's room, but Adelaide was past caring. She lowered herself to the bed and kicked at her shoes. They were firmly laced, thanks to Zilda. Lucie knelt and untied them for her, then briskly removed Adelaide's clothing. Adelaide burned with embarrassment. Nudity was not something she was used to and avoided it whenever possible. Lucie covered her with a sheet, then proceeded to examine her. Adelaide stared at the cracked ceiling, willing herself gone from this place.

"You are progressing nicely. I think we can give you a sponge bath before the child is born. That will relax you and make the birth easier."

Bath? Did she say bath? With warm water?

Lucie fetched a basin of water and gently washed Adelaide then toweled her dry and braided her hair. The pain had not ceased throughout the process, but at last, Adelaide was clean, and that made every contraction easier to bear.

ಙ Φ ಚ

The sky outside was darkening and Adelaide still labored. Lucie continued to reassure her with gentle words.

I'm never doing this again. I don't care how charming he is, no man will ever touch me again. It's not worth this pain.

She rode the waves of pain higher and higher and just when she was sure she couldn't continue, a burning ring of pain tore her open and her child was born. Lucie cut the umbilical cord and wrapped the infant with practiced, efficient movements. She placed the squalling red bundle in Adelaide's arms. "You have a fine, healthy boy, Madame."

Adelaide looked down at her son and burst into tears.

Lucie patted her shoulder. "You did well, madame. There's just a little bit left to do. Push now." She kneaded Adelaide's belly like a loaf of bread. More cramping and pain. The baby quieted and nuzzled at her chest, distracting Adelaide from the pain. Blinking through tears, she stared down at her son.

I have a son.

She touched his tiny cheek with one fingertip. He turned his head to suckle on it briefly, then closed his eyes. Adelaide watched, entranced, as his eyelashes fluttered and his rosebud mouth pursed.

"Madame, I need you to push. The afterbirth is still inside you."

Adelaide grimaced, not sure what was happening. Hadn't she just been pushing for hours? What more did she have to do. At that, a deep cramp gripped her and she gasped. A flood of liquid gushed out of her. Lucie frowned and reached for the clean bundle of rags she had prepared. She shoved the rags between Adelaide's legs and pushed hard.

"What are you doing? That hurts." The absurdity of that statement struck Adelaide as funny and she snorted a laugh.

"No, don't laugh. Hold still. You're bleeding too much."

Coldness filled her. Bleeding too much? That didn't sound good. She held herself as still as she could, but could feel the blood leaking out of her, drenching the rags that Lucie held in place. The metallic tang of blood filled the small room. The midwife's face was pale and drawn. "I need to get help. Don't move." She got to her feet and ran from the room.

Adelaide looked down at her sleeping child. Was she going to die, leaving him alone with strangers? She caressed his head, noting idly that his hair was already dark and curly and his skin a rich brown. Like Henri. He'd be a beautiful boy if he took after his father. The room darkened and she grew cold. She tightened her grip on the child, not wanting to drop him, and he woke with an angry cry. Her arms felt like lead weights and the rest of her body was numb. Exhaustion washed over her and her eyelids fluttered closed.

A commotion at the door woke her and she peered at the trio of nun-nurses, their robes and headdresses looking like dove wings. Lucie stood behind them. "She's lost too much blood and it won't stop. You need to help her. Please, Sisters."

The nun-nurses regarded Adelaide and her wailing child. One of them shook her head. "We've not been trained in childbirth, Madame Azoulay. I don't know if we can help."

Another nun-nurse stepped into the room. "Nonsense, Sister. We will simply pray for guidance and the Holy Spirit will fill us with Their power." She came to stand over Adelaide and raised her arms in supplication, whispering a prayer. The other two nun-nurses followed their sister's lead. Lucie watched, swaying with the rhythm of their prayers, her face slack.

What are they doing? Praying over me? Am I going to die?

Warmth filled Adelaide's body and she felt as if a weight had lifted from her swollen, aching body. The women's voices droned and Adelaide felt the vibrations move through her, easing the pain. She drifted into darkness.

ఠ Φ ⋒

Adelaide was drowning. Icy, dark water soaked through her clothing, dragging her down. She clawed for anything that might help her stay afloat, and her hands found something soft and warm. She clutched it tight and woke with a start as the baby gave a sharp cry. She looked to the bassinet next to her bed. Her hand was wound up in the rough linen swaddling her child. Only his curly head was visible. Adelaide sat up and a wave of dizziness hit her.

She rubbed her forehead and took a deep breath. She felt weak and empty. The baby continued to wail so she leaned over to pick him up. Black spots swam through her vision and she laid back, leaving her hand over his brow, rubbing softly. "Hush, little one, I'll be there in a moment. Just give me a little time to breathe." The infant's screams grew louder. The ancient woman in the bed next to Adelaide grumbled under her breath. Adelaide darted a look at her. "Sorry. He's probably hungry or wet or something. I don't know." She peered over the side of her bed at the baby, trying not to move her head too much.

A nun-nurse scampered to her bed, her young face creased with worry. "You must tend to your child, Madame. Or are you still too unwell?"

"I'm very dizzy. I felt as if I would faint when I leaned over to pick him up."

The nun-nurse nodded. "You are blood deficient, madame. It will take some days for you to regain your strength." She reached into the bassinet and picked up the sobbing baby. "Now, now, stop that fuss, little one. Here's your maman." She handed the baby to Adelaide. "He'll want to nurse, then I will take him and clean him."

Adelaide took the warm little body in her arms and marveled once again at his tiny head. He quieted, his face solemn like a little old man. He gazed back at her with eyes a dark shade of blue-brown. They were ringed with thick, curly lashes, so unlike her own sparse ones.

"What am I going to do with you, little one? You don't even have a name."

The nun-nurse hovered next to Adelaide's bed. "It is your first child? You should name him for your husband.

Oh Madame, your husband will want to know about his child! Should we send word to him that you are here?"

Adelaide bit her lip, not meeting the young woman's eyes. "There was a fire. Our house was destroyed, burned to the ground. There is no one to send word to."

The young nun's eyes filled with tears. "Oh, Madame, I am so sorry for your loss. But your son is safe, as are you. And that is even more reason to name the boy for his father."

Why did I make her think that I had a husband who died in the house fire? I shouldn't care what she thinks. They won't throw me on the street if they find out the child is illegitimate. Or will they? I don't know what creed these nuns follow. Still, the boy has to have a name, and Henri is common enough.

Adelaide attempted a smile but it wavered. "Yes, of course. In my grief, I hadn't thought of that. His name will be Henri. Henri Coumain."

Giving her son the artist's last name seemed a little too presumptuous, even if the man was in exile.

The young nun-nurse nodded her head happily. "A fine name, honoring His Majesty as well as your departed husband. I'll let the registrar know so she can write it in our records."

At that, Adelaide had to stifle a snort. Why had she not stopped to consider that? The idea of honoring the man who had outlawed Science! And as for the artist Henri being departed, she knew only that he had departed the shores of France, not the earthly plane. But it was too late now. The nun-nurse was already trotting out of the ward to complete her duty.

The midwife Lucie was Adelaide's next visitor. "Good morning, Madame. How are you feeling? The baby is looking well. Has he nursed?"

Adelaide shrugged and held the baby out for the midwife to examine. Lucie examined the infant, smiling at him as she turned him this way and that, hefted him as if to gauge his weight. Seemingly satisfied that all was well, she returned the child to Adelaide, who held him close to her bosom. She then gritted her teeth and concentrated her attention on the rhythm of her and her son's breathing, while Lucie conducted an under the sheet examination.

"You will need to stay here for a few days to regain your strength. Have you family to go to afterwards? You said your house burned down and the sister has just told me that your husband did not survive, you poor dear." Lucie patted Adelaide's hand.

Adelaide swallowed down her sudden panic. "I have nowhere to go. No family. I don't know anything about babies." A tiny sob escaped her.

"There, there. None of us knows anything about babies with our first. But you know, many Parisian mothers send their children for fostering in the country. Since you have no home for the child, that may be a good thing. Just until you find yourself a new home."

Fostering the baby had sounded like a good plan when it was suggested at the farmhouse, while she was still pregnant. But now, with her son nestled in her arms, every fiber of her being rebelled against the idea. "Send him away? To strangers? I don't know if I can do that."

Lucie nodded. "You're still raw from the birth. Those feelings will settle down, madame. You'll see the practicality of fostering. You have nowhere to go. Will you wander the streets with a tiny babe at your breast, begging for food?

Or enter him into an overcrowded creche where he would sicken? Let the sisters find a foster home for him since you are currently under their care. You can reclaim him in a couple of years when you are back on your feet."

Adelaide bit her lip, blinking back tears. The baby woke and wailed his hunger. Adelaide clumsily tried to nurse him but the baby grew more frustrated. "What am I doing wrong?"

"Nothing. You have no milk yet. If the foster mother comes, she will already have milk flowing. That would be better for the little one, no?"

Adelaide's arms were weak and heavy but she clutched tighter to her child. "It wouldn't be permanent? I can have my son returned to me when I'm established?"

Lucie assured her. "Indeed, madame. The foster mother will bring your child back once he has reached two or three years of age. That is most often what occurs." She finished with a sideways glance, as if holding something back.

"What else occurs? Lucie?"

"It is nothing, madame. Nothing so important as the blessing you hold in your arms."

Adelaide scrutinized the midwife's face, seeking for the truth she was not revealing, but Lucie merely smiled again, and gazed down at the child. Adelaide found herself following the midwife's lead, and studied her son's face, trying to memorize the details. Fostering was truly her only choice now. She could not survive on the streets with him requiring her constant care and attention. She could barely imagine surviving out there by herself.

Little Henri gave a cough, and gurgled some spittle onto Adelaide's gown. The midwife quickly wiped away the mess with a cloth and a dish of water kept by the bedside.

"I will fetch the sisters, madame, and you can let them know of your decision." Lucie said, and then she was gone.

Adelaide stroked Henri's back, patting him and feeling the warmth and weight of his tiny body. If she let him go, when would she see him again?

Ten

Baby Henri howled, his face red with frustration. Adelaide adjusted her grip and tried to hold him closer to her exposed breast. He swung his head back and forth, mouth gaping. She shifted her torso to move him closer, but the pillow slipped from under her arm. The baby's head slipped away from her proffered breast. His screams grew more shrill. Adelaide winced and shot an apologetic look at her neighbor in the next bed. The wizened old woman smiled vacantly and coughed, the wet, raspy sound coming from deep in her chest. Adelaide gazed down at her baby and bit her lip, tears slipping down her cheeks. This wasn't going well at all. Henri was four days old and Adelaide hadn't been able to nurse him. Would he starve before the foster mother arrived? She tried again to latch him on. He suckled for a few seconds then pulled away, screaming his frustration. Adelaide ran her fingers through his soft curls and made shushing noises, trying to soothe him.

"Here, this will help." Lucie had approached the bed without Adelaide noticing. The midwife held out a glass bottle filled with cloudy liquid; a rubber nipple attached to the top.

Adelaide heaved a sigh of relief. "You're an angel. Is that a feeding bottle? Where did you find it?"

Lucie shrugged. "Not at this hospital. Never mind. Offer it to the baby. Sit him up a little so he doesn't choke on it."

Adelaide squinted at the proffered bottle. "That's not milk. What is it?" She frowned at Lucie. "It's not that awful tea, is it?"

Lucie snorted and pushed the bottle into Adelaide's hand. "It's barley water. I made it myself. I wouldn't trust the milk in Paris. Who knows what's in it. The barley water will keep him going until the foster mother gets here."

Adelaide took the bottle and offered it to the baby. He suckled at the nipple, eyes closed with contentment. Adelaide sighed, her body relaxing. "Thank you, Lucie. I'm not sure we could have stood any more of his crying."—

The baby stopped sucking at the bottle. His head slumped back over Adelaide's hand and he seemed to be sleeping. Lucie sat down on the cot next to Adelaide. She sat the baby back up and thumped his back. "You need to get the wind out or he'll have cramps."

Adelaide nodded. Henri's body was warm and heavy and she adjusted him so that he rested against her. She closed the bodice of her nightgown. He wouldn't be needing her for sustenance anymore.

"When will she be here to take him from me?" Adelaide caressed the baby's head with a gentle hand. His soft breathing soothed her and her breathing slowed to match his.

"Some time today ... ah, it looks like she's here now." Lucie stood to greet the plump young woman in a tidy traveling dress and cloak crossing the ward.

Adelaide jerked, disturbing the baby who woke with a wail. So soon? She had hoped for another day or two before giving him up.

Lucie introduced the foster mother. "Madame Coumain, this is Madame Joubert. She will be your baby's foster mother."

Madame Joubert didn't smile. "Good morning, madame. And this is the child?"

"Yes. His name is Henri."

"I just call them all Baby. Saves confusion."

Adelaide shot a look of concern at Lucie and tightened her grip on the baby. Lucie shrugged, a look of apology crossing her face. Madame Joubert reached down and plucked baby Henri from Adelaide's arms.

"We need to go now. My husband is waiting outside in the cart."

Adelaide surged forward, reaching up for the baby. "No, please, don't take him yet. Just a few more moments."

Madame Joubert's expression softened. The baby stirred and she sat down and unbuttoned her dress. "Well, perhaps he can nurse a little before we go. We'll stay a little longer so that he can eat."

"Thank you." Adelaide whispered. Dizziness swept through her. She shouldn't have moved so quickly. She settled back on the lumpy pillows of her cot and watched her baby nurse at another woman's breast. Jealousy tore at her. She should be the one nursing her child. Baby Henri's eyes closed in satisfaction as he suckled. Adelaide clenched her hands, willing herself to be silent. He needed the milk. It didn't matter who provided it. She knew that but she hated it, feeling less of a mother because she was allowing another woman to feed her child. Baby Henri finished nursing and Madame Joubert raised him to her shoulder, patting his back until he burped.

"There you are, all done, Baby. Good boy." She rose with the baby resting in her arms, a move that looked practiced.

"How many children do you have, Madame Joubert? You seem so easy with my baby."

Adelaide hoped to delay the woman with a little conversation. Just a few more minutes.

Madame Joubert wrinkled her nose in a frown. "Does it matter? I have three little ones. Don't you worry, madame, I have plenty of milk for Baby here."

Adelaide tried not to wince. Couldn't she at least try to call him by his name? "I thank you, madame."

"It's my job, madame. We're off. I suppose we'll see you in a few months when we bring Baby in for the nuns to see him." She strolled away, hips swaying under her skirts.

Adelaide suppressed her anguished cry with a hand to her mouth. She watched the foster woman carrying away baby Henri until they passed through the ward door. Only then did she let her tears fall. Adelaide hid her face in the rough grey linen pillow. Lucie's gentle hand rubbed her back.

"I know it's hard to let him go but it's for the best."

Adelaide raised her head. Her face was wet and felt swollen. "But what if she neglects him? She wouldn't even say his name."

"The foster mothers are all registered by the municipal employment bureau. If she neglected her charges, they would find out and not pay her. And she'll be back with him in a couple of months for the nuns to do their inspection. Try not to worry."

Adelaide sniffled and dragged a hand across her nose. "I know. But I can't help but cry all time. I hate being so irrational. I never cry."

Lucie chuckled and patted Adelaide's back. "You'll feel better soon, I promise."

Adelaide flopped over onto her back. The weakness still lingered. "I hope so. Oh, Lucie, did I really do the right thing? I can't help but think he should be with me. It hurts that he's not here."

    Lucie smiled but her eyes were sad. "I know."

Eleven

It had been a week since Adelaide had watched the foster mother take baby Henri. The comings and goings of the nun-nurses and their orderlies were Adelaide's only source of entertainment as she lay in a narrow cot recovering from Henri's birth. Her chest was wrapped with layers of tight bandages to suppress her milk flow. A physical longing for her baby filled her and tears constantly threatened. The other patients on the ward all seemed to be coughing their last. Rather than feel sympathy for the ill and dying, Adelaide could only resent their raspy breaths and moans of pain.

Her newborn son was lost to a strange foster mother, and her mechanical child destroyed in a fire. She knew she was fortunate to have survived the birth but her grief overwhelmed her. Lucie had voiced concern, but no amount of sympathy could stop the darkness from filling Adelaide. She tried to distract herself by diagnosing her fellow patients. Despite her losses, at least she could think like the scientist-doctor she was. Many of them probably had the coughing sickness, their cheeks bright with fever. Despite that, Adelaide had seen no doctors in the week she spent there, just the nun-nurses praying over their patients.

Do they take the patients to a different part of the hospital for treatment? Or have they given up on these women?

One of the orderlies, a young woman with a pocked face, served Adelaide a bowl of thin gruel with odd leaves and chunks of unidentifiable meat. The midwife had told her it was supposed to tonify the blood and strengthen her after childbirth, but it left an acrid taste on her tongue. Adelaide took the opportunity to question the orderly. "Mademoiselle, why do the doctors not treat the women in this ward?"

The girl's mouth dropped open and her eyes widened. "Hush, madame. We do not talk about the doctors. They're all gone. It is only the sisters now."

No doctors? What kind of hospital was this? No wonder I almost died.

"There are no doctors at all here?"

The young orderly shook her head. "Just the director, Dr. Dutrochet. She runs the hospital. But they don't let her treat the patients anymore. It's against the new policy." A nun-nurse entered the ward and the girl ducked her head and shuffled away, not looking back at Adelaide. Adelaide gaped after her. Sequestered in the countryside, she had not heard that the king's laws had prohibited the practice of medicine. How would people manage without proper medical care? She looked down at the gruel. Were they hoping this concoction would heal them?

The nun-nurse approached Adelaide's bed, a tight smile on her wrinkled face. "Madame Coumain, the midwife tells me that you are well enough to be discharged."

Adelaide's heart sank. She knew this was coming but she was no nearer to a solution to her homelessness. The idea of begging for a home with her Scientist colleagues didn't seem like a promising idea after all. And even if she were to do so, how might she find them? "Sister, I wonder if I might speak to the director about employment?"

The nun raised her eyebrows. "You want to work here at the hospital? To be sure, we always need more help but

I'm not sure that a woman of your status would be willing to do what we need."

"Perhaps I can talk to Dr. Dutrochet? She might be able to find something for me. I have skills that might be useful. Please, I don't know what to do now that I've lost everything." Tears blurred her vision. She was still too sensitive, and it gnawed at her that every utterance presented a challenge to her calm.

The nun sighed and rolled her eyes. "Very well, madame. Get dressed and I will take you to the director's office." The nuns had provided a dress for Adelaide since the one she wore when she arrived was destroyed. Adelaide pulled on the new dress over her linen nightgown, wincing at the itchy wool fabric. The dull grey dress hung on her like a burlap sack full of sugar beets. There was no corset to constrain her waist or soft petticoats caressing her legs. She missed the swish of taffeta,

No one at the Palace would recognize me looking like this.

She ran her finger along the high neckline to ease the roughness rubbing against her skin. At least the dress was clean and didn't smell of smoke. She smoothed back her frizzled hair and considered rebraiding it, but the nun waited nearby, arms crossed. Adelaide stood up straight and threw her shoulders back. She lifted her chin, emulating the haughty nobles she'd served what seemed like an eternity ago. "I'm ready to speak to Dr. Dutrochet now. You may lead me to her office."

The nun-nurse blinked at Adelaide's imperious tone but without hesitation gestured for her to follow. Adelaide smoothed the rough wool over her still protuberant belly. How long would it be until she looked and felt herself again?

The checkered marble floors and lofty ceilings of the corridors reminded Adelaide of Versailles. Through the high arched windows, she glimpsed greenery. Was there a garden beyond these walls? She suddenly longed to walk amongst flowers, inhaling their fragrance. She would investigate the courtyard later, if she managed to secure employment here.

The hospital director's office was tucked away under a curving staircase. Its wooden door was ajar and a woman's voice echoed from within. "Nurse Emard, I am troubled by the incidences of fever on your ward. Do your assistants wash their hands before attending the patients?"

A sharp voice retorted, dripping with disdain. "We don't hold with the philosophies of Science, Madame Director. The Holy Spirit cleanses us as is needed. The worthy patients are healed and the sinners suffer."

Adelaide threw a sideways glance at the nun-nurse who had escorted her. Her face was blank of expression. She clasped her hands at her waist and seemed to be willing to wait as long as needed for the director's time.

"Very well, sister. You may return to your ward. And perhaps you could say an extra prayer or two for the fevers to abate?" The woman's voice sounded weary and defeated.

Nurse Emard swept out of the office, a smug smile tracing her lips. Upon seeing Adelaide and the nun-nurse who accompanied her, Nurse Emard furrowed her brow, as if trying to place Adelaide in memory. She moved past the pair without a word. Adelaide remembered her all too well. Her second impression of the woman was no better than the first.

"There you are, madame," her escort said. "The director appears to be free now. I'll leave you to it." The nun-nurse walked away without a second glance.

Taking a steadying breath, Adelaide approached the office door and tentatively knocked. "May I come in, Dr. Dutrochet?"

"Enter. And who might you be?" The woman sitting at a cluttered desk looked kind but harried. Her gown was fashionable and made of rich green wool. Her black hair was pulled back in an elaborate braid but ringlets had escaped to hang down around her face. She dragged her hand across her hair. "Well? I haven't got all day."

Adelaide flushed and gripped her hands in front of her. "I find myself in a predicament, Madame Director, and wonder if you could be of assistance."

Dr. Dutrochet sat back in her chair as far as her bustled dress would allow and waved a hand. "Please, don't hover at the door. Come in and sit down, madame. Tell me of this predicament."

Adelaide sat in a rickety wooden chair that creaked when she lowered herself into it. "Thank you, Madame Director. I am Adelaide Coumain. I recently gave birth, here in your hospital, after losing my home in a fire. I have no one to turn to, so the nuns arranged to send my child to be fostered. But I am at a loss. I need a job and somewhere to stay. I trained as a doctor and a surgeon, among other things, although it seems my skills are no longer needed in the current climate."

"Adelaide Coumain?" Dr. Dutrochet hissed through her teeth and a look of concern creased her face. "Close the door if you would, madame."

Adelaide hoisted her lumbering body off the chair to push the door closed, then returned to sit. Why did Adelaide's name cause the director so much concern?

Dr. Dutrochet sighed and leaned forward; her green eyes fixed on Adelaide's. "My dear Madame Coumain, you must realize that it is not safe to be a Scientist in today's France, and especially not at this hospital. You would be wise to not to speak of your training outside this room. I am only here on sufferance because my uncle is on the board of regents. Even as the director, I am not permitted to practice medicine. I simply supervise the nun-nurses and orderlies and make sure they feed the patients." Her tone was bitter. "So what need do I have of a doctor or surgeon?"

Adelaide sank lower into her seat and grimaced. "One of the orderlies told me there were no doctors permitted here. And the nurses were all dismissed as well?"

Adelaide could almost hear Dr. Dutrochet grinding her teeth. "Yes, all of them were dismissed. The new regime believes that all ill health is due to impurity and can be resolved with prayer. That is why the king allowed the Sisters of Mercy to take over the hospital. They perform their prayers to heal the patients. But they can't be bothered with the merest amount of hygiene so too many patients become ill with fevers and infections. And for every success they can boast of we lose at least twice as many to preventable sickness."

"How far we're reverted. I had no idea what was going on in the hospitals until I was admitted for my confinement."

"I'm surprised that you gave birth here. Most women stay home now. It is safer for them and their babies. The Sisters are not proficient in childbirth, it seems. Oh, but you said your home recently burned down. And you were unable to secure new lodgings?"

Dr. Dutrochet raised an eyebrow, and Adelaide for a moment worried she would be turned in to the new Police Secrète. Would the doctor do such a thing? She seemed sympathetic, but would some benefit await her should she inform the new regime of Adelaide's presence?

With a shaking breath, Adelaide attempted to calm her nerves, cursing her fragile state yet again. And now, with desperation clouding her thoughts, she found herself unable to contain the truth from Dr. Dutrochet.

"The—the house was not my own. Nor my husband's. I was staying there with my colleagues when it was burned."

"When it was burned. So the fire was set on purpose, Madame Coumain?"

Dr. Dutrochet's tone awoke something in Adelaide. A familiar feeling of being spoken to as both colleague and friend. "The king's soldiers came. The day before my child was born. My colleagues were arrested, but I was allowed to leave. They assumed I was a loose woman, not a Scientist. I made my way here, thinking a modern Parisian hospital would be superior to a dirty hovel somewhere. But I almost bled to death. The nun-nurses came to pray over me. I thought I was dying and receiving last rites."

Dr. Dutrochet's mouth twisted into a frown. "They were trying to heal you with their prayers, not send you into death. They heal through mysticism, not Science. But in your case, it seems to have worked. Or maybe you were merely lucky, and now that luck has given the Sisters another success to rally around." She shrugged. "Madame Coumain, I'm not sure this is the right place for you."

Adelaide felt unruly tears spring to her eyes. "I don't know that anywhere is the right place for me. But I'm here. Perhaps I could work as an orderly?"

Sadness filled Dr. Dutrochet's face. "A trained doctor and surgeon emptying bedpans and wiping the chins of derelicts? It seems a shameful waste of your skills."

"Indeed, but what else is there for me to do? I am a Scientist in a country that abhors Science."

"Hush, don't speak so loudly. I'm not sure where you've been for the past six months but all those who publicly declared themselves to be Scientists have been imprisoned or executed." She regarded Adelaide and silence settled in the room. Dr. Dutrochet stood and walked around the desk. She leaned over and took Adelaide's hands. "Madame, I don't want you to end up in prison too. I'll keep you safe here. You can work as an orderly and live in the women's dormitory. Just promise me that you will tell no one of your background."

Adelaide nodded. The director's hands were warm and comforting. Relief washed over her. She could do this. She shuddered at the thought of dealing with human filth, but she would have somewhere to stay and food to eat. Then, once she had regained her strength and saved some money, she could reclaim her son and move on.

ఠ Φ ଓ

The ward was still dark when Adelaide reported for duty on her first morning. The corridors from the dormitory had been cold and deserted. Was she the only orderly on duty so early? She rubbed the sleep out of her eyes and yawned. Not even a cup of tea had greeted her in the women's dining room, just more of the tonifying gruel. She thought longingly of the breakfast trays at the Palace, loaded with fresh pastries and good strong tea. She had taken them for granted, most days ignoring them altogether. Now she would dearly love just a morsel of a croissant.

Some of the patients were already awake, their eyes blinking at her in the dim light cast by the single lantern. Adelaide waited in the doorway for her new superior. Dr. Dutrochet had asked her to work in the veterans' ward under Nurse Emard. She had admonished Adelaide to not neglect hygiene despite what the nun-nurses might tell her. The director hoped that better hygiene would reduce fevers and infections in that ward. The stench of urine drifting from the room warned Adelaide that she had plenty of work to do in that regard.

"I've got a new orderly, the director tells me." Nurse Emard appeared behind Adelaide without warning. Adelaide jerked in surprise and turned to regard the nun-nurse. The woman's gangly frame was clad in the grey robes of the nun-nurses but to Adelaide's practiced eye, hers was made of a finer fabric than most.

"Nurse Emard. Good morning. I am indeed your new orderly, Adelaide Coumain."

The nun-nurse sniffed in disapproval. "What is a cultured lady like yourself doing here? I won't go easy on you, you know. You'd best work hard on my ward, Coumain. Can you do that?"

Adelaide raised her chin, staring down her nose at the nun-nurse but Nurse Emard was taller than her by several centimeters so the effect wasn't what Adelaide had intended. "You have no need for concern, Nurse Emard. I'm not afraid of hard work."

Nurse Emard snorted, her mouth twisted in disdain. "I don't know about that. You just birthed a child, right? We'll see if you're as tough as you say. Come along, first thing you do every morning is empty the bedpans." Her beady eyes pinned down Adelaide, watching for a reaction. Adelaide's stomach turned at the thought of the bedpans but she kept her face carefully neutral. Nurse Emard grumbled under her breath and stalked into the ward. Adelaide dutifully followed.

Nurse Emard directed her to take the full, stinking bedpans to the ward's only bathroom. Adelaide suppressed her gagging and carried two at a time, careful not to spill any of the contents. The facilities were lit by oil lanterns hung haphazardly on the winding, ornate pipework. The build-in gas lamps were not in use. Adelaide puzzled at that. Were they broken? She dumped the bedpans into a grimy toilet and pulled the lever but no water flowed. She leaned over to inspect the workings and saw that the water valve was turned off. She shrugged. No wonder the toilet was so filthy, they were meant to flow with water. Adelaide turned on the water and flushed the toilet.

"What are you doing in here?" Nurse Emard spoke behind her. Adelaide uttered a small shriek. The woman moved like a cat.

Adelaide held out the empty bedpans. "Doing as you directed, Nurse Emard."

The nun-nurse peered at the toilet. "I heard running water but we had these pipes turned off. We don't allow technology."

Adelaide gaped at her. "Not even running water? Even the Romans had running water and that was millennia ago."

Nurse Emard sneered. "Romans? A bunch of pagans to be sure. His Majesty has decreed there is to be no use of technology and these pipes and mechanisms seem to be technology to me."

Adelaide spluttered. Where did these bizarre nuns with their rigid views come from? Had they been in hiding all along or was this something new? "How do you expect to keep a city hospital clean without running water? We're not in the countryside with clean streams to wash away the filth."

Nurse Emard fixed her with a baleful glare. "You're an orderly, Coumain. I don't know what you did before you came here, with your fancy accent and attitude, but in this ward, I'm in charge. You don't use this unholy technology. Do you understand?"

Adelaide nodded. She would have to be careful to keep her efforts at sanitation secret from the nun-nurses.

Nurse Emard bustled out of the bathroom. "You have to work quicker, Coumain. There's a lot to do this morning. My other orderly won't be here until midday. Feed the patients, then I'll show you how to change bandages. I doubt you know how."

Adelaide almost spoke up. The words were on her tongue, but she bit them back, remembering Dr. Dutrochet's warning.

Tell no one of your background.

Adelaide followed Nurse Emard, squinting at the sunlight streaming in through the high windows of the ward. It revealed the faces of patients marked with sores and misery. Adelaide moved quickly to remove and dump the remaining bedpans. This was not going to be her favorite part of the day. She was careful not to flush the water while Nurse Emard was in earshot but determined to turn the water back on when she was gone. Adelaide washed her hands with a bucket of water, sighing at the waste of a perfectly useful sink that was also turned off. She dumped the dirty water into a toilet and carried the bucket back into the ward.

"Nurse Emard. This bucket of water will need to be refilled. Where am I to get more if I can't use the taps in the bathroom?" She worked to keep her tone civil but found herself clenching her teeth.

The nun-nurse stared at her balefully. "Go to the courtyard. The outside pumps work."

Outside pumps? Am I back in the wilds of Picardy?

Adelaide hefted the wooden bucket. Apparently metal was too modern for the nuns. At least she would have an opportunity to investigate the courtyard.

The sunlight glowed with the richness of autumn when she stepped outside. For the first time in what felt like months, Adelaide breathed in fully, inhaling the fragrance of a garden in its last gasp of summer, overblown rose blossoms and decomposing leaves mingling to delight her nose. She closed her eyes and relaxed, a smile across her face.

"I see that I'm not the only one who enjoys the garden."

Adelaide's eyes flew open. Dr. Dutrochet was seated on a stone bench, half-hidden behind shrubbery. She smiled at Adelaide, smile lines gathering at the corner of her eyes. "No need for concern, my dear. There's no harm in being here. The adoration of Nature is one of His Majesty's highest ideals after all. No one can fault you for lingering in the gardens and enjoying the plants and birds."

Adelaide ducked her head, a shy smile tugging up her mouth. "I've always loved flower gardens. It's one thing I really miss about ..."

She shook her head. No need to bring up her time at Versailles. It would only lead to awkward questions.

"About what? Your past is mysterious, Madame Coumain. Were you once a noble lady before things changed?"

Adelaide snorted. "Noble lady? Not I. I merely served."

"Served who? The old Court? The gardens at Versailles are stunning but I rarely visit. Were you in service there?"

Adelaide closed her eyes again, picturing the lush rose garden where she used to walk daily. Where she first encountered Henri, the man who would give her the child she just birthed. She knew better than to reveal that detail, but perhaps she could share her memory of the gardens safely. "I loved being able to wander through the gardens of Versailles. I haven't seen them for a long time. My life has changed."

"Indeed, as have all our lives, Madame Coumain."

"Indeed, as you say. Now I must fetch water since Nurse Emard does not allow the use of indoor plumbing." Her tone was sarcastic, drawing a chuckle from Dr. Dutrochet.

"Well, Nurse Emard does sometimes leave the ward, you know. I'm sure you're resourceful enough to manage her ... eccentricities."

The women exchanged a sly smile. Warmth stole through Adelaide's body. It seemed there were some good things about this hospital. Bidding the director farewell, she located the pump, filled her bucket, and headed back to the reeking ward.

Nurse Emard was waiting for her, foot tapping with impatience. "You're too slow, Coumain. I sent you for water ages ago. Were you napping in the sun?"

Adelaide smiled in return. She wasn't about to let this bitter nun-nurse steal her serenity. "No, simply enjoying the grandeur of the morning. The courtyard flowers are still in bloom."

Nurse Emard growled, a sour expression twisting her features. "Grandeur? You're not here to enjoy yourself, Coumain, you're here to work. Do you want to keep this job or should I tell the director to get me an orderly who will work? You're here as a special favor to Dr. Dutrochet, but if you won't work, you're out. Got it?"

Adelaide swallowed her fear. She needed this job, as menial as it was, until she could establish herself again. "Yes, ma'am. I understand. I will work as you require." Her arms ached from the weight of the full bucket but Nurse Emard still regarded her with her stony gaze. "May I go?"

Nurse Emard waved her away. "The patients are still waiting to break their fast so make it quick."

The bucket bumped against Adelaide's leg and sloshed onto the floor as she hastened to the bathroom. She grimaced at the puddle. At least it would be an excuse to clean the floor. If she could find some soap and cleaning cloths in this squalid place. The patients watched her as she passed, ready to be fed. The floor would have to wait. She washed her hands again then reported back to Nurse Emard.

"The pot of gruel is over there on the sideboard. Bowls are there too." She pointed to one corner of the ward. "Those patients need to be spoon fed. The others can manage themselves."

The gruel looked no more appetizing than what she'd had herself in the dormitory. It was probably the same stuff, full of bitter herbs and cheap meat. She slopped it into chipped porcelain bowls. The men didn't seem to care how appetizing the food was. They slurped and chewed through their portions before she had served all of them. That left those who needed to be spoon fed. She approached the corner of the room on slow feet, hesitant to approach the drooling, stinking babies age and illness had made of these men. Adelaide gulped and sat down next to one of them, a wizened little man with wispy white hair sticking out in all directions. His eyes were milky white with blindness but he turned his head at her approach. "Is it my breakfast? About time, I'm starving."

"I apologize for the delay, monsieur. I am new to my duties."

He harrumphed and opened his mouth like a baby bird waiting for a worm. She spooned the gruel into him. He smacked his lips loudly after every bite, then burped when she'd finished feeding him. She wiped his mouth with a stained napkin, mentally noting the need to find clean linens. The veteran grinned a toothless grin and Adelaide moved on. The last veteran in the little cohort was much younger than the others. His dark hair was overlong and plastered to his sweating face. He appeared to be tall but much too thin. His cheekbones jutted out and his neck muscles stuck out like rigid cords under his skin. Adelaide murmured a greeting but he ignored her, staring straight up at the domed ceiling. She settled down next to him on a low stool and held out a spoonful of gruel.

"Don't want it."

Adelaide frowned. No wonder he was so emaciated if he was refusing to eat. What was the matter with him? He looked feverish, so she leaned forward and placed a hand on his forehead.

"Don't touch me. What are you doing?" His scowl turned to her. She noted that despite his ill-kempt and emaciated appearance, he was a handsome man.

"Checking you for fever." Her tone was calm, her standard approach to dealing with upset patients.

"Why? You're not one of those nun-nurses. You're just a servant."

A flare of anger triggered her snappish response. "And you're a rude boy. You don't seem to be feverish, just petulant. Why are you refusing to eat?"

He turned back to his regard of the ceiling. "What's the point of eating? Just prolongs the pain."

Adelaide scanned his figure under the blankets with a physician's eye. He seemed to be intact with no bulky bandages. "Where is the pain, monsieur?"

"Legs." He threw back the covers, revealing brass and leather where his legs should have been.

Augmented. He's one of the Augmented soldiers. I might have been an assistant at the surgery that replaced his healthy young legs with these prosthetics, all to make him a faster, stronger soldier.

"Ah. I see. They pain you?"

"Ever since I was discharged and didn't have the benefit of regular maintenance by the army scientist-doctors. And now that all of the Scientists are dead or in prison, there's no hope that someone can fix them and stop the pain."

"Can't the nun-nurses pray away your pain?" Adelaide's tone was half-mocking.

He fixed her with a suspicious look, one eyebrow raised. "Don't you believe in our Sisters of Mercy and their holy powers?"

She shrugged. He guffawed and pulled the covers back over his mechanical legs. "They won't touch me. I'm too tainted by forbidden technology. So here I am, too weak to get out of bed and the pain worsening every day."

Adelaide reached out and touched his shoulder. "Not all the Scientists who survived the purge are in prison."

He shot her a wide-eyed look, then glanced around the room. Nurse Emard was at the nurses' station, frowning as she scrawled in her notebook. He lowered his tone. "In hiding?"

She nodded.

The young veteran clasped her hand. "Madame, I would be forever your slave if you could find one to help me." He kissed her palm, his lips hot against her skin. She pulled away, her heart thudding and a queasy feeling filling her belly. He reminded her of Henri and his seductive endearments.

Adelaide got to her feet, catching Nurse Emard's scowling regard. "No promises. I'll do what I can." She scurried from his bedside, carrying the bowl back to the serving area.

I'll need to find tools and some quiet time to examine him. I didn't even think to ask his name.

His name didn't matter but his need for her skills filled her with new hope. Perhaps this job was exactly where she needed to be. Repairing the Augmented veterans who ended up here could be a way for her to use her skills, as long as Nurse Emard didn't find out and report her.

Twelve

Henri sat in Gleyre's airy dining room and sipped at a bitter cafe au lait. Isabelle always over brewed the coffee. He smiled across the mahogany table at his sleepy wife. She had dark smudges under her eyes and her skin looked ashy. Mornings were difficult for her. She picked at her pastry, her coffee untouched. She sighed then met his eyes. "What are your plans for today, cheri?"

Henri lowered his cup to the saucer with a clink. "I thought to head to Versailles. It's about time I visited the king, let him know we're in Paris."

She brightened up. "Excellent idea. You can ask him for your fee for his paintings you did in England. I still think it was rude of him to return to France without paying you first."

John entered the dining room, overhearing her last sentence, and laughed. "I think being crowned king might have been a little bit more pressing."

Henri and Isabelle looked up at him with smiles. Isabelle shrugged. "I suppose."

Henri waved John over to the table and offered him the basket of pastries. "I'm heading out to Versailles today. Would you like to join me?"

John's face fell and he shuddered. "No. I don't want to go to Versailles. I don't think I'll ever want to go there again." He sat down next to Henri and reached for a pastry. "Any more coffee?"

Henri winced. Of course John didn't want to go. He hadn't been back since Marie-Ange had died in front of him in a corridor at Versailles. "But the king will wonder why you're not coming to present yourself at Court."

John didn't look at Henri. He poured himself a cup of coffee and stirred sugar into it. "I'm not French. I don't have to serve the king."

"But you'll get more commissions at Court. You were always very popular there."

John shot a sideways glance at Henri. "Plenty of rich socialites in Paris. I don't need to go to Court again. I'm surprised you want to go."

"He needs to collect his fee." Isabelle grabbed the empty coffeepot and stood. "Do you want another au lait, cheri?"

Henri shook his head. He could barely get down the first one. "I can't be choosy about commissions now. We need the money. I'll go and ask Arthur for a train timetable. I think I spotted him walking in the garden when we came down."

John craned his neck, trying to see out of the window into the garden. "In this rain?"

Henri lurched to his feet and the chair scraped the parquet floor. "Rain during the day! Glorious, is it not? Nature untrammeled. But it's only drizzling. He won't melt." He sauntered to the window and peered out. "Yes, he's out there. Be right back."

Rain spattered his face as he stepped through the French doors into the garden. He shivered. Water dripped from the lush greenery, leaving the flagstones slick. Henri looked up at the drizzling sky and decided not to go further. He was in his shirtsleeves and didn't want to get damp before going out. Arthur stood close to a bush, peering down at the branch he was cradling.

"Arthur! A moment of your time?"

Arthur jerked, his mouth open, and squinted over at Henri. "You startled me. I was examining the intricacies of this leaf. What do you need?"

Henri beckoned him closer. "I don't want to get drenched."

Arthur raised an eyebrow. "It's barely raining. Bit chilly though." He approached Henri. "Better? What do you need?"

"I'm just looking for a train timetable to Versailles. Do you have one handy?"

Arthur frowned, cocking his head to one side. "Train timetable? None that would be useful. Your Naturalist friends shut down the train system. There are no trains running."

"No trains? At all? But … how do people get around? Don't tell me horse carriages are all that's left? That's so antiquated. I mean, I was never a fan of steam omnibuses in the city, but trains are so much faster to get out to Versailles."

Arthur shrugged. "I don't go out much."

Henri screwed up his forehead. "You must be wrong. Perhaps they just reduced the services or something. Have you been to the rail station? Are you sure that the trains have been stopped?"

"No, I haven't been to the station. Didn't bother." He turned and wandered back into the garden.

Henri spoke to his retreating back. "Well I need to get to Versailles and I don't want to take another bone-rattling journey in a carriage. I'm going to the station to see about a train." A giant raindrop plopped on his head. He glowered up at the dripping vine that crawled up the wall and stepped back inside.

Isabelle and John were talking in low voices over their breakfast. Henri didn't stop to wonder at the topic. Probably money, or their lack of it. The sooner he sorted out his train and got to Versailles, the happier he'd be. "Going over to the train station for a timetable. Arthur seems to think that there aren't any trains running."

"No trains?" John's bemused voice followed Henri's progress out of the house. He snatched his overcoat and hat off the coat rack by the door and tromped down the steps and out into the bustling street. Passing by were all manner of Parisians—midinettes on the arms of elderly gentleman friends, suspicious-eyed policemen, veterans on crutches, and street vendors hawking their wares. The street echoed with clattering carriage wheels and clomping hooves from carriages racing along the Rue Ortolan. Henri took it all in with a smile. He breathed in the smells of Paris and grinned. It was good to be home. He sauntered along with his fellow Parisians, exchanging nods and smiles with the pretty trim-waisted women.

The Gare de l'Ouest was a long walk from Gleyre's house and Henri was cold and footsore by the time he arrived. A row of carriages lined the road in front of the massive stone building. The crowds thinned as he approached the station. Beggars sat on the damp pavement, hands out. A police officer stood at attention on the steps into the station. The doors behind them were boarded shut. Henri's heart pounded, the sound of blood rushing in his ears drowning out the stamping and snorting of the waiting horses. Perhaps there was another door. He spotted a grisette lingering nearby, a hopeful smile on her young dirty face. He waved her over. "Bonjour, mademoiselle. Can you tell me why this station door is boarded shut? How am I to get to the platform?"

She guffawed and hit him on the arm. 'Why would you want to get to the platform, monsieur? There are no trains."

Henri felt a chill steal over him that had nothing to do with the drizzling rain. "No trains? You're sure?"

She looped her grubby arm in his. "No trains. Not for months. But you could take a carriage ride with me instead." She tugged him towards one of the waiting carriages. He resisted, pulling back, and she turned with a frown. "You were funning about the trains, right? Just an excuse to come down and see who's here?"

Henri spluttered a denial and the grisette laughed in his face, her mouth full of yellow teeth. He saw movement out of the corner of his eye. It was the police officer. He tried to disentangle his arm but the young grisette held on.

"Bonjour, monsieur. And what brings you here today? Looking for illicit company perhaps?" The stern-faced police officer tapped their baton on their leg, looking as if they would prefer to rap it on Henri's head.

"No, no, I'm married." Henri protested, his face flushed.

"Ha, that doesn't seem to stop you men from keeping company with other women. Marie-Louise, haven't I told you I would lock you up next time I saw you soliciting here?"

The grisette hung her head as if taking a scolding from a headmistress and pulled her arm away from Henri's. How old was she? Under all that grime it was hard to tell. She slipped away and the police officer turned back to Henri. He cowered beneath their steely gaze. "Perhaps a few days in jail would teach you a lesson."

"Please, officer, I was just looking for a train. I didn't realize that the station was closed. " The thought of jail turned his insides to jelly. He trembled as if palsied.

"The king ordered all of the train stations closed six months ago. How did you not know this?" They stepped closer, baton held away from their body, ready to strike.

"I have been abroad. Just returned. I didn't know the trains weren't running."

The police officer cocked their head. "You want a train? You sound like a Science supporter. That is treasonous. Perhaps you need to be taken into custody and interrogated."

Henri clasped his shaking hands and held them up, begging. "Please, I had no idea. I need to get to Versailles to see the king."

The police officer laughed. "What makes you think the king would give you an audience?"

Henri drew his shoulders back and tried to stop shaking. "I painted the king when we were in England together last year. I am quite certain His Majesty would see me."

That stopped their laughter. "I see. Not a Science supporter then, Too bad, I would've liked to interrogate you. You'll need to hire a carriage to get to Versailles, monsieur." They sauntered back to their post on the steps.

Henri looked over at the waiting carriages. No, a carriage ride all the way to Versailles now didn't appeal. He wouldn't be there until late in the day. He strode away on shaky legs. What had happened to France? He had been a fervent Naturalist when technology had intruded on his life but this? It was too extreme.

Thirteen

Adelaide trudged into the laundry room. Her shoulders slumped when she spotted the giant pile of unfolded sheets she'd been sent to fetch. With a weary sigh, she reached for a sheet and tugged it out of the pile. Folding them all was going to take a long time. And Emard would be sure to criticize her for being tardy when she returned with the sheets.

Footsteps clattered on the marble floor behind her and Adelaide turned to see Lucie, the midwife, entering the laundry room. "Adelaide! How are you feeling these days? Goodness me, you look exhausted. Here, let me help you with that. Folding sheets alone is awkward, is it not?"

Adelaide smiled her thanks and handed the end of the sheet to Lucie. "I'm better. Still very tired. How long will it take to regain my strength?"

Lucie cocked her head, assessing her. "You should be feeling almost back to normal by now but I think you're probably working too hard and not eating enough. Yes?"

The heat in the laundry room was oppressive and Adelaide wiped her forehead with the rough sleeve of her dress. "I'm trying to make Nurse Emard happy. I don't want to lose my position. And the food here. It's hard to eat. It's not exactly haute cuisine, is it?"

Lucie giggled, an incongruous sound from the grey-haired woman. "It's not tasty but it is healthful. You should try to eat more. You won't be as tired. That Nurse Emard.

She is an absolute tyrant. I'm sorry you were stuck with her."

Adelaide laid the folded sheet on a counter and reached for another. "She seems to hate me. What have I done to earn her enmity? I barely know her."

"I think she hates everyone. Especially mothers. And loose women. I heard that her fiancé left her for another woman when she was young. That's why she became a nun."

Adelaide sniffed. "I hardly think that's good reason to hate everyone. And why hate mothers? That doesn't make sense."

Lucie smoothed the crease on the sheet they held between them. "Perhaps because she never had the opportunity to be one."

A black cloud descended on Adelaide's mood. She had given birth but hadn't been able to mother her baby. His every cry and coo were watched by another woman, his needs met by her, not Adelaide.

Her change in mood must have shown on her face.

Lucie gently asked, "Are you missing your babe, Adelaide? I'm sure he's well. The foster mother we found is a good woman. He'll be returned to you once you're back on your feet and can manage him."

Adelaide took a deep breath to calm herself. "I know. She seemed very competent. I just—I didn't know how much I would love him until he was born. And then I almost died. It was all so confusing. What happened at his birth, Lucie?"

Lucie lowered her eyes, her mouth drawn tight. "You did almost die. You were bleeding too much and I couldn't stop it. The nuns came and prayed, then the bleeding stopped. I don't know. It all felt unreal to me. The tea they give everyone. It's supposed to be healing but sometimes it makes me unsure of what's really happening."

Adelaide stopped folding. "The tea? That bitter brew they make us all drink? I've noticed that too. I feel woozy after drinking it. I wonder if it has hallucinogenic properties."

Lucie frowned, a crease appearing between her eyes. "That makes sense. I wonder if all that praying is just hope and hallucinations. But I've seen the prayer work. Well, I think I've seen it work."

They folded in silence for a few moments, Adelaide's thoughts drifting to her plans to repair the young veteran's Augmentation. She needed to find some tools. Hopefully there would be something she could use in the old Robotics wing but it was blocked off.

Casually, Adelaide broke the silence. "Lucie, this hospital is so busy and it seems like every bed is occupied, but I noticed that there's a whole wing that's blocked off. Is it too damaged to use? Perhaps there was a fire?"

Lucie shrugged. "I know the wing you mean. The nuns closed it off to contain the impurity." Adelaide raised her eyebrows and Lucie giggled. She lowered her voice. "It used to be a surgery wing for Augmentations. Forbidden technology now. They took out all the furniture and equipment and made a giant bonfire of it. Fire cleanses, I suppose. And then they shut the wing."

Adelaide frowned. "That seems like a waste of space. But nothing these nuns do makes sense to me."

Lucie shushed her just as one of the nun-nurses entered the laundry room. They were all so quiet on their feet. Was it something they were taught in their convent?

Adelaide took the pile of folded sheets, thanked Lucie for her help, and headed back to the Veterans' Ward. If

Lucie was correct, chances were slim that Adelaide would be able to find anything of use in the Robotics wing. She needed to explore for herself, after everyone had retired for the night.

ಸಿ Φ ೞ

Later that night, Adelaide made her way down an empty, dark hallway of the hospital, her footsteps echoing on the dust-covered marble floor. A draft whistled through the tall windows and she shivered in the dank night air. The dust lay thick in this part of the hospital, the area she remembered as the surgical unit for robotics. Most of the rooms she had so far explored were empty of even a chair. Even the big operating theater had been gutted, and left an empty shell of a room. Adelaide had held hope of finding something, anything at all in the robotics wing of the hospital. But as she moved from room to room, her hope faded. Whoever had ransacked and emptied this part of the hospital had been thorough in their work.

She entered what had probably been an office. Elegant wooden bookshelves lined the walls. All of them empty, standing like tombstones against the far wall. Adelaide turned to leave but a glint of metal caught her eye. She crossed the room to investigate and found a piece of metal attached to one shelf. It seemed to be an ornate curlicued bookend. Adelaide pulled it to take a closer look, but it didn't budge. Adelaide tugged harder. The whole shelf swung out, forcing her to step backwards into the room. Stepping closer, she spied a handle on the wall behind the bookshelf. Heart hammering with excitement, Adelaide turned the handle, and a section of the wall opened inward, revealing a dark cavity. Adelaide took a quick glance behind her then stepped through the portal and into a cluttered room lit only by a tiny window high on the wall. Glassware and metal instruments glinted in the moonlight.

Someone's private workroom. And from the looks of it, the revolutionaries didn't find it during the purge.

Adelaide grinned to herself and wandered from cabinet to cabinet, mentally cataloging their contents. Drawers full of brass connectors and coils of copper wire. A whole cabinet of Augmentation parts. It had been a robotics workroom. Exactly what she was searching for. She bumped into a crate full of rattling glass tubes and a vision of her Versailles laboratory flashed across her memory. She had loved that room, full of automaton parts, even as she had berated her assistant for the continual clutter. Adelaide picked up a wrench, toying with it as she remembered Zoe, her young assistant who had sabotaged Adelaide's work. After catching her, Adelaide had sent her to be executed for her crimes against Science. She winced, remembering the panic in the young girl's face as the soldiers dragged her away. Had her death been worth it, now that the old monarchs were in their graves and the Automated Dauphin a melted pile of rubble? Tears burned in Adelaide's eyes. She'd been so sure of herself, so convinced she would save France with her brilliant technology. And now she was relegated to furtive repairs of the Augmentations she had once invented. She tightened her grip on the wrench, trying to quell the ache in her heart with the pain in her hand. Adelaide bit down on her lip.

Enough self-pity. At least I wasn't executed like Valmont. How he must have regretted accepting my old position. He couldn't keep the old Queen functioning. The Naturalists were waiting their chance for power and took it after she died. Everything that remotely resembled the Old Monarchy has been swept away.

She shuffled around the room, trying to dodge the clutter. The tools she needed to fix the injured veteran's Augmentations were simple but specific. Not just any screwdriver would do. A drawer in one of the cabinets held a carefully arranged display of exactly the tools she needed. She cast about for a case to carry them in. It wouldn't do for the tools to be visible as she carried them through the hospital. She found a leather satchel and placed the tools inside, then added a few spare parts. She didn't know what she would need to fix the young veteran's legs and didn't want to risk returning here too often.

Adelaide took one last look around the workroom and returned to the office, closing the bookshelf behind her. It swung closed with a creak. She grimaced at the noise. A little oil on the hinges might be in order. She crept to the office door and peeked out. A lantern bobbed at the end of the corridor. It was the night watchwoman on her rounds. Adelaide ducked back into the office and stood behind the open door, out of sight.

Please don't come in here. Please pass on by. There is nothing of interest in here.

The heavy tread of the watchwoman's feet neared, then paused at the open doorway. She reached out and pulled the door closed, leaving Adelaide in darkness.

☙ Φ ❧

Adelaide waited in the darkness for endless moments, counting her heartbeats to track time. When she reached two hundred, she slowly cracked the door open and listened. Seeing and hearing no sign of the watchwoman, Adelaide slipped out and carefully pulled the office door closed. She scampered through the empty wing, moving as quickly as she dared, with the case of tools tucked under her arm. She'd need a pile of linens to disguise her contraband once she got to the occupied part of the hospital. Adelaide scoured her memory for the location of the linen cupboard. Where had Nurse Emard said it was? Near the kitchens? She headed in that direction, pausing at corners to be sure her path was clear. Her throat was dry and she swallowed. No-one wandered the hallways late at night like this. Was it forbidden, or were the others too exhausted by their labors to stay awake? Heart in her throat, Adelaide stayed to her course until she located the linen cupboard. She grabbed a bundle of sheets to hide the satchel underneath and returned to the veterans' ward.

The patients all appeared to be sleeping except for the young Augmented soldier. He stared at the ceiling, just as he had all day. Adelaide approached him on soft feet, hoping not to disturb the other patients. He was biting on his lip, sweat glistening on his forehead. He turned his head when she sat down on the stool next to his bed. "A little late for changing bed sheets, is it not?"

Adelaide pushed the sheets to the floor at her feet and held up the satchel. "I found tools I can use to work on your legs. I'm sorry it took so long."

He stared at her. "You were serious?" His voice raised in hope.

She shushed him and nodded. She kept her voice low so she wouldn't wake the other patients. Who knew if they would tell the nun-nurses about Adelaide's midnight visit. "I told you I would try to help. Now let's take a look at those Augmentations."

She pulled back the covers and squinted at the mechanisms. The dim light made it difficult to examine them properly. She looked around and spotted an unlit lantern on the central nurses' station. Adelaide retrieved it and spent several long moments trying to light it. It had been so easy to simply turn on the gaslight or switch on the electricity in her workroom at Versailles. She'd almost forgotten how to properly light an oil lamp. When she finally succeeded, the light it cast was enough for Adelaide to see the workings of the Augmentations. Some of the wires had come loose and the servos were jammed with grease and hair. She fell into a quiet trance of work as she tightened connections and cleared the stuck servos. When she'd finished repairing the obvious problems, she glanced up at the man's face. "I never asked your name."

He grimaced. "Boulet. Axel Boulet."

"Does that feel any better, Monsieur Boulet?"

Axel shrugged, sweat still glistening on his forehead. "It's eased some but that jangly pain that goes right up my back is still there."

Adelaide scowled. He had been Augmented with one of the inferior models. It had been designed for speed and strength with no thought for the user's comfort. The sensation he described was typical of that model as it aged. "I am afraid there's little I can do for that. I could try to disconnect the legs altogether but that is a dangerous surgery and would leave you an amputee."

Axel's face dropped. "I don't want to lose my legs altogether, madame. Is there nothing you can do?"

Adelaide propped her chin up with her hands and stared at the wall above his head. She had theorized a solution to this faulty mechanism but had never had the opportunity to attempt it. "There's something I can try. But it may not work and it has the potential to render the legs useless."

Axel let out a long sigh. "Madame, the pain is driving me mad. Can you try on one of them? If I am only left with one leg, at least I will have that. Better to be crippled than unable to walk at all."

She pushed a wisp of hair back off her face then dug into the satchel for the spare parts she'd tossed in at the last moment. "I'll do what I can. It may pain you more when I switch the connections, but that will be temporary."

"Go ahead." He clenched the covers with his hands, knuckles white with tension.

Adelaide got to work, ignoring her patient's grunts of pain. There was no way to make this pleasant. Once she was finished, she sat back and looked at Axel. His breath was ragged but as she watched, it eased. He opened his eyes and gaped at her. "It worked. Madame, you are a genius, an angel. The pain in my spine has eased. Please, please, fix the other one?"

She grinned and turned to the other leg, screwing and unscrewing wires and bolts with practiced ease. Axel watched her avidly and flexed his leg. Adelaide frowned up at him. "Be still. I'm not finished yet."

After completing the repair, she sat back, stretching her arms and shoulders. Axel lay on his cot, breathing deeply and grinning like a boy with an ice cream. "No pain. No pain at all. I can't believe this. Madame, I am forever in your debt. If there's ever anything I can do to help, I will do it." He snatched her hand and tried to press it to his lips but she pulled it away.

"I am pleased that I could help. Now try to sleep. Your nerves need to recover from the shift in current. Rest and food will be your best medicine. Good night, Axel."

His blissful smile answered her. She stood, gathering her tools into the satchel and adding the pile of sheets. She walked past the blind man who whispered, "Good night, madame."

Adelaide's guts clenched. How much had the old man heard? Would he tell Nurse Emard? She swallowed and exited the ward on trembling legs. Nurse Emard stood there in the dim hallway.

"Nurse Emard. Good evening."

"Coumain, why were you in the ward after hours? You should be in the women's dormitory, not wandering around."

Adelaide stuttered and blushed. "Sheets. I was changing sheets."

"At midnight?"

"One of the patients wet his bed and asked me to change his sheets when I peeked in to see if they were in need of anything." Even to Adelaide's ears, the excuse sounded weak.

"The night orderly will be back from his supper momentarily. He would have taken care of that. It is not your job to interfere with the ward at night. Are you sure you weren't visiting the handsome young veteran who refuses to eat?"

"Monsieur Boulet? No, er, of course I wasn't."

Nurse Emard sneered and hatred dripped from her voice. "Seducing the patients under our care is the act of a weak, immoral woman, Coumain. I won't stand for it."

"Seducing? What? Me? I would never..." Adelaide's stomach turned at the thought but remembered Axel's passionate kiss on her palm. Her face grew hot.

"If I discover that you are engaged in immoral acts, you will be immediately dismissed. Is that clear?"

"Of course, Nurse Emard. Good night." Adelaide trotted away, clutching her contraband under the bulky linens. She could almost feel Nurse Emard's gaze burning through her back.

Fourteen

Rain dripped off the trees in the courtyard, freshening the air. Adelaide breathed in, enjoying the cold, clean scent. The roses had faded, their browned petals littering the slate pathways. Winter was coming and Adelaide would need warmer clothing if she wanted to spend time outside. But she received only a pittance for her work. Nurse Emard had explained that she worked for the cost of her food and lodging. Adelaide sighed, thinking of the few coins she had saved. It would be years before she could afford even a tiny garret. How could she hope to support her son? How did he look now, two months after his birth? Was he healthy and thriving? Or was the foster mother neglecting him?

Adelaide shivered in the cold and returned to the interior of the hospital. Nurse Emard would be wondering where she had disappeared to, no doubt. That woman never let up. Adelaide trod the echoing hallway back to the Veterans' ward, exchanging nods with passing nun-nurses. None of them were particularly friendly but at least they didn't scowl at her like Nurse Emard did. Why did that woman hate her so? Was it because Dr. Dutrochet had asked for her to be assigned to Nurse Emard's ward? As if summoned by her thoughts, Dr. Dutrochet stepped out through a doorway as Adelaide passed by.

"Good afternoon, Madame Coumain. Are you settling in to our ways?" She smiled at Adelaide, a genuine look of warmth.

Adelaide stopped and stood in front of the director, resisting the urge to take her hands in greeting. Odd how comfortable she felt with the director of the hospital. "Dr. Dutrochet. It's good to see you. I fear that our paths do not cross as often as I would like." She felt her face grow warm. Was she too bold?

The director broadened her smile. "Agreed. Would you like to sit and have a cup of tea with me? Or are you about your duties? Nurse Emard works her orderlies rather hard, I've been told."

Adelaide shrugged, a mischievous grin dancing across her face. "I'll tell her I was needed in the laundry. I would love a cup of tea. All I get in the dining room is that awful herbal stuff. It's so bitter."

Dr. Dutrochet laughed and tossed her head back. "Ah yes, the nun-nurses' special tonic. It's quite wretched, isn't it? I have some nice Assam I sneak in when they're not looking. Come into my office and we'll indulge."

Adelaide followed her into her office, feeling like a schoolgirl skipping school. "Thank you, Dr. Dutrochet."

"Please, call me Mireille." Her eyes were warm.

"Mireille." Adelaide liked how it sounded in her mouth. "Then you must call me Adelaide."

The women settled onto a sofa, a pretty tea service beside them on the occasional table. Mireille poured the golden-brown liquid into a delicate china cup then handed it to Adelaide. She inhaled the aroma of the tea as the steam wafted off it. "I can't remember the last time I had a good cup of tea; this is heavenly. Thank you so much, Mireille."

Mireille sipped her own cup, her eyes on Adelaide. "My pleasure. You've been in dire straits since the Naturalists took power, I think."

Adelaide sighed. "Before that, I'm afraid. My life took a wrong turn a year ago and I've been struggling ever since. I didn't intend to have a baby."

"Your husband pressed the issue?"

Adelaide leveled a look at her. "Will it shock you to know that there was no husband? My son was conceived in a moment of madness. The father fled to England after escaping prison. The prison I sent him to."

Mireille sat back, her eyes widened. "Adelaide. You are a woman of depths I had no idea existed. Perhaps you will tell me your story?"

Adelaide shook her head. "Not today. I must return to work before Nurse Emard has a fit. Thank you so much for the tea, Mireille."

She got to her feet more easily than she had just a few weeks ago. The hard work was helping her regain her figure. Mireille stayed seated, regarding her with sharp eyes. A smile tugged one side of her mouth up. "Off you go, my lady of mystery."

Adelaide left the office, wishing she could stay and bask in the warmth of Mireille's regard. But perhaps it was best that she had to go. Why had she divulged her secrets? Could she trust Mireille? She wanted to trust her and the growing rapport between them but it could all go so wrong.

༄ Φ ༅

When Adelaide returned to the ward, Nurse Emard and one of the other nun-nurses stood over the bed of a patient, a man who complained all day about his numb, unmoving legs. Their arms were raised in supplication and they prayed aloud in a language Adelaide didn't know. She drew closer, curious about their supposed healing powers. The man groaned. Adelaide peeked around the nun-nurse's billowing sleeves but couldn't see anything.

Nurse Emard's voice rose to a bellow and she switched to English. "Begone, evil!"

The man gasped, then sat up and placed his feet on the floor. He stood, grinning, and gestured to his legs. "I can stand again! It's a miracle! Thank you, sisters. You've given me back my legs."

Adelaide stepped back, intending to flee but Nurse Emard turned to her, fixing her in place with her intense gaze. "You're back finally. How much did you see?"

Adelaide opened her mouth to speak but couldn't make a sound. What had she just seen? Had the man's paralysis really been healed? She stared at Nurse Emard with a gaping mouth, fighting the urge to run from the nun-nurse and what had appeared to be a terrible power.

The porter appeared at the doorway of the ward. "Nurse Emard, you have a new patient." A thin man clad in a ragged uniform stood next to him, wavering on his feet.

Nurse Emard glared at Adelaide for another moment, then strode to the doorway. She examined the thin man. "What is wrong with you, monsieur? Fever? Pain?"

The man didn't respond. His eyes rolled up in his head and collapsed at Nurse Emard's feet.

"Coumain, get over here and help move this man into a bed."

The porter and Adelaide hoisted the man with almost no effort. He was so slight, so weak and frail. They carried him across the ward. Adelaide felt the familiar metal and leather mechanisms of an Augmented leg under her hand as she settled him into a bed. She removed his shoes before covering him with a light blanket.

Nurse Emard waited for Adelaide to finish then pushed past her. She placed a hand on his forehead. "He seems feverish. Could be la grippe. Coumain, fetch some tonic for him."

Adelaide knew she meant the bitter tea the nuns prescribed to all of the patients. She poured some from the pot that sat on a little wood stove all day, growing more concentrated and harder to choke down. She brought the mug back to the man's bedside and offered it to Nurse Emard.

"Wake him up and get him to drink it. I have more important things to do."

Like practicing your sorcery on paralytic patients?

Adelaide wasn't sure what she had seen. Had the man really been paralyzed? She hadn't examined him since he wasn't Augmented. It must have been some trickery the nun-nurses performed, but Adelaide knew better than to suggest that aloud, much less in the presence of her superior. She didn't want the nun-nurse hating her anymore than she already did, or have more cause to turn her in to the Police Secrète. But she could not still the revulsion that stirred within her at the thought of what trickery these nun-nurses might be capable of.

Nurse Emard sneered at Adelaide, her enmity a tangible presence. She took her leave, turning away from the ill man almost in disgust. Adelaide shook herself as if to clear her mind of any dangerous thoughts. She sat with a thump on the bedside stool next to the feverish veteran. She rubbed the man's shoulder with a gentle touch. "Monsieur, wake up? I have some medicine for you."

He opened his eyes, bright with fever and pain. "Are you Madame Coumain?"

She drew back and scrutinized his face. Did she know him? Perhaps he had been a Palace guard during her time there? "Yes, I am, but how did you know that?"

He exhaled a sigh of relief. "The angel who repairs broken soldiers. A friend told me of you and your miracle."

Adelaide's heart thudded with fear. Bile rose to her throat. She leaned over him, spoon to his mouth. "Hush, not so loud. These are illegal activities you speak of. I could be arrested if someone thought I repaired Augmentations."

He swallowed the proffered tea and grimaced. "Ahhggg, what is that poison you're feeding me?"

She smirked. "It's meant to make you well. The nun-nurses brew it for all of the patients, regardless of their affliction. Now quietly, who told you to ask for me?"

"Someone from my old regiment, Boulet. He said you fixed his legs. Maybe you could help me too?"

Adelaide stole a look around the ward. Nurse Emard stood outside, talking to another nun-nurse. "Maybe. What's the problem?"

"The leg seizes up sometimes. Especially when it's raining out. Can't predict the rain anymore y'know, so sometimes I get caught out in it."

She nodded her head. "It's a very common problem. Probably rust. Do you oil your leg?"

The man looked shamefaced. "Well, not as often as I should, I suppose."

"Coumain, you're supposed to be giving the patient tea, not indulging in conversation."

Adelaide jumped, spilling the concoction onto her dress. Had Nurse Emard heard what she had told the veteran? She looked at the nun but her typical sour expression adorned her skinny face. Adelaide turned back to her patient, spoon at the ready. "Yes, Nurse Emard."

Emard rolled her eyes, her mouth turned down in disdain. Adelaide watched her leave the ward before turning back to the veteran. "Let's take a look at your leg before she gets back to berate me again."

She pulled back the covers and lifted the man's trouser leg. As suspected, rust corroded some of the mechanisms. She scraped at the rust with a fingernail. "It doesn't appear to be too deep into the metal. I think I can get it off but I'll need to get my tools. Not now. I'll do it tonight after they're all asleep."

"Would that be wise, my dear Adelaide?"

Adelaide yelped and whirled around. Mireille hovered behind her, a look of worry creasing her face. "If you're going to talk about illegal subjects, you should probably face the door so people don't sneak up on you."

Adelaide attempted a smile but it wobbled. "Are you going to turn me in, Mireille?"

The director shook her head. "For what? Aiding a patient? All I saw was you giving this poor man a drink. Come to my office when you're done."

She strode out of the ward as Adelaide watched. Mireille was so unlike the nun-nurses here. They moved as if bent to some ill task, all plodding and stern, each step a statement of their devotion and piety. And none more so than that harridan Nurse Emard. But Mireille moved with a gliding grace, almost swanlike. Free and unthreatening. Yet despite that impression of grace, Adelaide was still not convinced that Mireille wouldn't notify the authorities that Adelaide was breaking the law. How would she explain her activities to the director? Would she admit to being a roboticist, capable of repairing the malfunctioning veterans who came to the hospital? Would she lie?

The veteran lay on his cot, watching her. "I'm sorry I came. I wasn't thinking. You could be arrested for helping me, madame. Why would you do it? Not that I wouldn't be grateful for the help."

Adelaide let out a breath she hadn't realized she was holding. She cocked her head to one side. "Why? It's what I trained to do, monsieur. It's what I'm good at. Do you think emptying bedpans and feeding sick men foul-tasting tea is the sum total of my ambition? If I'm lucky, I'll avoid the notice of the police for a time. And maybe the king will relent and allow repair of Augmentations." She laughed, a short bitter laugh. "I can dream, right?" She rose to her feet. "Well, I'd better go and see the director, and hope the police aren't waiting in her office for me."

She passed Nurse Emard in the corridor and nodded to her. "The director wants to see me."

The nun-nurse merely scowled in return.

ஓ Φ ℭ

Mireille's office door was ajar and Adelaide could see her at her desk, writing in a notebook. The office appeared empty of anyone else.

No police. I'm not being arrested immediately.

She knocked on the open door to get Mireille's attention. The director looked up and smiled when she saw Adelaide. "Come in, my dear. Shut the door behind you."

Adelaide entered and took a tentative step toward the desk. She stopped a few paces away and let her arms hang by her sides. A sudden feeling of defiance filled her and she lifted her chin before speaking. "You haven't summoned the Police Secrète. Am I to be spared for now? And what are your conditions for this silence?"

Mireille frowned. "You don't trust me. I'm not calling the police, Adelaide. Why would I do that? Aren't we friends?"

Adelaide relaxed her shoulders, and chewed on her lower lip. Friends? A cup of tea didn't make someone her friend. Letting her breath out, but maintaining her defiant posture, she said, "You heard what I said to that veteran. I'm capable and willing to repair his Augmented leg. That's illegal. It's a foolish law, but it is the king's decree. One word from you and I could be in prison. But you say you won't turn me in? Why?"

Mireille stood and walked around the desk. She reached down and took Adelaide's hand. "You must know how much I admire you, Scientist-Doctor Coumain."

At the sound of her former title, Adelaide felt a wrenching pain. She hadn't been called that for months. "How did you know? Have you known the entire time I've been here?"

"Yes, my lady of mystery. I recognized your name immediately, but was waiting for you to confide in me. I followed news of your career for years until you were dismissed from Court. You were a brilliant young Scientist, Adelaide. Your invention, the artificial heart that produced no pulse. Such a promising technology. And then you disappeared. What happened?"

Adelaide withdrew her hand from Mireille's and covered her face with it. "I feel stupid even talking about it. In retrospect, I overreached. I didn't have the support from my superiors for my ambition." She looked up at Mireille with eyes blurred with tears. "I had such dreams. I was going to bring true democracy to France, but I failed. I wasn't capable of finishing the project alone, and now it's been destroyed. It was all for naught. It might have been better if I had still been the Royal Scientist-Doctor when the revolution came. I would've been executed. Not stewing in regret. Not mother to a child I only held for moments before losing him as well." She dashed the tears from her eyes and clenched her jaw.

Mireille rubbed a finger across Adelaide's roughened knuckles. "I'm glad you weren't executed. We would never have met. And the Augmented veterans who come to the hospital wouldn't have anyone to help them." Mireille's voice was warm and soothing but her eyes were drawn together with worry.

Adelaide twisted her mouth with irritation. "I used to create those Augmentations. I was an inventor, an innovator. Now at best I'm a mechanic and could be jailed for my work. Or worse."

"You're a doctor, Adelaide. A scientist-doctor. And your skills are still needed by those men. Would you abandon them to a lifetime of pain and malfunctioning limbs because of your pride and self-pity?"

Adelaide sucked in a breath. Self-pity? She rebelled at the thought. That didn't sound like the person she thought she was. And was she really too proud to help those who needed her? She thought of Boulet's gratitude when she had repaired his legs.

"You're right. Helping the veterans is not inconsequential. But how can I continue? I can only sneak around so much before I'm sure to be caught. Nurse Emard watches my every move. She seems convinced I'm up to no good. She even accused me of seducing a patient when she saw me leaving the ward after I repaired one of the Augmented veterans."

Mireille chuckled. "Seducing a patient? The very idea. Nurse Emard has some strange views, that is to be sure. She sees immorality everywhere."

Adelaide rubbed her rough knuckles, reddened from washing the patients' laundry. "She and I were once more similar, I think. I was raised to be a celibate Scientist, took vows just as she did. It used to be easy to tell good from evil. Now, all I see is shades of gray. Am I immoral because I gave birth out of wedlock?"

Mireille shook her head, her dark ringlets swinging across her face. "You are the most moral person I think I've ever met. Emard is narrow-minded. I will help you avoid her when you work on the Augmented veterans. I know this building better than she does. I know the hidden passages. I have keys to all of the rooms."

Adelaide sat back in the creaking chair and looked around at the office walls with a closer eye. "Hidden passages? How medieval."

Mireille smoothed down a ruffle on her dress, a dimple appearing on her cheek. "I suppose so. The building is ancient. I spent a lot of my childhood exploring when my uncle was the director here. He has no children of his own so liked to spoil me. He let me wander freely."

"And Nurse Emard doesn't know of these passages? Do any of them lead to the veterans' ward?"

Mireille nodded, a mischievous smile playing on her lips. "From the bathroom. I can show you the entrance. That passage leads to a storage room off the main corridor of that wing. No one would notice an orderly fetching supplies from a storage room and if she happened to stay in there for a while, who's to know?"

"What if someone came into the storage room while I was working?"

"I'll give you a key. You can lock it from the inside while you're in there. And if you want to keep your tools there, you- can lock the door to the main corridor."

Adelaide beamed. She would be able to work in peace, without the fear that Nurse Emard would discover her. She grasped Mireille's forearms and gazed at her. "Thank you so much, Mireille. This means the world to me."

Mireille clasped Adelaide's arms and drew her closer. She brushed her mouth against Adelaide's then leaned back. "I'm delighted to be able to help."

Adelaide drew a ragged breath. Her insides felt like they'd turned to hot liquid. What had Mireille meant by that kiss? Was it just a friendly gesture?

Mireille stood up straight, acting as if nothing more than a friendly secret had passed between them. "Let's see if we can sneak past Nurse Emard and show you the entrance to your secret workroom." She winked and pulled Adelaide to her feet.

Together they walked to the veterans' ward. Adelaide fought the urge to link arms with Mireille. She was surprised to find she wanted the other woman's arm against her side, to feel that closeness they had just shared in the office.

Nurse Emard sat at the nurses' station, laboriously writing in her large notebook. She looked up at their approach then stood when she spotted the director. "Madame Director. Is there a problem with my orderly? She's been gone for quite some time."

Mireille waved a hand in dismissal. "No problem at all, thank you, Nurse Emard. I was discussing some of Madame Coumain's skills. She may be able to assist me with some tasks."

Nurse Emard's eyes narrowed. "She's got no skills I can see. What do you mean?"

Mireille shrugged. "She has a tidy hand and can spell even the most technical terms."

The nun flushed. Adelaide could see the spotted, messy pages covered with Nurse Emard's cramped handwriting. "Don't know where she picked that up. Maybe in her fancy house that burned down. Funny that no-one's come looking for her, wouldn't you say, Dr. Dutrochet?"

Adelaide tilted her chin up. "Nurse Emard, I don't see why my lack of family should interest you."

"Well, maybe your family don't want you. Maybe you were some noble's doxy tossed out when you got with child. Maybe you made up your story of a fire."

"Nurse Emard. That is enough. You have no reason for this shameless speculation. I'll have no libelous talk among my staff." Mireille's tone was sharp.

Nurse Emard cringed but shot a dark look at Adelaide. "As you say, Madame Director." The nun gathered her skirts and scurried for the door. As she passed Adelaide, she paused. "I know something's not right with you. I'll find out what it is."

Adelaide and Mireille watched her leave the ward. Mireille sighed. "You've got an enemy there, Adelaide. I don't know what it is about you that she doesn't like. Watch yourself around her."

Adelaide followed along beside Mireille, knowing that she hadn't needed the warning. Nurse Emard was dangerous, and just how dangerous Adelaide did not wish to find out.

Fifteen

Henri leaned back in the wrought iron chair on the patio of the Café de Flore and grinned at his three companions. "It's good to be back home at last. And with daytime rain." The little patio on the pavement of the Boulevard Saint-Germain was deserted except for their group in the chill afternoon air. The empty tables and chairs were spotted with raindrops.

Isabelle huddled into her wool cloak. Her curly hair frizzed out around her head, disheveling her carefully arranged coiffure. She quirked a smile at him. "If you say so, cheri. But look at my hair. Ruined. I'll have to re-do it before the reception at Gleyre's tonight."

Henri leaned over and kissed her pouting lips.

Arthur brushed raindrops from his well-tailored wool overcoat. "Must we sit out here in the rain, Henri? My toes are freezing off."

John chimed in, his nose red with cold. "I've had enough drizzling rain after ten months in England. I was hoping for drier weather. I suppose they must have shut down the Weather Machines when the new king took over?"

Arthur scowled and leaned forward. He lowered his voice. "They've been off for months. I heard that it hasn't stopped raining in Picardy since. Most of the barley has rotted in the fields which means no beer for Paris. There has been some unhappiness about that."

John raised an eyebrow and regarded Arthur. "Unhappiness?"

"Oh you know, marching on the government at the palace, lots of shouting, breaking shop windows. There's no free bread either. People aren't used to paying for their own bread but the government says the grain reserves are too low to give it away."

Henri grumbled and looked across to the pavement at the people passing by, their shoulders hunched against the drizzle. "No matter. The free bread didn't taste like anything. I'd rather pay for my bread. That was one good thing about England. The bread and butter were delicious." He licked his lips at the thought of it. "Maybe we should have some bread to go with our wine? Where's that waiter?"

Arthur shook his head. "Bread is very expensive right now, Henri. Better not order any."

Henri frowned and opened his mouth to protest. Isabelle jingled her reticule at him. "We're low on funds, cheri. No bread from here, eh?"

Henri turned to John to appeal to him. "Mon frere, you'll buy me bread since my wife is holding tight to my purse strings, won't you?"

John chuckled. "I've already bought you wine, now you want me to feed you?"

Henri exhaled a long dramatic sigh and slumped in his seat. "We're supposed to be celebrating the triumphant return of the great artists Henri Desjardins and John Saylor to Paris! Not penny pinching like a bunch of worried housewives. No, this is unacceptable." He sat back up and waved the waiter over. "A bottle of '77 Champagne! This is a celebration, not a funeral. Isabelle, don't look so worried. I'll have commissions filling every day as soon as I meet with

His Majesty. We'll be popular, wealthy, not a care in the world."

They all wore identical expressions of bemused indulgence. Henri grinned, looking around at them. He took a deep breath of the cold, damp air and watched the people walking by on the pavement. Unmistakably Parisians, their attire so much different than the English. He admired the bustles and nipped in waists of passing shop girls, midinettes carrying hat boxes. Henri ignored the frown Isabelle shot at him across the table. Then a woman, thick around the middle and clad in a rough woolen gown and cloak trudged by along the pavement. The turn of her head reminded him of someone. Had he painted her? As she drew closer, she turned her head and stared right at him across the patio. Her heavy, dark eyebrows drew together in a frown of recognition. With a start, he realized who she was. Or rather who she had been. It was Adelaide Coumain. The Royal Scientist-Doctor. But hadn't she been executed? John had said that he'd read of her execution in one of the newspaper articles covering the French regime change. Ice crept through his veins.

"Henri? Cheri? You look like you've seen a ghost?" Isabelle's worried tone cut through the fog.

Henri broke eye contact with Adelaide and faced Isabelle. "Pardon, chérie? Is our champagne here yet?" He stole a glance towards the pavement but the figure in grey had disappeared into the crowd. He swallowed hard. She was supposed to be dead. If she was alive, she could report his presence in Paris to the police. He was a known fugitive, escaped from imprisonment in the Bastille. So far, no one had realized that but with her around, there was no telling how long it would be before his presence was noted.

John's voice broke into his thoughts. "Henri? Something is bothering you."

"Just the wait for my Champagne. You know, it is getting a bit chilly. We should move inside after all." He rubbed his hands to warm them and got to his feet.

Once they settled themselves inside the cozy bistro, Isabelle snuggled next to him. "Henri, did you see someone you know out there? You can't lie to me, you know."

He gazed down into her lovely hazel eyes, drawn together with concern. She knew him too well. "It's nothing, no need to worry."

John leaned closer to the couple. "Who did you see out there? We could be in danger if someone from the old regime recognizes us and reports us as fugitives. Remember what the police commander at Calais said?"

Henri waved a hand in dismissal. "Everything has changed, John, it's why we returned. The crimes we were accused of were committed in support of King Henri and the Naturalist cause. The old officials are gone, swept from power. Right, Arthur?'"

Arthur shrugged. "The chief of the Police Secrète was removed. I've heard the new one is no better. Takes bribes. Enforces the law when it benefits them."

The waiter chose that moment to bring the Champagne. Henri sipped the cold wine, its bubbles tickling his nose. A pall of gloom had dropped onto the little group and the Champagne's effervescence failed to cheer them. The tall windows of the bistro allowed a clear view of the people passing outside. No sign of Adelaide. Had she really recognized him? Was she going to fetch a policeman to arrest him? The wine soured in his stomach. He lurched to his feet, knocking the table. The glasses sloshed their contents onto the tablecloth and his companions looked up at him with wide eyes. "Need to use the facilities." He dashed to the back of the bistro and locked himself into the diminutive toilet, breathing hard. He ran a shaking hand across his forehead, wiping the sweat away. He sat until his stomach calmed down then wound his way back through the crowded tables to his companions. The buzz of the crowd enjoying pre-dinner cocktails had increased, echoing off the high ceilings of the bistro. Isabelle turned her worried face towards him as he approached, then took his hand and drew him down next to her. "Tell us what's worrying you, cheri. It's no use pretending that all is well."

Henri cleared his throat and sighed. "I saw Adelaide Coumain out on the street."

Arthur frowned in confusion. "Who?"

John answered for Henri, his face pale. "She was the Royal Scientist-Doctor at Versailles when I was painting the old queen's portrait last year. We thought she was dead."

Arthur looked from John to Henri and back again. "Why does that matter?"

John grimaced. "She was Henri's accuser. Her word to the Palace Guard was responsible for his arrest. She claimed he was speaking sedition against the monarchy. There was no trial, just the Bastille."

"But the old regime is gone. They have no more power in France." Arthur looked baffled.

Henri's tone was bitter. "If they're gone, why is she still free to wander the streets of Paris? Who knows what's really going on? This new chief of police … is he still arresting people for sedition against the old king and queen?"

Arthur shook his head, deep in thought. "They're arresting enemies of the current king, not the old one. But a prominent Scientist, still free? She must be in hiding, Henri.

They were all rounded up months ago. I remember the reports of the trials."

Henri stared at Arthur. If that were true, it meant that Adelaide was the fugitive, not John and him. But could he really trust that? What if the police still hunted for him? And what if Adelaide reported his presence anonymously? He was still in danger if she was around. He needed to talk to her, find out what she intended to do about his presence in Paris. But how would he be able to locate her?

Sixteen

Adelaide marched along the boulevard towards the Jardin du Luxembourg, her jaw clenched. Other pedestrians stepped out of her way, her glowering face warning them to stay clear. She ground her teeth. Her first free afternoon since she'd started working at the hospital and she had to encounter Henri Desjardins. What was he doing back in France? He had just sat there on the bistro patio looking like he owned the place, surrounded by his cronies. Adelaide had thought he wouldn't dare to come back so soon after he escaped the Bastille. Or perhaps he thought that the records had been destroyed during the regime change. And he had seen her, recognized her. What did he know about the current politics of France? Did he know she was a wanted woman? Her jaw ached and her head started to throb.

Carriages clattered by her. She dodged around one to reach the gates of the Jardin du Luxembourg. The rows of trees crowned with yellow and orange leaves distracted her from her worry. The tension in her head eased. The fountain de Medici danced with water as she approached, the splashing sound almost musical. This was why she'd left the hospital on her free afternoon and walked, despite her aching feet. Adelaide sank onto one of the benches near the fountain and let her body relax against the back of the bench. It was a novel sensation, no corset to hold her back stiff and straight, just short stays. The seat was wet and the rain continued to drizzle but at that moment, she didn't care. She watched the water in the fountain, tracing it back to its source.

That pump must be powered by a water wheel over on the Seine. There's not enough of an elevation change to move the water through gravity. I wonder if the King realizes that this fountain owes its water flow to mechanical workings?

She snickered to herself. These Naturalists were ignorant, not seeing the benefit of Science even when it gave them this beauty. And when the fountain pumps broke, who would fix them? Maybe the king would care about Science when its absence affected him.

A ragged woman approached her, a small child clinging to her skirts. The child looked up at Adelaide with huge, dark eyes. Adelaide felt a pang of longing for her own child. The beggar held out her hand. "Spare change for a bit of bread, madame?"

Adelaide looked into the woman's grubby, desperate face then down at her child. "Can you not acquire free bread from the bakeries, madame?"

The beggar shook her head. "Not anymore. Baker says the government stopped that. We've always had free bread. What are we supposed to do now? My husband can't work since he got back from the war, with his legs that don't work anymore."

Adelaide frowned. No more free bread? That meant the grain supplies were already low.

"Sorry to bother you, madame." Her frown must have discouraged the beggar.

"No, wait! I have a few sous. Here, take them."

The woman looked down at the proffered coins. "I thank you, madame, but that won't even buy a roll. Maybe you need the money more than me." She dragged her child away, heading deeper into the park.

Adelaide put the coins back in her pocket. Just a year ago, those coins would have bought an entire loaf of bread. These Naturalists and their idiotic ideals were going to cause the people of France to starve. The memory of Henri Desjardins and his friends feasting at the bistro while that poor woman struggled to feed her child burned in her mind.

Murderers.

First they'd murdered her beautiful Marie-Ange and now indirectly, the unfortunates of Paris.

She knew it had to be one of those artists who killed Marie-Ange. She had found a paintbrush near the girl's body. Henri and his artist friends must pay for their crimes but if Adelaide herself turned them in, wouldn't she reveal herself as a Scientist? There must be some way to claim her vengeance.

Adelaide looked around the garden, seeing the buildings of Paris rising behind the trees, She knew Henri was in the city now. She could wait and see what mischief he and his friends got up to. When the time was right, she could anonymously report him for his crimes.

The tiny face of their child filled her mind. But what if Henri found out about the baby? Would he try to claim baby Henri? Adelaide pulled herself to her feet and continued her walk along the tree-lined path. Little Henri was safe in the countryside, far from the clutches of his father.

Seventeen

Henri stood up from the bistro table. The Café de Flore felt too public, too exposed. "Let's go home. I can't stay here. What if she comes back with the police? I can't go back to the Bastille."

Isabelle got up and placed a hand on his arm. "Don't worry so, Henri, she's more at risk than you."

Other customers eyed them curiously and Henri lurched away from the table. "We have to go now. The police could be here at any moment." He headed to the door, Isabelle still on his arm. The freezing air slapped him when he stepped outside and he drew a shaking breath, Henri scanned the street, full of people and pushcarts, but no police. John and Arthur caught up and they made their way back to Gleyre's house. Henri's shoulders were rigid with tension.

After what felt like an age, they arrived back at the house and sat in the parlour. John wore a look of despair and he rubbed his hand across his face. "Henri, I don't think you are the one the police would be interested in. You were arrested for speaking out against the old monarchs. They would be more likely to investigate the murder of a noblewoman."

Henri started. "You mean Marie-Ange? What does Adelaide Coumain have to do with her?"

"Marie-Ange brought my art box to me after I left it in the Queen's Rooms. The bomb went off while she was holding it and it killed her. She was Augmented."

Henri huffed an impatient sigh. "I know all that, John, but what does that have to do with Adelaide?"

John dropped his head into his hands. "I think her laboratory was near where Marie-Ange died. Coumain must have been the one to find her body then moved it. Which means she saw my art case before I went back for it. I'm the one they're going to arrest, Henri, not you."

Henri shook his head. "No, it's me she hates. She'll pin the murder on me. I need to find where she's hiding and convince her not to turn me in."

Isabelle stood and flung her hands in the air. "You two are ridiculous. This woman is in much more danger than you. She will not be approaching the police with any reports. Henri, you just need to stay away from her. It will only lead to trouble if you go looking for her. And I'm sorry, John, but I don't think anyone is investigating the murder of an Augmented noble."

John winced and lowered his head back into his hands. Henri looked at her and nodded, his face gloomy. He had dreamed of being back in Paris, his beloved, comfortable home once more, but his idyll was proving to be illusory.

Eighteen

The massive Palais du Luxembourg dominated this side of the park and Adelaide wondered at her daring to be walking so near the central government's building. Gravel crunched under her boots, and for a moment she feared her next step would betray her. She circled the Grand Basin and the sight of a child sailing a toy boat with a bright red sail made her smile. Perhaps someday, she could bring little Henri here to sail his own toy boat. But that would assume she would be reunited with her son, and right now, after seeing the boy's father in Paris again, Adelaide could not bring herself to feel anything like hope.

She headed towards the less manicured English garden to the south. The apple orchards had been overgrown the last time she visited there, branches spilling from their espaliered forms. Her mouth watered at the thought of a tart apple. The drizzling rain lightened to a mist and Adelaide moved further from the few people lingering in the gardens. The orchard surrounded her, ghostly branches stretching as if to grasp her in the dim November light. She walked closer to the row of trees, hoping for a stray fruit, but the branches were bare of both leaves and fruit. It had been a cold wet autumn and the trees had dropped their leaves early this year.

A stocky man appeared from behind a garden shed and stopped short when he spotted her. He stood on the grass next to the shed, holding his body rigidly. He clutched a large toolbox in one hand. A look of dismay crossed his tawny face, to be quickly replaced with a polite smile. "Good afternoon, madame. I didn't expect to see anyone back here on such a dismal day. Are you lost?"

He looked familiar and Adelaide squinted at his face. Where did she know him from? She was sure she'd seen him before. Had he been a patient at the hospital? That didn't seem right. He looked too fit to be one of her wounded veterans. "No, not lost. Just looking for a little solitude. I'm sorry if I startled you."

The man sketched a short bow, one hand to his chest. "Please do not concern yourself." He shifted his toolbox to the other hand. "Good day to you, madame." He set off towards the nearest gate. His profile triggered her memory and she knew who he was.

She held up a hand to halt him. "Hamidou? Monsieur Hamidou? Is it really you?"

The man froze but didn't look at her. She remembered him now. Monsieur Hamidou had been the Scientist-Engineer at Versailles. He had overseen maintenance of the Weather Machine at the palace, keeping the weather perfectly fine, no clouds or rain in the daytime to inconvenience the nobles of the Court. They didn't encounter each other often but had shared an occasional word.

"You don't recognize me, do you? I'm Adelaide Coumain. We worked at the Palace together."

Hamidou swiveled to face her, eyes narrowed as he scrutinized her. "Adelaide Coumain? The Royal Scientist-Doctor? I thought you were dead, executed during the revolution."

Adelaide dropped her chin and shook her head. "I lost my position at Court just before the old monarchs died. I wasn't at Versailles when the new king arrived and started his purge. But you were still there. How did you get away with your life?"

The man continued to eye her with suspicion but then shrugged. "I suppose they didn't notice me. I never wore the Scientist blacks, you know. They would've been ruined on the machines when I worked on them. But is it really you? Adelaide Coumain? I can't believe it. How did you escape when the Police Secrète raided all of the laboratories and arrested everyone?"

Adelaide looked away. "After losing my position, I—I was already in hiding when they came looking for Scientists. I found refuge in the countryside, somewhere I could continue my work."

His eyes brightened and he moved a few steps closer. "You mean your work with automatons? I remember the lecture you gave about the future of automatons. It was truly inspiring, madame. Were you able to complete your project out there in the countryside? Is that why you're back in Paris, to present your automaton and convince the king and the senate to allow Science to be practiced?"

Adelaide's body quavered and while Hamidou's tone convinced her she could trust him, a wave of fresh grief threatened to choke her as she remembered the Automated Dauphin succumbing to the flames. She lowered her gaze to her tightly gripped hands and bit the inside of her cheek. It had once been her dream to present her automaton to the king and senate. Now it was ashes. She looked back up at Hamidou, her face rigid. "No. I was unable to complete the project."

A look of confusion passed across his face. "But then why are you here? You must know that Paris is dangerous." He gestured in the direction of the Palais du Luxembourg.

"The senate meet just across the park at the palace and the Police Secrète have their headquarters nearby."

She gripped her hands tighter. "I know. I couldn't stay in the countryside any longer. I had reasons. But why are you here?" She gestured towards his toolbox. "Not illicit work, here under the very nose of the government?"

He grinned, his face almost boyish. "You know there's a Weather Machine here? It wasn't completely destroyed when they shut it down. I might be able to repair it, if I can find the parts."

Adelaide snorted. "Parts for Weather Machines? That's unlikely. Unless..." Some automaton parts were compatible with Weather Machines. The hidden workroom she'd discovered at the hospital could have the parts that Hamidou needed.

"Unless? Do you know where I can find parts?"

She shook herself. What was the point of repairing the Weather Machines, just for them to be destroyed? She didn't want Hamidou meeting the same fate as Doctor Gregoire and the rest of the Scientists at the farmhouse. "Why do you want to repair the machines? It's illegal to run them."

Hamidou gestured with his free hand, his voice strong with passion. "Parisians are miserable in all this daytime rain. They grumble and complain to the senate at every opportunity. They want the predictable weather back, I'm sure of it. I think if we could make them happier, the king would be more favorable to Science. We must somehow convince the king to open his mind to the use of technology. These so-called Naturalists have no idea what they are espousing. They think that Nature is holy, to be left untouched, and they call that Naturalism. It's a bastardization of Deism, really. They sound like Deists but reject natural reason. But what we do in our pursuit of Science is truly Naturalism, madame. We study what is visible and real. We reject the Supernatural and pursue what can be proven."

Adelaide unclasped her hands and fixed him with a steady gaze. "I agree with you. We're the real Naturalists. But I must confess, I've seen things at the hospital that I can't explain with Science."

"Tricks of the mind and clever sleight-of-hand, I'm sure."

Adelaide frowned. Was that true? Were the nun-nurses tricksters, pretending to heal with their prayers? Had it been a hallucination? Or coincidence? She didn't know and it shook the core of her beliefs. "Perhaps. They seem to have strange, unexplainable powers. I've witnessed unusual events."

Hamidou cleared his throat and shifted the toolbox in his hands. "But why are you at a hospital? Are you ill?"

He thought she'd lost her mind and was institutionalized. Adelaide drew her eyebrows together in a scowl. "I work there. As an orderly. It's the only work I could get. They don't use doctors or real nurses anymore, just nuns."

His mouth hung open, revealing his yellowing teeth. "An orderly? But you are a trained doctor, a surgeon."

Shame encompassed her. How low she'd fallen. This man had known her at the height of her acclaim and now saw her laid low. She ran a hand across her belly, clad in rough wool, so unlike her black taffeta Scientist garb. "I am in hiding, Hamidou, as are you. I took the work I could get. I need to eat, you know."

His face darkened. "France can't survive this way. Without doctors, people will die needlessly, prematurely. And with the rain uncontrolled, there will be floods, failed harvests, famine. We need to do something about it, madame. Won't you help me repair the Weather Machine?"

She'd refused to help the Scientists in Picardy with their work because she wanted to focus on her own. Now she didn't have that excuse, nor could she claim the obligations of motherhood as reason for avoiding Hamidou's plea. Helping him restart the banned technology was dangerous, even more dangerous than her repair work with the Augmented veterans. But if it could help convince the king to be more tolerant, perhaps she would be able to work on automatons again, even create a second Automated Dauphin. "I'll help you. I don't have the strength to do all the needed work on the Weather Machines but I'll look for parts. Tell me what you need."

Hamidou named a few pieces, items Adelaide was familiar enough with to recognize on sight. She didn't recall any of them from her cursory search of the hidden workroom, but that didn't mean they could not be found.

"I will bring what I can find, and it may require some innovation on your part."

Hamidou shook her hand, a grin wreathed across his face. "Thank you, madame. Great things will come of this, to be sure. Shall we meet here again next week?"

She nodded and returned his smile. He traipsed away, lugging his toolbox and she watched him go. Would restarting the Paris Weather Machine really sway anyone to their cause, or would it be the final death knell on her work as a roboticist?

༂ Φ ༃

Adelaide let herself into a side entrance of the hospital, stamping her feet to warm them after her long walk. Her cloak was damp and she slipped it from her shoulders. It was still early enough that she had free time before feeding the patients dinner. She headed to the locked storage room that served as her makeshift workroom. Some of the parts Hamidou needed might already be there. Otherwise, she'd have to sneak into the robotics wing tonight to find them. The hidden laboratory she'd discovered only held so much. Hopefully there would be enough for her Augmentation repairs and the Weather Machine. The veterans who needed the repairs continued to find her. What would happen if she ran out of the necessary pieces to fix their Augmented limbs? Hamidou's project needed to be completed before that happened.

The corridors bustled with nun-nurses and orderlies and Adelaide worried that she wouldn't be able to slip unnoticed into the storage room. She hovered near the door, waiting for the hallway to clear of people.

Mireille discovered her there, a concerned look on her face. "Good afternoon. Did you enjoy your free time?"

Adelaide blushed like a child caught stealing a sweet. She hadn't exactly enjoyed herself but she chose a polite response. "Yes, Madame Director. It was cold but the gardens were still lovely."

"You still look chilled. Would you like a cup of tea to warm you?"

Adelaide hesitated, scanning the corridor for Nurse Emard. She didn't want her superior to know anything about her friendship with Mireille. There was no sign of the nun-nurse's gaunt form. "That would be lovely."

Mireille smiled into Adelaide's eyes. They proceeded to the director's cozy office and Adelaide hung her damp cloak on the cloak rack then settled on the divan with a sigh. She wiggled her toes, cold and cramped in the ill-fitting boots. Mireille handed her a steaming cup of tea and sat down next to her. "How's your work with the veterans? Is the arrangement working?"

Adelaide glanced at the closed door. Why was Mireille being so circumspect? No one could overhear their conversation. "It's harder than I expected." She had struggled with the repairs to the veteran's leg. The rust had penetrated deeper into the metal than it had first appeared and several components had cracked under her fingers as she worked. She gave up after the veteran's moans of pain had threatened to betray their presence in the storeroom.

"Can I do anything to help?"

Adelaide shook her head, warming her hands on her cup. "Not unless you can find a more competent Scientist, someone who actually knows how to repair machinery. I don't know if I can fix these Augmentations. Perhaps the first success was a fluke."

Mireille sipped her tea and watched Adelaide from under her eyelashes. "Do you really believe that? Are you giving up already?"

Adelaide gulped her tea, burning her mouth. Rather than looking at Mireille, she gazed across the room at the books arrayed on a shelf. "I seem to have forgotten my skills. My hands feel clumsy. I know I assured you that I could do it but now, I don't know if I can help the veterans."

Mireille snorted. Her cup clattered in its saucer. "Of course you can. You kept the Queen alive for years and that must have been far more complex than the Augmented limbs you're working on."

"I was only her physician for two years and she died just after I left. Not long enough for Valmont to do that much damage."

Mireille leaned over and patted Adelaide's hand. "My dear, you are too hard on yourself. Drink up your tea and tell me about your free afternoon."

Adelaide half-smiled then remembered Henri. Her face fell. "It would've been a fine time despite the cold, but I saw someone I hadn't expected to see."

"I take it from your expression that it was not a happy reunion?" Mireille's sympathetic look loosened Adelaide's tongue.

"No, that is, it wasn't a reunion. I just saw him sitting at a bistro." She twisted her lips at the thought, a bitter taste filling her mouth.

"Who was it? A fellow Scientist from before?"

Adelaide cringed. She hadn't already mentioned Hamidou to Mireille, had she? She pushed the thought away. "He's an artist. At least he was an artist the last time I saw him."

"You're being mysterious again, Adelaide. Do tell me who this artist is and why you weren't happy to see him."

Adelaide faced her. "Why do you care? I don't understand, The tea, the cozy chats. Why me?"

The director looked uncertain and her words were soft and gentle. "I care, Adelaide. I care about you. You seem so unhappy and alone. I thought you might need a friend."

Adelaide regarded her for a long moment. Friends? Friends were dangerous people. You let them see your vulnerability and they stabbed you there. "That is kind of you." She sounded stilted and stiff, even to her own ears.

"Won't you let me in, Adelaide? Tell me your troubles. This artist who upset you just with his unexpected presence, who is he?"

What did that secret matter? Adelaide's voice was low. "The father of my child." Her stomach turned at the thought. She'd never intended to be a mother or even have a lover. Henri had seduced her in a moment of weakness. She squashed the memory of that afternoon.

Mireille nodded. "Ah. I see. That would be upsetting. You parted on less than amicable terms. And now that you know he's back in Paris, what happens? Will he come looking for your child?"

Adelaide exhaled a deep sigh. "He doesn't know about the child. He'd have no reason to look for me. I think."

"Then you have no need for concern, my dear." She sat back and sipped her tea, still watching Adelaide.

"But he does know of my former position. He knows I was a high-ranking Scientist, personally serving the King and Queen. He could report me to the police."

Mireille sucked in a breath. "Ah. that could be a problem. We'd best make sure he doesn't find out where you are living. Perhaps a different route when you take walks?"

Adelaide nodded her agreement. She still didn't know what inspired this friendship, this loyalty from Mireille.

How in good conscience am I going to steal parts from her hospital for Hamidou? What if someone catches us and traces the source back to her? Who deserves my true loyalty, Hamidou or Mireille?

"You're still worried. There's something more, isn't there? Is it Nurse Emard?"

Adelaide placed her empty teacup on the little table beside her. "No, there's nothing more. I have nothing more to tell you."

Mireille put her arm on the back of the divan and turned her body towards Adelaide. "Adelaide, don't lie to me. I can tell you're keeping something from me."

Anger flared in Adelaide. Who was this woman to demand all of her secrets? She had never promised to tell her. Her tone was sharp. "I said, no. I have nothing more to tell you."

"You don't trust me. After all I've done for you, you still don't trust me. My situation is just as precarious as yours. If someone found out that I had given you the key and shown you the hidden passageway, I could be in deep trouble."

Adelaide got to her feet and glared down at Mireille. "I didn't ask for you to put yourself in that situation. You volunteered."

Mireille stood and placed a hand on Adelaide's arm. "I'm just asking you to trust me as I have trusted you."

Adelaide shook her head. "I trust no-one. It's safer that way." She gulped back a sob then stormed out of the room, her cloak abandoned.

ೞ Φ ೞ

Adelaide sorted machine parts in the locked storeroom, fighting the urge to slam the pieces onto the shelves. She could hear people outside in the corridor. Too much noise could draw their attention. Her jaw ached with tension. Had she just ruined her friendship with Mireille? Did she even want to be friends with the director? Or was there something more between them that she had squashed? And now she had to go back to the director's office to retrieve her cloak.

She fingered a metal part that could be useful for Hamidou's Weather Machine. She had promised to help him by finding parts but was it the right thing to do? Taking the parts from the hospital was technically stealing but was stealing the right thing to do? The end result was a restored France. How much would she do to achieve that? Stealing parts seemed minor but what if a veteran needed the part to repair his Augmentation? What other crimes was she willing to commit? She'd already deceived Mireille.

Adelaide leaned against a wall and stretched her weary back. She hadn't just deceived Mireille. She'd lied to her and now guilt ate at her guts. Adelaide winced at the memory of the hurt on Mireille's face.

She's shown herself to be my ally. She has trusted me and I am lying to her.

She huffed out a breath, disgusted with herself. She'd go to Mireille's office to get her cloak and tell her about Hamidou and the Weather Machine tomorrow morning. Feeling a little lighter, Adelaide left the storeroom to feed the patients dinner.

Nineteen

The Palace of Versailles sparkled despite the overcast sky. Henri followed a liveried servant through the tall golden doors leading into the palace. He tried not to gawk at the soaring ceiling, decorated with gilt carvings and frescoes. He'd been to the magnificent public gardens but never set foot in the palace. His shoes clattered on the marble floor as the servant led him to the king's reception room. Two guards bowed and opened the towering, carved wooden doors. Henri stepped into the bright chamber, lit with what seemed to be hundreds of candles. He glanced at the massive oil paintings hung on the brocade walls then around the room, taking in the sight of a crowd of richly dressed people, all courtiers no doubt. King Henri V stood in the midst of them, talking with expressive gestures.

A beautiful noblewoman smiled at Henri from the crowd of courtiers surrounding the king. She reminded him of Isabelle, with her golden-brown skin and dark eyes. Her brunette hair was swept up from her delicate cheekbones, then fell in loose coils around her silk-clad shoulders. The noblewoman's smile deepened at his scrutiny, dimples appearing in her cheeks. Henri could see why John had so enjoyed painting the noble beauties at Court although it seemed pure white skin was no longer in fashion. He flashed a seductive grin at her, his loins stirring. He adored Isabelle but monogamy was proving to be difficult. He wrenched his eyes from the noble beauty and focused on the king. He was here to laud the new monarch, not seduce his courtiers.

"Ah, Desjardins, so you finally made it out to Versailles to see me!" The king had spotted him and waved him closer. "But where is your delightful wife? Don't tell me you deserted her in England?"

Out of the corner of his eye, Henri saw the noblewoman's smile turn mocking. "I dared not bring her here, Your Majesty, where she could so easily succumb to your charms. She is tucked away safely in our little garret in Paris."

The king guffawed and smacked his fleshy lips together. "Yes, just as well, she is a tasty morsel and my courtiers would be hard pressed not to gobble her up." He grinned at his own jest.

Henri clenched his jaw. Tasty morsel? As if she were someone's mistress? Henri bared his teeth in a grin. "Then it was best for me to bid her to stay home. She's not comfortable in such grandeur."

And detests the game of seduction played at Court.

The king's gaze wandered around the elegant reception room, examining the courtiers gathered there. "Well, without your wife in tow, you are free to make the acquaintance of the beauties who fill my court. It's so good to be here, surrounded by all of this magnificence, don't you agree?"

Henri stole a glance at the flirtatious noblewoman, who looked boldly back at him. "It would be my honor to make the acquaintance of all of your courtiers."

The king shot a mischievous look at Henri then at the noblewoman. "Francoise, do come and be introduced to my favorite painter." She sauntered to the king's side. He placed his arm around her tightly corseted waist. "Henri

Desjardins, this is the Duchesse de Fronsac. She has long been a patron of the arts, have you not, chérie?"

The duchesse's voice was low and husky. "Indeed, sire. I have commissioned a number of portraits in the past. It is always my natal day gift to myself."

Henri bowed over her hand and brushed his lips across her soft hand. No gloves? How daring of her. "I believe your name is familiar to me, madame." This flirt had to be John's duchesse. Should he mention John's name? Or would that bring up the Marie-Ange tragedy?

Her laugh was a sultry purr. "Have you heard about me from other painters? Only good things, I hope?"

He shot a look up at her, a wry smile tugging up one side of his mouth. "Only the best of things." He released her hand.

"Excellent. Enchanted to make your acquaintance, Monsieur Desjardins." She dimpled a smile at him and turned back to her circle of friends, dismissing him. Henri raised an eyebrow.

A voice behind Henri spoke. "Quite a minx, that one. Her husband has let her run wild for so many years, it would be impossible to rein her in now." Henri turned. A quiet, pale courtier stood there. Was this her husband? Or an interested bystander?

"There you are, de la Fontaine!" The king strode to de la Fontaine's side and placed his hand on the courtier's shoulder. He beckoned to Henri, rings flashing on his fingers. "Desjardins, you must meet my chief advisor, the comte de la Fontaine. This man was responsible for me being able to ascend to the throne as is my rightful place."

De la Fontaine shook his head in denial. "You have many loyal subjects, Your Majesty. I can not claim to be responsible for your ascension, although I did aid the effort."

He wheezed as he spoke. Henri didn't see the telltale red cheeks of the consumptive but the man did not look well. His greyish pallor reminded Henri of the nobles of the previous court with their hereditary heart weakness. He had heard that they had all died without the care of the Royal Scientist Doctor and her fancy medical devices.

Henri bowed to the king. "France has benefited already from your monarchy, Your Majesty. It feels so much more real to stroll the streets of Paris in the rain at noon. And no clanking policemen or spy machines."

The king looked up at the high ceiling, painted with clouds and a blue sky. "I am pleased. Nature is in the ascendant."

The comte nodded, his face grave. "France is becoming more pure as we rid ourselves of these unnatural devices. And those who perpetuated the atrocities are being punished as they deserve."

The memory of Adelaide, walking free along the Rue de la Cite, sparked Henri's curiosity. "Have you managed to capture and punish all of the Scientists?"

"Scientists?" The king grimaced as if the word pained him. "My soldiers have located isolated groups of them, with the help of loyal citizens. Many of them are imprisoned. The most diabolical were executed. De la Fontaine, have we a plan for those in prison? We don't want the burden of feeding all of those traitors, do we?"

De la Fontaine coughed, a harsh bark that sounded painful to Henri. "There was talk in the Senate of rehabilitation, Your Majesty. Perhaps as soldiers or farm laborers. The country needs more farmers. Our crop yields are down. The Minister of Agriculture has suggested clearing land to plant more next spring but that would require more laborers."

Scientists, reduced to mere farm laborers? Henri had a difficult time picturing the proud Adelaide Coumain plowing a field. It might change her mind about the importance of respecting the natural world though. He must have made a sound because the king threw him a sharp look.

"Something amusing about farm laborers, Desjardins?"

"I was merely picturing proud Scientists having to plow fields."

The king scowled. "It would be fine justice."

De la Fontaine shrugged and placed a hand on the king's arm. He leaned in to the king. "Perhaps but they could rebel against their new role. I'd be more inclined to execute them all, sire. A clean slate as it were."

Henri cleared his throat. This was certainly not the compassionate king he had expected. "That could be seen as somewhat brutal, sire. The French wish for justice, not tyranny. And I've heard that the shortage of grain is causing unrest."

The king pulled away from De la Fontaine, his scowl deepening. He drew himself up to his not-impressive full height. "I don't care to be lectured on what the French wish for. I am the King of France and my decisions shouldn't be questioned."

Henri knew he should stay quiet but the words burst from him. "Your Majesty, France is ruled by a democratic monarchy, not a tyranny. The people's voice must be heard."

De la Fontaine shook his head at Henri, hand over his mouth. The king narrowed his eyes. "Why is an artist lecturing his king?"

Henri's face grew warm. "I apologize if I gave offense, Your Majesty. I spoke out of turn."

The king nodded his head once, then stalked away from Henri and the comte.

De la Fontaine stepped closer to Henri and lowered his voice. "That was not wise of you to criticize him, Monsieur Desjardins."

Henri drew his brows together. "Monsieur le comte, it's 1881, not 1581. The world has changed since the feudal days. People expect their voices to be heard by their government. We thought our new king would lead the way into modernity, not become one of the despot kings of the past."

The comte nodded, shifting his weight from one foot to the next. He glanced around at the courtiers but no one seemed to be paying attention to their conversation. "He's still not sure of himself. All those years in exile, he wasn't trained to rule a country. Be patient."

Henri looked across the room at the king, surrounded by fawning courtiers. "But all this talk of mass executions? You can't be serious."

The comte's face was grave. "The country needs to be purified, monsieur. We must rid ourselves of the abomination that is Science so that the Holy Spirit will bless us. Grain will then be in plentiful supply."

Henri smiled politely. All this talk of purification made him squirm. His feet ached in the unaccustomed dress shoes and his stomach growled with hunger. He was ready to go home. He surveyed the room again but couldn't see the Duchesse de Fronsac. Isabelle would be disappointed that he didn't have any new commissions or even the fees owed him from the English paintings he'd done of the king but he had endured enough sycophancy for the day. He bowed and excused himself.

ಬ Φ ೞ

Isabelle burst into the apartment at the top of Gleyre's house and shook water off her purple and gold parasol. The silk was spotted, stained beyond cleaning. She frowned at the sodden parasol, then caught Henri's eyes and smiled. "Cheri, you're back. Did you get caught in this blasted rain? Look at my parasol, it's ruined. What I need is a parasol that won't get ruined in the rain. Oh. I suppose that would be an umbrella. I need an umbrella. I'll have to pick one up next time I go shopping."

Henri scratched his nose and shifted in the lumpy chair he was reclining in. "No new expenses yet, ma chère, alright?"

Isabelle paused as she was unclasping her cloak and shot him a sharp look. "The king didn't give you your fee, did he?" She dropped the cloak onto the coat rack and sank into a nearby chair with a sigh. Her eyes were wide with reproach.

Henri shrugged. "No, not yet. He's very busy, you know. Lots of affairs of state and other kingly things. The subject didn't come up."

Isabelle snorted and shook her head. One of her ringlets bounced free of her coiffure and clung to her damp forehead. "Of course he's too busy for a little thing like paying for his portrait. Henri, monarchs have people who take care of their business. You must apply to them, not the king, for payment." She leaned against the back of her chair, her corset holding her awkwardly upright.

Henri shifted in his own uncomfortable chair. "Of course. I didn't think of that. I'll have to go back to Versailles and ask the king's advisor for payment. "

The image of the flirtatious duchesse flitted across his mind.

"Henri, what are you smiling about? Did you get some new commissions?"

Perhaps the duchesse would commission me to paint her natal day portrait.

Henri got to his feet and wandered to the grimy window overlooking the lush, overgrown garden. None of Arthur's students were painting outdoors today so the garden was empty. "New commissions? No, not yet. A possibility perhaps."

Isabelle swayed over to him and wrapped her arm around his waist. "Cheri, you do need to go back out there to Versailles. You'll have to hire another carriage."

He leaned on the windowsill, away from her embrace. "Why am I even trying to paint the Court? I don't flatter my subjects. You know that. My work has always depicted real people, common folk. Not rich aristocrats."

Although I could be tempted to paint a certain duchesse if she were willing to show her skin.

Isabelle rested against the wall next to the window and looked up at him. "Common people can't pay to commission paintings."

Henri threw his hands up in disgust. "Isabelle, I don't want to be a portrait painter. I'm not John. I'll contact my old clients, the ones who used to buy my work when I lived here. I could convince them to advance me the fee so I can buy fresh paints and canvas."

"And pay for the roof over our heads. We can't continue to rely on Arthur's hospitality. He's barely able to support himself. And our expenses are going to increase."

He shook his finger at her. "I said no more fripperies, chérie."

Isabelle drew his hand to her mouth and kissed it. "I'm going to need new dresses."

Henri pulled her close and ran his hands down her back, feeling for her laces. "I just bought you a new wardrobe when we got married. Have you already tired of your dresses?"

She gazed up at him, her hazel eyes glistening. "They're beautiful. You know I love them, but in a few months, they won't fit anymore."

Henri's heart seemed to skip a beat. His fingers stilled. "Isabelle? Are you...?"

"Having a baby." The threatening tears spilled over onto her tawny cheeks.

His blood hammered in his head and he couldn't breathe, then a rush of unexpected joy filled him. He crushed her to him. "My darling, my love, this is amazing, I can't believe it ... a baby. Our baby." He pushed thoughts of the duchesse from his mind and kissed Isabelle's wet face.

"I know it's not the best of times..."

Henri caressed her hair. "Don't worry, ma chère. It'll be fine. I will take care of you and our baby. Whatever it takes."

If painting insipid portraits of inbred nobles is what it takes to support my wife and child, that's what I'll do. Even if I hate every minute of it.

Twenty

Adelaide traipsed across the bridge over the Seine, the Hôtel-Dieu towering behind her and in the distance behind it, the cathedral. She walked in the opposite distance, not wanting to be drawn into the church services by the nuns streaming in that direction. Foot traffic on the bridge moved against her, more parishioners headed over to Notre Dame for the Sunday mass.

Adelaide hadn't paid attention to people attending church services in the past. She'd never known any churchgoers since the only people she knew were Scientists. Now, working in a hospital staffed almost entirely by nuns, she realized that they regularly attended church services along with residents of the area.

People in their Sunday best stared at her going against the flow. Adelaide looked away from their accusing faces, over the balustrades of the bridge. The waters of the Seine flowed by, brown and muddy. The little boats flitted back and forth, carrying passengers up and downstream. Carriage rides were expensive especially for a long trip through Paris. The boats were cheap, although uncomfortable and liable to tip their passengers into the frigid water.

Adelaide stopped and peered over at the passing boats. What if Henri was riding in one? She needed to know where he was staying. The better for keeping an eye on him. What was he doing here in Paris? She didn't know if he was a native. Did he return to visit family? Was he back to stay? She was frustrated that she knew so little about this man who had fathered her child. For the millionth time, she berated herself for bedding him. What a stupid, weak choice that had been. There had been pleasure, certainly, but her life had gone into a tailspin afterwards. She couldn't imagine how much worse her life could be, Well, except for being dead. Not being Royal Scientist-Physician after the old Queen had died had saved Adelaide's life. She wondered if the Queen had noticed her absence after the Scientist President had dismissed her. The Queen had always been inscrutable to Adelaide. Her face had been so heavily enameled, it was all but a mask. She rarely spoke, conserving her flagging energy and had ultimately been too weak for the planned heart transplant. Adelaide had ordered her an Archimedean heart from the master machinist but it had remained in its packing box in Adelaide's workroom at the Palace. Adelaide wondered what had happened to it after the regime change. The new king had abolished all augmentation work so it may have been destroyed, A pity, It had been such a lovely thing, all precious metals carved into symmetrical anatomical forms.

    Birds wheeled in the air above Adelaide, startling her out of her daydream with their wing beats. Her feet had turned numb from the cold as she stood there musing. She continued her walk. She had at least a couple of hours to herself before the nuns returned from Mass. Nurse Emard had worn her usual sneer as Adelaide had left the hospital and made a snide comment about the loose morals of people who didn't attend church.

    Adelaide turned onto the river promenade and made her way to the 5th Arrondissment. The Café de Flore was on the other side of the Jardin du Luxembourg. Logically, Henri was probably staying nearby. She pushed aside the little voice inside her head questioning why she needed to find out Henri's whereabouts so badly. Revenge. She craved revenge. He had killed Marie-Ange somehow, she was sure of it. He deserved to be punished for her murder. But how did he kill her?

She thought back to that dreadful day almost a year ago. She'd discovered Marie-Ange unconscious and not breathing on the floor outside her workroom. There had been an explosion, one of several that week. The Naturalists had infiltrated the Palace and set off bombs to terrify the monarchs into surrendering to their terms. Adelaide couldn't forget Marie-Ange, lying on the marble floor in a cloud of billowing petticoats. The girl's chest was bruised and swollen. Her Archimedean heart, the only one Adelaide had managed to install before her dismissal, had been damaged somehow. Adelaide had guessed some kind of concussive blast had stopped the clockwork mechanism of her heart. But how? Had Henri been carrying a bomb? Adelaide frowned as she paced the cobblestone streets. She didn't remember seeing Henri at Versailles, except in the gardens. But she knew a painter had been responsible for the blast. She'd spotted a wooden case near Marie-Ange's body but it had been removed while she was trying to revive the girl. All that had remained when Adelaide went back to the corridor had been a paint-encrusted brush. Had Henri been painting one of the nobles? Or had there been another painter? Adelaide stopped short and a person behind her bumped into her, cursing under his breath. She flushed and murmured an apology. Another painter? Yes, there had been another painter in the palace. She chewed at her lip. So perhaps Henri hadn't been the murderer? No, it must have been him. He was a Naturalist after all. His seditious words to her had been enough for her to report him to the Police

Secrète. The inspector general had told her that he'd been arrested and imprisoned in the Bastille. But then he had escaped and fled the country. She had asked in his old neighborhood of Montmartre and that was what she'd heard. Montmartre. Could he be living there again? So why would he be in this neighborhood? She had reached the Café de Flore. The chilly day had forced all the patrons inside. Did she dare go inside to see if he was there? She didn't want him knowing where she was living. It was a dangerous game she was playing. He could easily report her as a fugitive Scientist. She would have to stay hidden and observe him covertly. Adelaide scanned the area. There was a small church nearby. The doors were shut and the sound of singing emanated from inside. She stepped up into the portico and withdrew into the shadows. She could stay there until the services ended, watching to see if Henri appeared. She stamped her feet and blew onto her hands. She wasn't sure how long she'd be able to keep watch here in this weather.

The door to the bistro swung open, a bell tinkling. Two people, chattering, muffled their faces with heavy scarves. Adelaide squinted, trying to see if she recognized them. They didn't look familiar. She slumped against the wooden frame of the portico. She didn't have much longer before she had to be back at the hospital and she was going to freeze to death if she stood here. Perhaps a walk around the neighborhood would be more fruitful. She wrapped her scarf more tightly around her neck and chin. She had no hat, just a woolen hood. She tugged that down over her face further, hiding her distinctive eyebrows, Adelaide wished she had an umbrella to hide beneath but since it wasn't raining, that would probably look odd. She didn't want to be conspicuous.

She looked both ways along the boulevard then stepped out of her shelter. A gust of wind tangled her skirts around her ankles and chilled her even more. She shivered. A pity she wasn't trying to find Henri on a more pleasant day but this close to winter, the cold would only get more intense. There were few people walking along the streets as she made her way around the neighborhood. She walked at a measured pace, head down, but darting her eyes from side to side. Watching for him. She found her heart beating too quickly. Was that fear or excitement? Or both? She sniffed and wiped her cold running nose. The houses on this boulevard belonged to wealthy people. They towered on either side, four or five floors of grand stone facades with elegant windows. Some had courtyards full of greenery, secreted from prying eyes behind sturdy gates. She longed to sit in those secret gardens, surrounded by lush foliage and blooms. They were tucked away from the harsh wind that continued to nip at her. Adelaide shook her head sadly. She'd probably never be admitted to those private, exclusive enclaves. And wasn't Henri a penniless painter? She remembered his decrepit garret in Montmartre. He had had little money then but perhaps now, it was different. He'd looked well-off when she spotted him at the bistro, his clothes well-brushed and in good condition. The woman he had been escorting had been clad in a rich olive-green gown and cloak. It struck Adelaide that she too had looked familiar. Was that the woman who had come to his garret when Adelaide had been tending his sprained ankle? She'd driven him home from Versailles in her private electric carriage that night. She wondered what had happened to that little vehicle. It had remained at Versailles after she was dismissed. Probably destroyed by the Naturalists when they took power. Adelaide sighed. She needed to help restore

France to modernity. This insistence on rejecting all technology was backwards. France would suffer while the rest of the world continued the march into the future. What would happen when the scientists who had fled France began working for other governments and advancing science there? Adelaide had rejected the opportunity to go to Vienna and work with the Austrian roboticists. Maybe she should have. The Automated Dauphin wouldn't have been destroyed. But he would have been co-opted by a foreign government. He might have become the Automated Kaiser. Adelaide couldn't accept that. She'd created him for France, not for another nation. It was just as well this way. Someday, when Science regained favor in France. she would create another Automated Dauphin. Her notes had been destroyed in the farmhouse fire, but the basics of his design remained in her memory.

She reached the boulevard that would take her back across the bridge to the Île de la Cité and turned towards the river. A gorgeous garden courtyard next to a spacious house caught her eye. It was the largest garden she'd seen in this area.

Who lives here? They must be immensely wealthy.

Voices from inside the house echoed into the street as the occupants opened the front door. Adelaide turned away, not wanting to be seen, and stepped behind the pedestal holding a statue of someone famous. Were those voices familiar? That laugh. It was him. Henri was standing on the front steps of that grand house, laughing at something someone inside was saying. Adelaide peeked around the pedestal. He and the woman she'd seen with him at the Café de Flore stood there, kissing. She felt a spasm of jealousy but quickly squashed it. Was the woman his wife? She turned away, intending to get away before he spotted her.

She scurried down the boulevard, in the opposite direction that she needed to go. It was getting late. She needed to get back to the hospital. Was that the bells, ringing for the end of services? In her haste, she bumped into a man and drew back, "My pardon, monsieur. I wasn't paying attention."

The man smiled kindly. "It's nothing, madame." He raised his eyebrows. "Good day to you, Madame Coumain."

She glanced at him with wide eyes. It was the other painter she's seen at Versailles. He was the same one that had been with Henri at the Café de Flore. She may have discovered Henri's domicile but now his friend had recognized her. She stepped around him without a word and stomped away, furious with herself for her clumsy attempt at surveillance.

༄ Φ ༅

Adelaide hurried through the streets, the bells of the churches ringing madly around her. People streamed out of the church doors, heading for their Sunday dinners. Her stomach grumbled. All that was waiting for her was gruel laced with gristly meat and bitter herbs. What she wouldn't give for some coq au vin with crusty bread to sop up the sauce. She sighed. If the hospital paid her more, she could stop into one of the little bistros filling up with people along the way and have a satisfying meal. She didn't have the money or time. Adelaide picked up her pace. She'd be needed to feed the patients soon.

The crowds parted before her vigorous trot but she pulled up short, a man on crutches in her way. She murmured her pardon as she dodged him but caught sight of his face as she passed. It was Axel Boulet, the veteran she'd recently helped. But why was he on crutches? She slowed to match his pace and turned her face towards him. "Monsieur Boulet? Is your leg bothering you again?"

He started and glanced at her. "Madame? Oh, it's you. As you can see, the leg stopped working." He glowered at her, his handsome face drawn with pain and fury.

Adelaide put her hand to her mouth. "Oh no. I'm so sorry. I don't know what would cause that." She felt incompetent and unsure of herself. She didn't know why the repair hadn't stayed working.

He crutched forward, his mouth grimacing with every step. "It doesn't matter anymore."

She swallowed a lump in her throat. "But it does. I thought you needed to be whole so you could help support your parents."

"I'm better to them dead. At least they wouldn't have to feed me and they'll get my army pension."

"Oh Axel, I know they don't feel that way."

He shook his head in silence, not looking in her direction.

She placed a timid hand on his sleeve. "I can take a look at it? Maybe there was something I missed. It worked at first, right?"

He snorted. "It worked until I tried to climb a ladder at the job I briefly had. Then it gave way and I almost fell to my death. I should've let go of the ladder and fallen."

Adelaide gulped, tears stinging her eyes. Guilt almost overwhelmed her. Her shoddy repair job had almost caused a death. Did she even dare to try again?

"Do you want me to look at your leg? You can't really mean to die and leave your parents alone. You're their only son, Axel."

He traipsed on, not responding. She kept up with him, worried about the time, but unwilling to leave him as he was. She was about to give up and go back to the hospital but he responded. "Alright. I'll give you another chance. I live over here."

They progressed down a dim, narrow street, Adelaide splashed through a puddle that smelled of human detritus. She flinched at the cold, stinking water penetrating her leaky boots. The house was tall and narrow, shutters half-hanging off the windows. It didn't look anything like the grand houses lining the boulevard. These back alleys and ramshackle houses were where the poor people of Paris huddled.

"In through here. Maman, I'm back." He ducked under the door frame and gestured for Adelaide to follow.

The hallway was dark and smelled of cabbage. Adelaide remembered Zilda and her cooking. Cabbage was always present in the kitchens of the poor. It was cheap. Axel led the way to a little sitting room, the brown furniture in it were scattered about. Nothing matched. The fire in the grate was out. Axel sat down with a thud on the rickety sofa and placed his crutches next to him. He rubbed his hands together and blew on them. He didn't take off his coat or scarf in the frigid room. Adelaide sat down next to him.

"Roll up your trouser leg and let me take a look,"

With a sigh, he lifted his leg up onto the sofa, sulky as a child told to clean his room. The leg's mechanisms weren't moving. They weren't reacting at all to his neural inputs.

She frowned. "That's not good. The mechanisms are completely quiescent. Tell me what happened when it stopped working. Was there any indication of a problem?"

Axel shook his head. "I don't think so. I don't remember much of that day. I fainted after I fell."

Adelaide made a hmming sound. "Are you sure you fainted after you fell, not before? Please try to remember, it's important. I'll need to get a closer look at the interface. Can you remove your trousers?"

A woman's voice came from the door of the sitting room, sounding shocked. "Remove his trousers? What's going on in here, Axel?"

Adelaide glanced at the door. An older woman stood there, with her arms crossed and a severe look on her face.

Axel gestured towards Adelaide. "Maman, this is Doctor Coumain. She was trying to help fix my leg."

His mother sucked in a breath. "A doctor? Who repairs augmentations? That is against the law."

Adelaide shifted in her seat, looking from Axel to his mother. "I was only trying to help, Madame Boulet."

"Haven't you helped enough? My son was almost killed when he fell off that ladder. If you hadn't messed around with his legs, he wouldn't have thought it safe to climb ladders."

Adelaide got to her feet, her knees wobbling. "I'm sorry, I'll go."

Madame Boulet glared at her. "Someone should turn you into the police. You're a menace."

The room seemed to spin and Adelaide struggled to breathe. "Please, I was only trying to help." She looked down at Axel, appealing him for help with her eyes.

Axel groaned and pulled his leg back to the floor. "It's no use. Please, just go away."

Adelaide edged past Madame Boulet and dashed from the little house, feeling the disapproval of the Boulets at her back. Why had Axel's leg stopped working? She wished she'd been able to examine the interface between the Augmentation and his leg. She remembered the sight of his mother's angry face. Would they really turn her in? Should she stop trying to repair Augmentations?

ಬ Φ ಆ

The bells of Notre Dame were ringing the noon hour as Adelaide dashed into the side entrance of the hospital closest to the veterans' ward, hoping to get there before Nurse Emard noticed her absence. Nuns and orderlies bustled along the corridors, carrying trays of bowls filled with the patients' lunch. The whiff of the herbs steaming off the gruel made Adelaide wrinkle her nose. Her own portion of the herbal gruel had made her woozy as always but the walk after her own lunch had cleared her head. She reached the door to the ward and peeked in. Nurse Emard sat at the nurses' station. She narrowed her eyes at Adelaide. "You're late, Coumain. The patients are waiting for their lunch, and now it will be cold. Where have you been all this time?"

Adelaide flushed and dropped her eyes. "I apologize, Nurse Emard. I went for a walk in the gardens and got turned around. It took me much longer to find my way back than I anticipated."

She looked up. Nurse Emard tsked, her thin lips twisted with disapproval. "Tardiness is not acceptable in this ward. I will report this to the director."

Adelaide nodded and moved over to the food station and ladled gruel into bowls. She walked around the ward, checking on the patients as she gave them their lunch. Her examinations had to be subtle so Nurse Emard wouldn't spot her. Adelaide's efforts at sanitation seemed to be helping some of the patients. The veteran whose leg had rusted gazed at Adelaide, his eyes filled with sadness. She wished she could fix his leg but it would require more parts than she had access to.

I'll have to look again in that hidden lab when I pick out some tools for Hamidou.

At the thought of the other scientist, she felt a pang of guilt. She was stealing parts from the hospital for Hamidou, for his project that might be destroyed as soon as he got it working. Parts that could help these veterans. But she needed to remember that they were trying to restore France, making their country successful and forward thinking again. These veterans were just individuals. Adelaide tried to convince herself that the big picture mattered more but she loathed seeing these miserable men with their defective limbs that she could help.

Except that her last two attempts at repair had failed. Was it her fault that Axel's leg stopped working? What had she missed when she rewired the mechanisms to stop the pain? She wished she could help him but she was sure that his termagant mother would prevent Adelaide from going to the house.

Adelaide finished serving lunch and carried the dirty dishes to the kitchen. She had a sudden urge to see Mireille, to sit with her in her comfortable office and drink tea. Nurse Emard thought she was washing dishes. Adelaide had a little time to sneak into the director's office and spend a moment or two.

She dropped the dishes in the scullery and scampered out before anyone noticed her. She didn't like shirking her duties but she felt compelled to see Mireille. Adelaide was astonished at her feelings but the director's consistent kindness had penetrated to her wounded heart. She slipped through the corridors, willing the nuns pacing by to ignore her. She made it to the door of the office, tucked away under a curving staircase. The door was ajar, Mireille's usual practice. Adelaide peeked inside. Mireille sat at her desk, resplendent in a deep wine-red wool gown, embellished with navy trim. She was always was beautifully attired, her hair caught up in intricate curls and braids. Adelaide felt a rush of warmth at the sight.

She must have a lady's maid. I suppose the director of a hospital is a lucrative profession. And she comes from a prestigious family. What does she see in a fugitive from a poor fisherman's family?

Adelaide stood, drinking in Mireille's lovely appearance.

Mireille must have sensed Adelaide standing there and looked up, one eyebrow raised. "Adelaide. I wasn't expecting you, ma chère. Please, come in. What can I do for you?" Her tone was warm, sending warmth throughout Adelaide's body.

"I wanted to see you." Adelaide blushed at her boldness and rubbed her hands down her grubby apron. She should have changed before coming to see Mireille, or at least taken off the apron.

Mireille got to her feet and circled the desk. "A social call? Or is something bothering you? Please, sit down. I'll make us some tea." She shut the office door and busied herself heating water, dispensing tea leaves and swirling the hot water in the tea pot.

The domesticity calmed Adelaide. She took a deep breath, the first it seemed like in hours. "Thank you. It's good of you to take care of me like this."

Mireille handed her a tea cup of steaming tea and sat down next to her. Concern was drawn on her face. "You look upset. Is it Emard again?"

Adelaide shook her head. She cocked her head and smiled at Mireille. "Can't I just stop by to see you?"

Mireille's smile deepened and she placed her soft hand on top of Adelaide's. "Ma chere, you are always welcome to sit and drink tea with me. But I know you better. You didn't just pop in for a cup of tea. What's wrong?"

Adelaide bit her lip. Mireille could read her, more than anyone else. "I was out for a walk and I spotted one of the veterans I repaired. He was using crutches. The mechanical leg had ceased functioning. I tried to examine him but his mother threatened to tell the police that I am a scientist."

Mireille patted Adelaide's rough hand. "And now you're blaming yourself for the malfunction."

"Yes. Mireille, he almost died falling off a ladder when the leg malfunctioned. I would have been responsible for his death."

Mireille shook her head and squeezed Adelaide's hand. "You didn't tell him to climb a ladder a week after his legs started functioning again."

Adelaide gulped her tea, the hot liquid scalding her tongue. Mireille stroked her hand with long, soft caresses. Adelaide suppressed a shiver of delight at the sensation. "Mireille, what if my skills have atrophied and I'm doing more harm than good?"

Mireille clicked her tongue. "We've had this conversation. They have no one else to help them. Perhaps you're out of practice since your Academy days but it will come back to you."

"There's something else." Adelaide's voice was low and Mireille leaned closer to hear.

"Something else is upsetting you?"

Adelaide peered into the bottom of her empty tea cup. How much should she tell Mireille about Henri? She looked at Mireille's face, so close that Adelaide could see the laugh lines around her eyes. "I think we should place the veterans in a separate building. They don't need healing; they just need somewhere comfortable to rest. And you know those wards are not comfortable. They're drafty. The windows aren't sealed well and the wood stoves do nothing to heat the room."

Mireille sat back and fixed Adelaide with an appraising look. "What do you have in mind?"

Adelaide swallowed, nervous now. "I've been walking over in the fifth Arrondissment, near the Jardin du Luxembourg. I spotted a large house. It's surrounded by the most beautiful gardens. I think it's being used as an artists' studio but almost no one goes in."

"An artists' studio? Of all houses in the area, why this one? Others have gardens too."

Adelaide put her cup down and twisted her hands together. "I think the hospital could buy it cheaply. The artists don't seem to be doing well. The house is grimy and not well-kept."

Mireille cocked her head to one side. "Do you know the artists who live there?"

Adelaide bit her lip, feeling a flush wash across her cheeks. "Um. Yes. I am acquainted with one of them."

Mireille quirked a grin. "It's that artist who fathered your child, isn't it? And you want me to buy the house and throw him onto the street."

How did she figure out Adelaide's motives so quickly? Adelaide nodded, miserable and guilty. "I know it seems petty but they're not sterling citizens. He and his friends were accused of crimes before they fled to England."

Mireille exhaled a soft sigh. "My dear, you're not the police. But you don't care about that, you just want revenge, don't you?"

Adelaide burst out, her voice cracking. "He killed my patient with some sort of bomb at Versailles. He needs to be punished for that."

Mireille sat back and wrinkled her brow. "Did he murder her before you sent him to prison? You said he was imprisoned for seditious talk, not murder."

Adelaide shook her head. "The day she was murdered, I received news that he had escaped prison but he wouldn't have dared come to the Palace. But he may have helped plan the attack, even if he hadn't carried the bomb himself. He was a Naturalist even then. And it was an artist who had the bomb, I'm certain of that."

Mireille looked away and was silent for a few moments. "Adelaide, do you really want this? Will it help you heal to know that you were responsible for throwing this man onto the street?"

Adelaide thought of the long, miserable year she'd just had, precipitated by Henri. She'd lost her position, her Automated Dauphin, even her child. It was all his fault. She clenched her jaw. "Yes. I want him punished."

Mireille reached up to brush a lock of hair off Adelaide's cheek. "I will make inquiries. It's true that our veterans do need a better place to rest. Most of them are never going home. I hope this will make you happy."

Adelaide smiled into Mireille's concerned eyes, but the smile felt stiff. "Thank you, Mireille. I need this."

Mireille stood and brushed a kiss across the crown of Adelaide's head. "You'd better get back to work. It wouldn't do for Emard to find you here again."

Adelaide left the room, not looking back. She didn't want to see the look of worry on Mireille's face. Her vengeance was underway.

Twenty-one

Adelaide looked down at the face of her baby. It was covered with a metal mask with a hole for a mouth. The body nestling in her arms weighed much more than a flesh child would. The child whimpered, an odd mechanical sound echoing from the mouth hole. Adelaide caressed his smooth, cold cheek and nose, the Bourbon nose already visible.

"When you grow up, you'll be the new Automated Dauphin." She smiled down at her child but a nagging feeling of wrongness tickled her mind.

Without warning, Nurse Emard appeared and snatched the baby from Adelaide's arms. "Abomination! This is what happens when women have loose morals! They birth abominations!" The nun's face was contorted with rage.

Adelaide cried out and reached for the child, but her arms moved with an impossible slowness. She could only watch as the nun raised the metal child into the air and threw him into the roaring fire in the hearth next to Adelaide's bed. Adelaide screamed in horror as the flames consumed the metal child.

She woke and sat upright, shivering in reaction. The women's dormitory was dark and silent. Adelaide tried to catch her breath but her lungs were tight with fear.

Only a dream. It was only a dream. Little Henri is fine.

Adelaide held her shaking hands to her face. She gulped for air then pulled her blanket up around her shoulder to stave off the chill of the room. It was a long time before dawn, but sleep would not visit her again that night.

Twenty-two

The mahogany dining room table was too big for the four of the them sitting around it. Henri was sure that the food at Gleyre's house in better days had been more elaborate but he was too hungry to complain. Arthur had dismissed the last of the servants last month, leaving Isabelle to cook for them all. Not for the first time, Henri wished that his grandmother had taught him how to cook. He missed her spicy Senegalese dishes. Grandmère. He wished he could help move her out of that squalid garret she lived in. The dinner that Isabelle had put together was basic with none of Grandmère's seasonings, but she always roasted chicken to perfection. They couldn't afford much more than chicken though. Not yet. Henri would have to visit his old patrons and offer his services. They were merchants and had probably done well in these days of no free bread. Portraits of merchants' wives and their simpering children loomed in his future.

He pushed aside his worries and raised his glass to his dining companions, smiling at them. John was brooding. He'd been unhappy for days but wouldn't tell Henri was wrong. Arthur looked pensive. He had been closeted up with Gleyre for hours that afternoon. The old artist didn't come downstairs much. He preferred to be alone. His mind wandered most days and staying up in his suite was more comfortable for him. Arthur would take him food after they had eaten even though he didn't eat much anymore.

Isabelle sat down next to him and squeezed his hand. He threw a smile at her. Was she already glowing with that maternal light? He raised her hand to his lips and kissed it. "Thank you for dinner, my darling. Delicious as always."

The other two men mumbled their thanks. She shrugged, an arch look on her face. "It's nothing fancy but it fills your belly."

Isabelle got up from the table to fetch the next course. She had warned them that the pot-au-feu would be a stew of mostly vegetables.

Henri opened another bottle of burgundy and poured wine for everyone. He had only enough money to purchase one bottle from the wine merchant and that had stayed with his grandmother. Fortunately, Gleyre's wine cellar was still allowing them wine with dinner, even if they had little money for expensive cuts of meat. Or any meat at all. Henri longed suddenly for some braised lamb or veal tongue. At least they could still afford peppered onion soup, his favorite. Isabelle was wicked with the amount of pepper, one of the few dishes that rivaled his Grandmère's seasonings.

Henri inhaled the aroma of the wine, closing his eyes in delight. "This is lovely, Arthur. Good choice."

Arthur frowned, a slight crease between his eyebrows. "Is it? I just grabbed the closest one I could find. It was very dusty. I hoped it hadn't gone bad."

Henri chuckled and examined the label. "It was dusty because it had been down there for decades. Very nice vintage." He felt the wine mellow him and he surveyed his companions, wondering why they both looked so miserable and uncomfortable. Isabelle returned with the stew and some crusty bread.

She winked at Henri. "Someone gave me a great deal on bread when she heard you were back in Paris. You have fans among the grandmères, ma cher."

Henri grinned. "Yes, the grandmères love me. I really must take you to visit my own grandmère. She still hasn't met you, my dearest wife. She'll be quite annoyed with me if she finds out I have married and not introduced my bride to her."

Isabelle served the stew and sliced bread for everyone. "You didn't mention me when you saw her last? We could go tomorrow if it's not raining too much. How far does she live?"

"Across the river. John, would you like to come too?" Henri was trying to shake John out of his glum mood.

John looked up from his meal. "But I don't even know her. She's not my grandmother."

Henri shrugged. "Doesn't matter. She'd like you. She likes pretty boys. And she knows about you, you know. She was always curious about you. You can come too, Arthur. My grandmère is an amazing cook. She was born in Senegal and combines French food with Senegalese." He didn't mention that they would need to buy all the ingredients for her.

Isabelle sniffed, an indignant little noise.

Henri squeezed her hand. "I have no complaints about your cooking skills, chérie."

She gave him a look, then relented and smiled back. "I never did learn much about cooking. My sisters were the ones who helped Maman in the kitchen. You're lucky I don't serve you undercooked and burned chicken."

Henri took a bite of the stew and nodded. "Your roast chicken is exquisite. Pass the salt, Arthur? Tell me, gentlemen, when are we hosting a studio next? Have we enough students to do so?"

Arthur bit his lip. "No, the students have all disappeared, it seems. I suppose they're all mad for someone new. They're not interested in what I can teach them."

John looked up at the ceiling, in the direction of Gleyre's apartment. "I suppose they all wanted Gleyre, not us."

Arthur nodded his agreement. "Students have been disappearing from the studio ever since Gleyre retired. I don't think I'm fashionable enough. And you two have only just arrived, so no one really knows that you've returned. You haven't announced your presence."

Henri put his spoon down and stared at Arthur. "We were unsure of our reception here. If we make our presence well known, we could attract the notice of the police. I don't know if John was ever charged of anything but I was in the Bastille."

Arthur drew his brows together in thought. "The newspapers must have been censored. I didn't read anything about you escaping custody. And there was no mention of John at all. I really don't think you have to worry. Getting your name out there would improve the studio's popularity. But I fear it's too late now."

Henri looked sharply at Arthur. "Too late? What do you mean?"

Arthur poked at his stew with his spoon then took a long draught of wine. "Gleyre has been talking about selling the house and moving to a little cottage on the coast, in the village where he grew up. He's talked about it before but he's been mentioning it more and more frequently of late. His solicitors were here with papers today."

Henri broke in, shaking his head wildly. "No! He can't sell the house. It's a gathering place for artists, has been for decades. Where would we go?" Henri's voice trembled with emotion. How could Gleyre even consider such a thing? Henri knew the old man was wandering in his mind but didn't he love this house? How could he think of leaving it?

Arthur dropped his head, sadness painting his face. "I know, it's a tradition, this place, but the younger students have forgotten about it. They go to other studios over in Montmartre now. They can't be bothered to trek all the way here." His tone was sarcastic, surprising to hear from the usual placid Arthur.

John sighed and sat back, twirling his glass around in his fingers. He watched the wine swirl. "As if Montmartre is such a great distance. We used to come over here all the time when we lived in Montmartre, didn't we, Henri? I loved that walk along the broad boulevards, watching the light play across the stones of the mansions and churches. Now the students just want to sit around and drink absinthe in the bars and pretend they're artists."

Henri threw his hands up, exasperated by his brother's placid reaction. "Who will buy this gigantic house? It's sure to cost more than most can afford with the gardens. Are the bourgeoisie doing that well now? Or has the king granted money to his loyal nobles?"

Arthur shook his head. "Neither. Apparently the Board at the Hôtel-Dieu is in need of a new building. They want to open a convalescent home for army veterans. This house isn't too far from the hospital and the gardens would be nice for invalids."

Henri placed his wine glass down with a thump and leaned forward. "A convalescent home? Arthur, you can't just be giving up? Can't you convince Gleyre to keep the house? We could try to recruit more students and I'm sure we'll get commissions soon to help pay expenses."

Arthur shrugged. "Gleyre seems to be sure of his decision. He likes the idea of helping veterans. It is a noble cause. Those poor men have been treated poorly by the current regime."

Isabelle sighed and looked pensive. She toyed with her stew. "The Naturalists abhor the Augmentations so the veterans are suffering. No one can repair their Augmentations any more."

Henri's lip curled. Augmented veterans? Here? "I don't think that's a good idea. Look at all these floors. It would be a disaster to have men with malfunctioning legs trying to get up and down stairs."

Isabelle smiled at her husband. She knew of his bias against Augmentation but he was being irrational. "Cheri, there's a lift. I'm sure they've thought of all that, am I right, Arthur?"

"Yes, I suppose they must have. Gleyre's solicitor arranged all the details and met with the hospital board. I wasn't consulted on any of this, you understand. I tried to convince Gleyre not to rush into it but he wouldn't listen."

The four sat in gloomy silence. Isabelle pushed her chair back and got to her feet. "Cheese board? I'll just go and fetch it."

Henri watched her leave. "Why does she always support those horrific mechanical men? I was so pleased to return to Paris and not see a single Augmented policeman,"

John pursed his lips, brotherly disapproval oozing from him. "Have you never asked her? It could be someone close to her was Augmented and she feels for them because of it."

Henri cleared his throat, feeling his face grow warm. "Um. No. We've never talked about it. I didn't think to ask why she cared so much. She has a large family. Could've been a brother." He felt like a heel for not even considering that Isabelle might have had a close connection to an Augmented person. He shuddered at the thought. Would he have to sit in her family's sitting room someday and try not to be sick at the sight of an Augmented brother, broken and miserable? That was another family visit they needed to make. And not one he was looking forward to.

Isabelle returned with the cheese board and sat down next to him. "Did Gleyre get a good deal on his house? Has he enough to buy his little cottage and live on? Since he won't have any income from the studio."

Arthur pursed his lips. "Apparently he sold the house for a song. As I said, he really believes in the validity of turning the house into a convalescent home. I just hope he has enough to live on."

Henri took a long swallow of Gleyre's fine Burgundy. Had he sold the cellar too? Would the nurses let their patients drink? He remembered a veteran, begging on the street for brandy money. The man had told him that brandy was the only thing that killed the pain from Augmentation malfunctions. Henri wondered if he could take the Burgundy with him or would Gleyre stuff it into his cottage? He pictured a fisherman's cottage, the rooms piled high with crates of wine and smiled to himself.

Arthur broke into his musings. "I don't think it's particularly funny. The old man needs enough to live on. Who's going to take care of him?"

Henri raised his eyebrows at Arthur and drawled a response. "You could always move to the coast with him and be his nursemaid. Since you're so concerned."

Arthur's nostrils flared and sat up straight, tugging on his waistcoat. "He was your mentor. I think you'd show a little more concern for him in his declining years."

John shifted in his seat and cleared his throat. Isabelle looked wide-eyed at the outburst from the usual placid Arthur. Henri gritted his teeth. "You're right. I do care about Gleyre. But I'm more concerned about where my pregnant wife and I are going to live after we're thrown out of this house."

John and Arthur gasped aloud. "Pregnant? Isabelle is having a baby?" John grasped Henri's hand and shook it, beaming. "Felicitations to you both."

Arthur run a hand over his curls. "A baby. Where will you go?"

Isabelle stood and stacked plates with a clatter. "We'll manage. We're used to not having a lot of money. I have family in Montmartre. We'll bunk in with them for a while until Henri gets some commissions. We'll be fine." She carried the dishes to the kitchen, her head held high.

Henri watched her go. "She always takes such good care of me. I still think the hospital is taking advantage of Gleyre. I'm going to go to that hospital over there and tell them so."

༶ Φ ༷

Henri stood on the pavement, staring up at the looming bulk of the Hôtel-Dieu. The wrought iron fences around the building jutted out of the concrete, baring teeth at him.

The windows were baleful eyes glaring down. He shook himself, trying to shake off the feeling of foreboding. The hospital had been there for so long, it had a presence. A pair of nuns trotted down the front steps, their grey robes fluttering in the gusty wind. They paid no attention to Henri standing there, shifting from foot to foot.

Time to move, Henri. Can't stand here all day.

The wind seemed to push him towards the portico of the hospital. He gazed up at the dark walls and climbed the stairs. His heart pounded. Who was he to demand anything from this massive institution? What was he doing here?

Isabelle. I'm doing this for her and the baby. All I need is for them to delay taking the house until I find someplace for us to live. Some place that is not with her family.

He winced at the idea of staying with Isabelle's large and boisterous family. He'd only met them once, a luncheon at a bistro near her parents' apartment but he had been stunned by how loud they were.

Isabelle was a quieter version of her mother. Henri wondered if she'd become louder once she became a mother. She was already bossy like her mother which Henri still found endearing. At the thought of her, he smiled, feeling the glow of love he always felt. Emboldened by the thought of Isabelle, he reached up and pulled the bell cord. He waited, tapping his foot. He jammed his hands into his overcoat pockets against the cold. His gloves were too thin for this weather. They were more for show than comfort. He checked the front of his overcoat as he waited. It looked tidy enough. Isabelle had given it a good brushing before she'd pushed him out the door.

The door opened with a creak and a man's head poked around the door jamb. "Bonjour, monsieur, can I help you? Are you a patient or a visitor?"

Henri shrugged. "I wish to speak to the director of this hospital. So that makes me a visitor?"

The porter grumbled and looked him up and down. "You got an appointment?"

Henri took his hands out of his pockets and flexed his shoulders, an unconscious attempt to look more intimidating. "Appointment? No, I have no appointment. Perhaps he has time in his busy schedule to slip me in? I only need a few minutes of his time."

The porter snorted. "Our director, Dr. Dutrochet, is a busy woman. I doubt she has time for you."

Henri felt the blood rush to his cheeks. A woman? What a stupid assumption he'd made, thinking the director was a man. He'd met plenty of women doctors in Paris. "I would appreciate it deeply if you could inquire?" Henri held out a hand, turned down to hide the coins he was handing the man.

The porter took the money and tilted his chin up at Henri. "I can ask. What is your business? Name?"

Henri coughed and his eyes darted to the staring windows of the building. "My name is Desjardins. I'm here about the Gleyre house." That was about as much information as he was willing to give the porter, who may or may not be discreet. Henri didn't want his intentions spread throughout the hospital.

The porter nodded, a sour look on his face, and closed the door. Henri looked over his shoulder at the people passing by. The trotting of horses drawing carriages sounded almost musical to his ears. Paris was quieter than it had been the last time he was here without the noisy steam omnibuses wheezing through the streets.

His toes felt frozen in the thin leather dress boots by the time the porter returned. Henri cleared his throat. "Well? Am I to be admitted?"

The porter opened the door wide enough to let Henri in. "This way, monsieur." He shuffled off along a wide corridor. Henri followed, his footsteps echoing on the marble floor. Nurses in grey robes and servant women in drab gowns scurried about, carrying linens and trays of food. Doorways, arched and high, were placed on one side of the corridor, while a lovely courtyard garden was revealed through the high windows along the other side of the corridor.

The light is fine in this building. I could paint the arcade with all these women flying about.

The hospital was expansive and Henri was beginning to wonder how long it would take to reach the director's office when the porter turned a corner. He pointed to a narrow door under a curving staircase. "Here we are. Director's office." He walked away without another word.

Henri watched him shuffle away then turned to the door. It was cracked open. He gulped. *Here we go, Henri. She's just a person.*

Henri tapped on the door of the director's office. "Pardon me? Madame director?"

The voice responding from inside sounded imperious. "Come in."

He pushed the door open further and stood in the doorway. The dark-haired woman at the desk clad in a fashionable burgundy wool gown was not who he expected. Weren't female doctors dowdy? He gave her his most charming smile. "Good day, madame."

She looked up from her paperwork, a pince-nez perched on her Roman nose that only emphasized her elegance. She was older than he thought from his first impression. She waved him into the room. "Don't just hover there. Come in and sit down, Monsieur Desjardins. Would you like a cup of tea?"

He sat on the edge of her damask sofa. "Thank you. Tea would be nice. It's rather chilly out there."

She bustled about, preparing the tea with practiced hands. He suppressed a thrill of excitement. He adored competent women.

Business, Henri, focus on business.

Dr. Dutrochet brought the tea tray over and placed it on the mahogany table. She poured him a cup of tea and handed it to him, a smile wrinkling her eyes. "Please help yourself to milk, sugar, lemon. Whatever you like."

He stirred in milk and added sugar lumps. "This is very kind of you, Madame director."

She lifted a shoulder in a shrug. "Your mission here was rather vague, Monsieur Desjardins. The Gleyre house?"

Henri slurped the rest of his tea and put the cup down. "The hospital board recently purchased a house, that of Monsieur Gleyre. He is a well-known artist, sadly declining. The house has been an artists' studio for many years."

Dr. Dutrochet gave him an appraising look. "Yes, I know about the purchase. We intend to use the house as a comfortable sort of place for our veterans who do not need constant ... healing but who need assistance. I don't understand why the house's former purpose is of interest."

Henri flailed for a moment. He needed to be rational or the director would simply show him out. He took a breath and smiled into her deep green eyes. "Well, you see, the artists who rely on the existence of Gleyre's studio are finding themselves at a loss. Some artists reside at the house and are having difficulties contracting new arrangements. Artists often struggle financially so this sudden sale is creating hardship." He paused, his smile fixed on his face.

She raised an eyebrow, not returning his smile. "Impecunious artists who take advantage of an old man's generosity hardly strike me as a reason for charity, monsieur. And you? Are you one of these artists in residence?" She glanced down at his hands.

Henri was relieved that Isabelle had insisted that he scrub ALL of the paint out from under his fingernails. "I am one of Gleyre's former students but I have been making my living as an artist for many years. I recently returned from England after painting the king and his court before he was crowned."

She drew back from him. Her expression grew hard. "Desjardins. Ah, now I recognize your name."

"I take it that is not in a positive light?"

Dr. Dutrochet pinched her lips together. "You could say that. Let's get to the truth. I don't know what you're asking of me. Why are you really here, Henri Desjardins?"

How did she know his full name? He was certain he'd only given his last name to the porter. What did she know of him?

He decided to bluff it out. "Madame, we're just asking for some time to relocate our artists in residence before you take over the house for your patients."

She glowered at him. "I see. Delay our plans? I am not inclined to do favors for you."

They stared at each other at an impasse. Henri nodded. "I don't understand what it is you've heard about me that prejudices you against me. There are others affected, madame. My wife is expecting a child. I worry that the move will prove difficult for her." If he thought that bringing up a baby would trigger a maternal reaction in the director, he was wrong.

"Your wife? Expecting a child?" Her voice was a trifle shrill although she quickly modulated her tone. "Such a blessing, to be sure. Although it would've been better for you to secure adequate housing before you decided to impregnate her."

Henri blanched at her immodesty, although she was a doctor and not as missish about human reproduction as most women. He opened his mouth, but didn't know what to say. A tap at the door attracted their attention and they both turned.

"I think we're done here, monsieur. Come in!"

A woman, clad in the drab grey-brown dresses typical of the hospital workers, stepped into the doorway and froze, staring at him, her face distraught. With a jolt, Henri recognized her. Adelaide. What was going on? Why was she here?

Henri stood, his knees trembling and threatening to drop him back to the sofa. "Adelaide. Is it really you?"

Adelaide shook her head and looked at Dr. Dutrochet. "What is he doing here?"

Dr. Dutrochet got to her feet and went to Adelaide's side. "I asked myself the same question. He was attempting to convince me to hold off on the conversion of the Gleyre house."

Henri watched the two women, standing close to each other. The director's face was bent towards Adelaide's, her expression tender and concerned. What was going on between them? "Why are you here, Adelaide?"

Adelaide turned to him. "I work here. I scrub bedpans and serve gruel to patients. Not exactly Versailles, is it? Do you see what you've dragged me down to?"

He grimaced. She did look wretched. Her gown did nothing for her figure and her hair was dragged back into a messy bun, a kerchief unsuccessful at taming the wisps around her face. "Dragged you down? But I had nothing to do with whatever got you here. Why are you blaming me?"

She hissed her response. "My life has been on a downward spiral since I met you, Henri Desjardins. First I lost my position, then my creation, and then my child. None of that would have happened if you hadn't ruined me."

Henri's guilt burned up in his anger. "You were the one who reported me for sedition. At your word, I was thrown into the Bastille. By rights, I should be the one angry at my treatment."

She shook her head. "You shook off those chains and went to join your beloved king in England. I was left here to suffer. Now here you are, begging for favors. Why don't you ask the king for what you need?"

Henri looked at the pain writ on her face, worn beyond her years. "Adelaide, I don't know what happened after I left France, but you must see it wasn't my fault."

She stamped her foot, her cheeks flushing with color. "You idiot, if I hadn't been pregnant by you, I could've escaped the king's revenge on Science and gone to Vienna with my automaton. Instead, I spent too much time mooning around Montmartre, searching for you."

Henri couldn't catch his breath. "Pregnant? I left you pregnant? But how? We only were together once."

Dr. Dutrochet broke in. "It only takes once. You artists and your lovers know how to take precautions. Adelaide didn't know about any of that. You seduced an innocent and deserted her, left her to suffer the consequences. Do you know what happened to Scientists who lost their virtue in the old regime? They were banished from the Academy, stripped of their rank."

Adelaide and Mireille faced Henri, wearing identical looks of disdain. He flushed, shame filling him. He had not even stopped to consider that he could have left her with child. "What of the child? Where is my child, Adelaide?"

Adelaide snorted and crossed her arms. She exchanged looks with Dr. Dutrochet. "Your child? You didn't even know he existed until a moment ago. And you weren't the one to carry him about in your belly, enduring the sneers of your colleagues. You weren't the one who nearly bled to death birthing him. Your child? Pah!"

Henri stood, his legs spread, his chest puffed up. "I want to see my son. Where is he?"

Adelaide shook her head in disgust. "Men, always wanting to claim their offspring even if they do none of the work. Henri is in the countryside with his foster mother."

Henri grimaced and shook his head. "You sent him away to be fostered? What kind of mother are you? Don't you know that few babies survive the care of their foster mothers? Is he even still alive? Have you seen him since you sent him away? Do you know who this woman was who took away our son?"

Adelaide's face grew pale. Her tone was frigid. "You know nothing of me nor of the decisions 1 have had to make."

"You're a cold woman, Adelaide. All you really care about is those wretched machines of yours. What do you care if our flesh and blood child is wasting away for want of his mother's love? Oh but you have no love to give him, that's why you sent him away. I see what happened. He was inconvenient, a burden."

She narrowed her lips and glowered at him. "I don't need to hear this from you, Henri. Why do you care?"

"Because he's my son! I care because I created a child and I am responsible for him, for loving him, for keeping him safe. Unfortunately, his mother seems to be an automaton who cares nothing for him."

Adelaide growled and stepped forward. Dr. Dutrochet placed a stilling hand on Adelaide. "Monsieur Desjardins, I think this conversation is at an end. I will not stand here and hear Madame Coumain insulted. Goodbye, monsieur."

Henri's blood was boiling. His breath came harshly and he ground out his words. "I want to know where my son is."

Adelaide sneered, her lips drawn back against her lips. "So you can kill him on the altar of Naturalism like you did Marie-Ange? Why would I trust you with his whereabouts?"

"Marie-Ange? What do you mean?" Henri was staggered. What did Adelaide know about Marie-Ange? He thought only he and John knew what had happened at Versailles that day.

"You might not have carried the bomb that killed Marie-Ange, but I know you and your Naturalist friends were responsible for it getting to Versailles. An innocent girl died for your beliefs, Henri. How could I possibly trust you with a babe?"

Henri shook his head, tears in his eyes. "I would never hurt a child."

She pounced on his omission. "Then you were responsible for that bomb? How could you? She was a child. Innocent. There was no need to attack her. Her death meant nothing to your cause."

Henri needed to get out. He pushed his way past them, not meeting their eyes. "This isn't over, Adelaide. I want my son." He rushed down the corridor, dodging nuns and orderlies. The tears in his eyes blurred his vision but he barreled on, needing to get back to Isabelle. She would help. She would know what to do. He couldn't allow his son to be raised by strangers. And he needed to talk to John and find out what had really happened when Marie-Ange was killed. How could Adelaide Coumain have found out who had been there?

Twenty-three

Adelaide stood in the director's office shaking. Mireille slipped her arm around her waist and guided her to the sofa. They sat down together. Mireille didn't remove her arm. Adelaide sighed and let her head fall to Mireille's shoulder. She felt safe, comforted although she knew the safety was an illusion. With Henri now aware of the child and Adelaide's whereabouts, she was no longer safe.

"I'm going to have to leave, Mireille. Now that he knows I'm here."

Mireille sighed and rubbed Adelaide's back. "It was unfortunate that you came to my office during his visit. It's such a large building, he would never have bumped into you otherwise. But don't be foolish, I won't hear talk of you leaving."

Adelaide suppressed a sob. Once again, her world was collapsing around her. Just when she had settled into a new life, she needed to uproot herself again. "But he knows who I am and he hates me. He has every reason to inform the authorities of my hiding place. For all I know, they're on their way to arrest me." Her breathing was shallow and rough. She gulped back tears.

Mireille shushed her, her warm breath tingling Adelaide's scalp. "Nonsense. Didn't you tell me that he was a fugitive? He can't just go to the police. And he was responsible for your patient's murder?"

Adelaide looked into Mireille's brilliant eyes. "Marie-Ange. She was a young courtier, a favorite of the queen. But no one cares about her death anymore. Henri was a fugitive from the old regime, not the current one. And if he didn't want to be exposed, he could write a letter anonymously or have one of his wretched Naturalist friends make a report. He could go to the King himself."

Mireille took Adelaide's face in her hands. "I'm afraid you're right. No one will stand up for a favorite of the old queen, not in these times. We need to convince him that this reporting you would be a terrible idea. He wants to see his son? Use that as a bargaining chip."

Adelaide drew back and Mireille's hands dropped to her lap. "It seems wrong to use my child as a way to bargain for my freedom. And I don't want Henri to have any contact with the child. He's not to be trusted." Henri had always been charming but what was he really like? Was he intemperate? Deceitful? Adelaide had no idea.

"He's the child's father. I think you ought to let him see the baby. What could it hurt? We'll be there. Nothing could happen to little Henri. Not with my fierce Adelaide protecting him." She smiled, her face at once indulgent and mischievous.

Adelaide blushed and returned Mireille's smile. "Why are you so kind to me, Mireille?"

Mireille shook her head, her curls dancing at her ears. "Why are you so astonished that I am? But we must decide on a course of action to deal with Henri Desjardins and his demands. I will hear no more of you leaving the hospital. You do good work here, Adelaide. And I would miss you."

Adelaide stared across the office at the painting of the hospital as it had been centuries ago. She still hadn't told Mireille about her work with Hamidou. Now didn't seem like a good time. "I don't know how much good I'm doing here. I've tried to repair two Augmentations and failed both times."

"You need to keep trying. The first one worked for a while. The second wasn't your fault. The mechanisms were too badly rusted."

Adelaide pursed her lips. "I suppose so. I wish Axel had let me try again."

Mireille took Adelaide's hand in both of hers. "So you'll stay?"

Adelaide regarded the director. "I'll stay as long as I can."

For however long that would be. Adelaide could make no promises.

Twenty-four

Henri lounged on the bed he shared with Isabelle and watched her comb her long, curly hair in front of the bureau mirror. He adored watching her, his painter's eye picking out the patterns and colors in her hair as she tugged and twisted it into a chignon. Jamming one last pin into her hair, she caught his eye in the mirror.

"You've got that artist look on your face, Henri. When will you start painting again? You know you're happiest with a brush in your hand."

He quirked a smile at her. "I have an artist look, chérie?"

She turned on the little stool to face him, an indulgent smile across her face. Was her face a touch plumper now? Her skin certainly looked brighter than it had for months. Isabelle nodded. "You do. So why aren't you painting?"

He shifted against the pillows and crossed and uncrossed his ankles. "I didn't want to ask you to sit for me in your delicate condition. I know it can be tiring to pose for hours."

Isabelle's laugh trilled into the air. "Delicate condition? Silly man, I'm not that far along. I feel fine. I can sit all afternoon if you wanted. As long as you don't want some athletic pose. Not really up for that."

Henri joined in her laughter. He had missed painting her. "This afternoon then."

She nodded her assent then looked thoughtful. "Just think, in five or six months, we'll have a little Henri for you to paint."

Henri jerked. "You want to name the baby Henri?"

Isabelle shrugged. "It's customary to name the first son after his son, non? And Henri is a lovely name. Why are you blushing so, cher? You don't have to be bashful about naming your child with your name."

Henri gulped and sat up on the bed. "I don't think ... that is ... we didn't do that in my family. I was named for a grandfather, not my father."

Isabelle shrugged and waved a dismissive hand. "I still think we should call him Henri. With all the trouble he's given me, I'm sure it's a boy." She made a playful pout but Henri didn't respond.

"I don't think it's a good idea. Too many Henri's. Everyone is naming their baby after the king."

Isabelle laughed again, shaking her head and setting her side ringlets dancing. "Henri, you are being ridiculous."

Henri stood up, his face flushing. He couldn't let her browbeat him into naming their son the same name as Adelaide's child. "No, Isabelle. He won't be named Henri."

She drew back in her seat, eyes wide with surprise. "Why are you so set against this? It makes no sense to me."

He paced across the room, crossing it in a few strides, and ran his hand across his curls. She wasn't going to let this go. He darted a look at her. "We can't name our child Henri because I already have a son named Henri."

Isabelle gasped, her face pale. Her eyes filled with tears. "What? You never told me ..."

He groaned and lowered his head. "I'm sorry. I just found out." Merde, Why had he let that slip?

"You just found out? Who is she? How old is this child?" Her voice shook with rage.

He raised his head to meet her furious eyes. "The baby was born while we were in England. Adelaide Coumain is the mother. "

She jumped to her feet and flew at Henri, her small hands clenched into fists. "You pig! You betrayed me with that mousy Scientist woman? How long was the affair?"

He grabbed her hands and drew her against him. She stared up at him, her face distorted by pain and anger. Henri's chest clenched. How could he have caused his lovely wife this pain? "I'm so sorry, Isabelle. It was a mistake. I was only with her once. I had no idea I'd left her with child."

She pulled away from him and shoved his hands away. She bit her bottom lip and looked away. "Now it all makes sense. I never could figure out why she turned you into the police. I thought you barely knew her, certainly not enough for her to know that you were working with the Naturalists. So, after you seduced her, she got her revenge by reporting you."

Henri gaped at her. Of course. How could he have been so blind not to realize that's what had happened. "You're right. But all that is over now. We're married and having a child together."

Isabelle shot a cold look at him. "Oh, Henri. You think it's so easy to just forget and move on? You betrayed me then. How can I be sure you'll stay true?"

Henri opened his mouth to reply and an image of the lovely Duchesse de Fronsac flashed across his mind. He shoved it aside. "I'm married now. I am loyal to you and only you."

She must have sensed his hesitation. She shook her head. "I'm going to my mother's. Don't wait up for me."

Isabelle left the room in a rustle of petticoats without a backwards glance. Henri gaped at her departing back. That had not gone the way he'd hoped. He hadn't even had a chance to ask her if she'd be willing to foster baby Henri but after her reaction, it seemed unlikely. Perhaps after she'd cooled off, she would be more amenable to the idea.

Twenty-five

Adelaide stuffed handfuls of bolts and screws into her leather satchel and glanced around the workroom, looking for more parts that could be used in Hamidou's Weather Machine. She racked her brain trying to remember the lectures she'd heard at the Academy on the construction of the Weather Machine. Didn't it use hydraulics? Maybe for repositioning the array? She grabbed some vacuum tubes and hoses just in case. Those were used in construction of the more elaborate Augmentations, not the Augmented limbs she was more likely to fix here at the hospital. The veterans wouldn't need them so Adelaide didn't feel bad taking them. Well, not exceptionally bad. She felt a twinge of guilt picturing Mireille's disappointed face if she ever found out that Adelaide was stealing from the hospital.

No one even knows these parts exists. They aren't good for anything the hospital needs. The nuns would just throw them away if they found them.

The rationalization didn't help her feel better. She buckled the satchel closed and exited the secret room with as much stealth as she was able. The satchel was heavy and banged against her hip, the metal parts inside clinking. Adelaide pulled the bookshelf back into place and tiptoed across the office to the door leading to the corridor. No one but the night watch walked the halls in this wing of the hospital, but Adelaide had always tried to operate from an excess of caution. She didn't want to get caught and have her secret stash of automaton parts discovered. The corridor was empty, echoing her footsteps back to her. She raised dust with her skirts as she walked and had to stifle a sneeze.

There's got to be an exit to the street around here. Logically, it should be where the doors are in the other wings.

She peeked into alcoves until she found the door. She tried the handle. It was locked. She bit her lip. She didn't want to walk through the occupied part of the hospital carrying a bulging bag full of clinking metal bits. She hadn't thought this through. Maybe someone had secreted a key near the door, for emergency exits. She squinted up at the lintel, the most logical hiding place. Something glinted up there. Cursing her height, she knew she couldn't reach it from where she was standing. The window next to the door had a wide windowsill that she could climb onto. She hoisted herself up and reached for the top of the door. Still too short. Adelaide ground her teeth, then her eyes caught the catch for the window. There was no lock, just a simple latch. She slid down from the windowsill and tried the latch. It was stuck tight. She pounded on it with the heel of her hand and it shifted. Adelaide pounded harder, wincing at the pain in her hand. The catch released and she pushed open the creaking window. Just enough for her to squeeze herself and her bag out. The drop to the ground was short although her petticoat got caught in a rosemary bush. Adelaide smiled to herself in triumph.

She was still on the hospital grounds so she followed the stone wall to one of the side gates. They were all unlocked during the day, she knew from previous excursions. Adelaide tromped through the gate and across the bridge to the Left Bank.

I hope Hamidou is still waiting for me. We didn't specify a time.

Adelaide's free afternoon had been scheduled to begin over an hour ago but Nurse Emard had insisted that Adelaide change sheets for all of the patients before she left. She picked up her speed, the satchel banging on her hip. She held onto it to stop it from swinging wildly.

A beggar on the steps of a church caught her attention with a gesture. "Please, madame. Have you a sou to spare?"

She paused and stared down at him. He wore the faded uniform of an army caporal. Was he Augmented? "Have you no one to take care of you, monsieur?"

He coughed, the sound rattling around his thin chest. "Family threw me out. Don't want no freaks in their house."

Adelaide's heart sank. Another Augmented veteran, discarded by their family because of Naturalist beliefs. She bent down to him and stared into his rheumy eyes. "You can go to the Hôtel-Dieu for care, monsieur. I work there. I can help you."

His eyes shifted away from hers to the people passing by. He spoke in a hushed tone. "Won't they throw me out because I'm not all human?"

Adelaide stiffened. "Don't say things like that. You're just as human as any one of us. You look ill, monsieur, and sitting on those cold stairs won't help. Please, go to the hospital. They have a ward just for veterans. Don't mention anything else, just tell them you are ill."

He examined her, a wary look on his face, then nodded. "Thank you, madame."

"Here, let me help you up." She easily hoisted the slight man to his feet and handed him the crutch that had fallen from his grip. The veteran limped off in the direction of the hospital. She watched him go, already planning how she would sneak him into her workroom to examine his faulty Augmentation.

Once he'd disappeared into the crowd, she turned and headed down the Rue de la Cite towards the garden. It was getting late. She wouldn't have much time before needing to head back to the hospital. Adelaide walked as quickly as she could without appearing to rush. The last thing she needed while carrying illicit machine parts was to attract the interest of the police.

Entering the park soothed her and she smiled as she stepped beneath the spindly, leafless trees, their branches tracing patterns against the grey sky. It wasn't chilly but very few people wandered in the gardens. She spotted gardeners raking leaves and pruning roses. They didn't look up from their work and Adelaide sped past them to the apple orchard. She circled the shed where she'd surprised Hamidou. The Weather Machine squatted in the midst of rows of espaliered apple trees, surrounded by a wooden fence. Her fellow Scientist was nowhere to be seen. She exhaled an irritated breath. "Oh bother, I've missed him." Adelaide approached the machine. Some of the fence slats were missing. People in Paris were cold as well as hungry and Adelaide guessed the missing slats had been used in someone's wood stove.

A dark head popped out from behind the fence. "Ah, it's you! You came!" Hamidou climbed out of the enclosure to shake her hand with his own grubby one.

She nodded in response and held out the satchel. "I brought some machine parts. I don't know if they'll be helpful at all."

Hamidou surveyed the orchard around them, then beckoned her to follow him through the fence. "This is greatly appreciated, Madame Coumain. I can't even find metal bolts anymore so really, anything is bound to help. Please, sit here on the stool, we need to stay out of sight of the gardeners. They've already finished with the trees but you never know."

He rummaged through the satchel, pulling out parts with snuffles of delight. He held the vacuum tubes up to the light and grinned. "Wonderful, wonderful, these are in excellent condition. I so appreciate this, madame. It will make our work possible. You said you don't have the strength to work on one of these beauties, but I can make good use of those clever hands of yours."

Adelaide felt a flush creep across her cheeks. Surely he didn't mean anything improper? He continued to examine the machine parts, oblivious to her discomfort. She stood up. "What do you need me to do?"

He drew her over to the machine and opened a panel. Wires fell out in a tangle. "The saboteurs pulled all the wires out, thinking it would destroy the machine. All you need to do is reconnect them. I'll work on repairing the vanes."

They worked in silence. Adelaide's fingers quickly went numb in the frigid air, since she couldn't wear gloves to do the work. She was on edge, sitting on the stool in front of the machine, certain that at any moment, someone would discover them working on the forbidden technology. After she replaced a few connections, the work soothed her anxiety and she worked smoothly, not aware of time passing. She screwed in the final connector and sat up, the muscles in her back cramped and complaining. "I'm finished here."

Hamidou poked his head around the machine. "Already? Excellent. I knew I had the right partner for this job. The repairs here are almost complete."

Adelaide stood and stretched her sore back. She peeked through a hole in the fence but spotted no one in the orchard, just a lone magpie perched on a leafless branch. It hopped to the ground and pecked at the grass then flew back into the tree.

Hamidou grunted with satisfaction. "There. I'm done here. Let's see if we can start her up." He joined her on her side of the machine and examined the panel she had been working on. "Power switch is here." He pointed at a toggle inside the panel. "We had a little sunlight yesterday. There should be enough energy stored in the machine to initiate startup."

"Sunlight? It feels like it's been cloudy for months. You're sure there's enough energy stored?"

Hamidou shrugged, a grin creasing his face. "Only one way to find out." He flicked the toggle. The machine whined then a slow whirring sound emanated from the base of the vanes. With what looked like great effort, the vanes started rotating, slowly at first, then speeding up. The whirring grew louder. Adelaide glanced over her shoulder. Was the noise loud enough to reach the gardeners' ears? She saw no one and looked back at Hamidou. He was watching the machine's movements intently, his head cocked as if listening to a bird's song.

A shaft of sunlight brightened the machine and Adelaide looked up. A patch of blue sky had opened up directly above them. She touched Hamidou's shoulder to catch his attention. "Look up. It's working." She felt a surge of exultation. Success. Their repairs had fixed the Weather Machine.

Hamidou looked up and whooped. "We did it!" He turned to Adelaide and shook her hand, grinning. "Well done, madame. You make a very creditable Scientist-Engineer, you know." He winked. Adelaide shuddered a little at the gesture.

They stood shoulder to shoulder, eyes fixed on the increasing blue patch of sky. The machine's whirring stuttered, then stopped. The vanes ground to a halt. Hamidou's mouth dropped open. "Oh no, what's happened?" He opened the panel and switched off the power. He peered into the depths of the machine.

Adelaide peeked over his shoulder. "Perhaps it ran out of power?"

Hamidou grumbled and poked the wiring, then got to his feet to examine the vanes. "Perhaps. I don't see any problems." He sighed and slumped against the now-silent machine. The air grew colder and the light faded as the clouds gathered. "It will self-generate power once it gets going, as long as there's enough sunlight. We'll have to try again on a sunny day."

Adelaide didn't respond. She didn't think she would need to be here just to switch on the machine. It was risky enough being here now, with the machine quiescent again. "We'd better go. We don't want to be seen near the machine. Someone might have heard it running." She clambered through an opening in the enclosure, pulling her skirts close to her legs. Fabric caught on the broken slat and she yanked it free, hearing a tear.

Hamidou closed the panel and took one last look at the machine. He patted it like it was his favorite horse then turned and climbed through the fence. His more practical clothing didn't get caught on anything. Footsteps crunched on leaves and the Scientists froze, looking around. A gardener approached from the other side of the garden shed, but she wasn't looking in their direction. Hamidou grabbed

Adelaide's hand and drew it through his own. "We're just going for a stroll in the orchards, madame. Just a stroll." His voice trembled, belaying his words. They moved away from the Weather Machine to the gravel path next to the apple trees. Adelaide was rigid with fear.

The gardener called out to them. "You two! What are you doing near that infernal thing? Don't you know it's forbidden?"

Hamidou waved a languid hand in return. "Good day, madame. We were just walking in the orchard. Didn't notice the machine. No harm done."

The gardener drew closer, scowling. "I heard something back here. Something... mechanical." She spat the word out as if it had a foul taste. "Did you two hear anything?"

Hamidou drew Adelaide closer and smiled down at her, the smile not reaching his deadly serious eyes. "We could only hear each other."

Adelaide suppressed her nausea and attempted a smile in return.

The gardener snorted and walked back to the central garden, calling over her shoulder. "Just stay away from that thing, you hear? I don't want to set the police after you."

They sauntered in the same direction, her hand still on Hamidou's arm. They needed to preserve the illusion of lovers out for a walk until the gardener was out of sight. Adelaide gasped. "I forgot my satchel! It's still got useful parts in it. I can't leave it out in the rain."

Hamidou twisted his lips and dropped her arm. "I'll fetch it. Duck behind that tree so she won't see you if she turns around."

He scampered back to the machine and reached an arm through the fence. Adelaide watched out for the return of the gardener. Hamidou returned with her satchel and presented it to her with a bow. "Madame, your satchel."

Adelaide took it with a nod and slung it over her shoulder. It was considerably lighter now. They had used many of the parts she had brought. "Will you need any more of these parts? You can keep them if you'd like." She held it out to him.

Hamidou smiled. "Thank you, madame. They certainly could be useful in future. But will you not continue to help me with my endeavors? We make a good team, no?"

Adelaide shrugged. "I see no need. I brought you tools and rewired the machine. What else would you have me do?"

Hamidou's face fell. "Do you ever really smile, Madame Coumain? Have you no need for company, friends, people who understand who you are and appreciate it?"

Her stomach felt sick and her heart fluttered like a trapped bird. Friends? That would mean trusting someone. "I think not." She pushed the satchel into his arms. "Farewell, Monsieur Hamidou. I must be going." She pulled her arm away from him and stamped off, not looking back.

Twenty-six

Adelaide spooned the last mouthful of gruel into the blind veteran's mouth. She wiped his mouth and started to stand but he grabbed her wrist, his bony fingers like talons. She sank back onto the stool. "What do you need, monsieur? Bedpan?"

He showed his blackened gums to her in what appeared to be a smile and cackled. "I know what you're up to. Sneaking around in here late at night."

Fear roiled up in her and she caught her breath. Nausea filled her belly. "What are you talking about?"

His bony grip tightened on her wrist. "You're fixing them, the broken men. I hear you telling them you'll repair them. I hear you take them out of here to the bathroom then when they come back, they're walking by themselves."

Adelaide swallowed. "I don't know what you're talking about. You must be imagining things. Dreaming."

He shook his head. "No, it's not my imagination and I'm wide awake when you sneak into the ward at night. Don't sleep much anymore. I could tell Nurse Emard. She's just waiting for an excuse to get rid of you."

Adelaide tried to pull her hand away from him but he was surprisingly strong. "Why would she believe such lies?"

He cackled again. "She hates you. I can tell by the sound of her voice. She'd believe me over you. All it would take is one word from me."

Tears welled up in her eyes. "What do you want from me? I've done nothing wrong."

"So you say. Fixing the mechanical men is against the law. You could go to prison."

Adelaide bit back her tears. "Why are you doing this?"

He released her wrist and laid back against his pillow. He snickered. "Not much entertainment around here. It's fun to listen to you squirm and beg for your life."

Adelaide's fear turned to fury. The evil little gnome was playing with her. He knew too much and was enjoying the power it gave him. Her hands shook and the spoon clattered in the dish. She stood up. "Good day to you, monsieur. Hopefully no one smothers you in the night."

She heard him gasp as she carried the dirty dish back to the service station. He wasn't the only one who could play games. She'd learned a few things while serving at Court. Nurse Emard looked up from her paperwork as Adelaide passed. "Is there a problem with that patient, Coumain?"

Adelaide didn't stop walking. "He seems to have an excess of spleen, Nurse Emard. Nothing serious. Perhaps he requires another dose of tea."

Adelaide gathered the dirty dishes from the patients' lunch and piled them on a tray for washing. That chore, while not pleasant, would at least get her out of the ward for a while. She carried the heavy tray out of the ward and headed down towards the kitchens. A dark-haired man on crutches sat on one of the benches in the hallway. She peered at him. It was Axel.

"Hello, madame. I've returned. Told the porter I was here to see you and he let me right in."

Adelaide stopped short, the cutlery rattling on the tray. "What? He'll think you're courting me. Oh, Axel, couldn't you have said you were ill?" She groaned and looked around. A nun-nurse was walking in their direction, her hands clasped in front of her. She appeared to be deep in thought and passed them without looking up. "I need to get these dishes downstairs to the kitchens for washing. Can you wait for me somewhere else?"

Axel's face was red with embarrassment. "I'm sorry, madame. I didn't mean to make trouble for you. Where should I go?"

She gave him directions to the hallway near the locked storage room that she used for repair work. "And don't talk to anyone. If anyone asks why you're here, tell them you're waiting for a family member to be discharged."

He nodded, chastened, and crutched away.

After cleaning the lunch dishes, Adelaide went looking for Axel. He was seated on a bench near the storage room, his malfunctioning leg propped up. She could see the strain on his face. He must be in pain again. Adelaide sighed. She needed to check those interfaces. She was sure that was the source of the problem. "Come on, get up, we need to go somewhere private."

He heaved himself to his feet. She beckoned him towards the door of the storage room. Adelaide surveyed the corridor. The same nun-nurse she'd seen earlier passed at the intersection with another corridor. Once she was out of sight, Adelaide unlocked the door and ushered Axel inside. With a quick glance around, she followed him in and locked them both in.

It was almost dark in the storeroom but Adelaide knew exactly where the oil lamp was. "Hold still until I light the lamp." She picked her way to the shelf that held the lamp and tinder. Matches. She would love some actual matches. Light filled the room and Adelaide turned to Axel. "Let's take a look at that leg. There's a chair over here."

He hobbled over and sat down with a thump. Adelaide drew a stool closer and propped his leg onto it. "Oh, right, I'll need to see the interface. Can you remove your trousers? Er, wait, here's a sheet to cover your, er, self."

She could feel the blood coloring her cheeks.

I'm a doctor, I don't need to be embarrassed at my patient's nudity.

She turned away and busied herself gathering the tools she needed for the examination. She could hear the shuffling of garments being removed.

"I'm ready, madame."

Axel had draped the sheet over his lower half and he too was blushing.

She sat down on a chair next to him and lifted the sheet. "Right, let's take a look, shall we? This interface between your mechanical leg and your flesh could be what's causing the problem here. I'll need to examine that area. What happened when it stopped working Are you in pain?"

I'm babbling. Yes, babbling. Shut up, Adelaide, you don't need to explain everything about Augmentations to your patient.

Axel shifted, his face drawn with pain. "It's a different pain than before. Like someone's stabbing me with a hot poker. My leg stopped working after the pain started."

She brought the lamp closer and leaned over. The interface looked inflamed. Adelaide shook her head. There shouldn't be infection here. The surgery had been completed years ago. She prodded the area and spotted a sore between the prosthetic and Axel's leg stump. "Have you been scratching the area?"

Axel coughed. "It was itchy." He sounded like a little boy caught stealing sweets.

She sighed. "Axel, you've injured yourself here. What did you use to scratch yourself with? A knitting needle?"

He squirmed in his seat. "Yes. I couldn't reach the itch."

She sat back and gave him a stern look. "You've managed to dislodge the connections and give yourself an infection. I haven't been able to find any carbolic acid in this place but you need to get some at a chemist and clean this area. Gently. I'm going to reconnect the wires so your leg will work but you need to be more careful. No more knitting needles."

He nodded, his cheeks still reddened. Adelaide got to work and reconnected the wires. Once she was done, she sat up and rubbed her back. "Move your foot." She watched as he turned his foot up and down. The mechanisms seemed to be functioning properly. She let out a sigh of relief.

Please let them continue to work. He'll be devastated if it breaks again.

Axel's smile was shaky. "It's working. Still hurts though."

She leveled a frown at him. "Infection, remember? I can't rewire that. Take care of that sore and the pain will diminish. You need to rest and not use the leg until the sore heals. Now, you'll have to pretend your leg is still not working when you leave here. It would be too obvious if you came to visit me with your leg broken, then left walking on it."

He clasped her hand. "Of course. Whatever you say. Thank you, madame. Please accept my apologies for my rude behavior before."

She pulled her hand free and got to her feet. "Yes, fine. Get dressed." Adelaide turned and busied herself reorganizing her tools. She heard him shifting and the swish of fabric behind her and waited until it ceased before turning back. She fixed him with a serious look. "Axel, I am in danger here. You know what I am doing for you is against the law. Please be careful who you tell about my work."

He stood up and gingerly walked from one side of the small room to the other. "It works. Thank heavens, it works. Don't worry, madame, I'll keep your secret safe. I'm going to tell my mother I went to Notre Dame and prayed to the Holy Spirit and it started working."

A stab of irrational jealousy pierced her. She knew it was too dangerous for her to publicly receive credit for her work but it irked her that some supernatural force was going to be lauded for it. "I suppose that's probably best. Let's go. I need to sneak you out of here."

He grabbed his crutches and walked with her to the door. Adelaide listened but the corridor outside was silent. She cracked open the door and peeked out. No one in sight. She motioned for him to move out into the hallway. He crutched out and she stepped into the corridor behind him, locking the door.

Nurse Emard's harsh voice echoed in the hallway. "Coumain, what have you been doing with this man in a locked room?"

Adelaide whirled around, her heart hammering. The nun stood at the top of the stairwell, glowering at her. She marched over to Adelaide and Axel, frozen in place and grabbed Adelaide by the arm. Her fingers pinched on the delicate skin of Adelaide's arm. "You and this man were engaged in unseemly acts, I know you were. And where did you get a key to this room? This is the last straw, Coumain.

We're going to the director about this." She yanked an unresisting Adelaide towards the stairs then looked over her shoulder at Axel. "You should be ashamed, young man. Take yourself over to the cathedral and ask for forgiveness for your sins."

Axel's mouth hung open. He balanced on his crutches as the nun dragged Adelaide away. Adelaide threw one more look back at him, silently begging him not to object. She didn't need any gallantry from him. That would just aggravate Nurse Emard even more and give her more reason to think that Adelaide and Axel were lovers.

Adelaide tried to keep her pace sedate but Nurse Emard barreled ahead, pulling Adelaide almost off her feet. Adelaide stumbled and tugged her arm away from the nun's firm grip. "Kindly remove your hand from my arm, Nurse Emard. I won't be treated like an errant schoolchild. I can walk to the director's office without being dragged along."

Nurse Emard stopped and glowered at Adelaide. Her bushy grey eyebrows were drawn together and her dark eyes flashed with anger. "You act like a child, I'll treat you that way."

Adelaide tossed her head in mock bravado. and curled her lip. Inside she was quaking with fear. "This whole situation is ridiculous. A complete misunderstanding."

Nurse Emard raised her beefy arm as if to strike her but stopped in mid air. She waved her arm in the direction of the stairs. "We'll see about that. Let's go."

She let Adelaide precede her down the stairs, her hot breath rasping in Adelaide's ear. Nurse Emard didn't touch her but Adelaide sensed that one wrong move would have her arm ensconced in that iron grip again. They passed other nuns and orderlies on the way to the director's office but none of them would look at Adelaide.

I hope Axel gets home safely. After his side trip to the cathedral, that is.

She suppressed a gleeful smile at the thought of him being ordered to attend church, as he had intended on telling his mother. She hadn't attended church since she was a small child and didn't miss the long, boring services and droning priests.

The director's door was open when they arrived but there was no sign of Mireille. Nurse Emard walked to the doorway and looked inside. "Madame Director? Are you here?" She shot a dark look at Adelaide, as if she was responsible for the director's absence. Adelaide stared back at her, her face expressionless. She wanted to giggle but knew that wouldn't go over well. Nurse Emard gestured to the wooden bench next to the office door. "We'll wait here. Sit."

Adelaide did as she was bidden. Her feet were sore so she was glad to sit down. Nurse Emard loomed over her; her arms crossed. Adelaide could hear the nun grinding her teeth. They waited without speaking for what felt like an eternity so when Nurse Emard spoke, Adelaide jumped in surprise. "You disgust me. Sneaking around with men."

Adelaide didn't want to lose her job so she tamped down the retorts that came to mind. She breathed deeply to calm her nerves. "I think you misunderstood what you saw. I have done nothing improper with any of our patients, current or former."

Before the nun could respond beyond her unchanged glower, the clicking of heels on the tiles announced the presence of the director. She approached the pair, a look of concern on her face. "Good afternoon. Is there a problem on the veterans' ward?"

Adelaide got to her feet, feeling some of the tension fall from her at the sight of Mireille. Nurse Emard stepped forward. "Madame Director, the problem is not on the ward, the problem is her." She jabbed a finger in Adelaide's direction.

Mireille looked from one woman to the other. "You'd better come into my office." She ushered them in and they took seats opposite Mireille's desk. She didn't offer to make tea. Mireille sat at her chair and clasped her hands on the desk. "What appears to be the problem?"

"She's immoral, a hussy, sneaking around with patients. I caught her with a patient coming out of a locked room. And where she got that key, I'd like to know. Stole it maybe." The nun fixed her dark stare on Mireille.

Mireille raised her eyebrows. "Nurse Emard. Are you sure you didn't mistake the situation? I don't believe that Madame Coumain is ... er ... a hussy."

Nurse Emard snarled. "She was making eyes at that pretty boy who was a patient and he came back today to see her. Saw them coming out of a locked room. Easy to imagine what they were up to in there."

Mireille turned to Adelaide who shifted uncomfortably in her chair. "Madame Coumain? Do you care to explain your behavior?" Her tone was stern and cold. Adelaide shivered at the coldness.

She tilted her chin up in the haughty noble pose she'd learned at Versailles. "Monsieur Boulet had returned to the hospital to give thanks to us for his treatment here. He had left a pair of socks behind and wanted them back. They were in the storage room."

Mireille unclasped her hands and sat back. "You see, Nurse Emard, a perfectly innocent situation that you misinterpreted."

Nurse Emard's shoulders were rigid. She snarled at Adelaide then faced Mireille. "Socks? Who comes back to the hospital for socks? Don't believe it for a second."

Adelaide cleared her throat. "They, um, apparently his mother had knitted the socks for him recently. She was quite put out that he had misplaced them."

Nurse Emard snorted at Adelaide then rounded back to Mireille. "And what about the locked room? Where did SHE get a key?"

Mireille and Adelaide exchanged looks. "I gave her the key. One of her new duties. Lost and found." She smiled at Nurse Emard although her eyes remained cold. "Are we through here, Nurse Emard?"

The nun dragged herself to her feet. "Need to get back to the ward. Who knows what's been going on there." She left the office, her face twisted. Her footsteps stomped away into the distance.

Mireille shook her head. "Be careful, Adelaide. I can only protect you so far. If she suspects what you're really doing..."

Adelaide got to her feet and laid a hand across Mireille's. "I know. Thank you for your help. I appreciate it more than I can tell you." She grinned and grasped Mireille's hand. "But I was able to help Axel with his leg. It's working again. Mireille, it felt so good to be able help."

Mireille leaned forward and brushed her lips against Adelaide's then smiled into her eyes. "I'm so glad. I knew you could do it. But please, please don't let Emard find out."

Adelaide nodded, her heart hammering from the kiss. "I must get back to work." She left the office on shaky legs. She'd managed to avoid Nurse Emard's wrath this time but Mireille was right. If the nun found out what Adelaide was really doing in that storage room, she'd go straight to the police.

Twenty-seven

Adelaide stood in front of Nurse Emard, hands behind her back, listening to another diatribe about her behavior. Apparently this time, she had been rude to one of the other nun-nurses. Adelaide couldn't remember the incident at all. She waited for Nurse Emard to wind down. A figure in the doorway caught her attention but she didn't look away from the nun.

"Don't know why I waste my breath on you, Coumain. Get back to work."

Finally. Adelaide nodded and looked fully at the person waiting at the entrance to the ward. With a sinking heart, she realized it was Henri. What was he doing here again? Stirring trouble, no doubt. "Pardon me, Nurse Emard, I think we have a visitor. I'll go and see what he wants."

Nurse Emard grumbled and plopped down into her seat. "A man. Find out what he wants. Let's hope you can keep your hands off that one."

Little did she know. Of all the men she accused Adelaide of toying with, here was the one who had actually known her. Adelaide squelched the memory of that long ago afternoon. She needed a clear head if she was going to deal with Henri again.

His face was calm and his body was relaxed as she approached. He watched her as she drew near. "Adelaide. We need to talk."

Adelaide glanced back at Nurse Emard. The nun stared at them, unblinking. "Not here. Come to the courtyard with me. I don't want her to overhear us."

Henri quirked an eyebrow and glanced over her shoulder at the fearsome Nurse Emard. "Quite a dragon, I'd say. Looks like she'd eat me alive given half the chance. Who knew the nuns would move in here so quickly?"

Adelaide glowered at him. "You know they got rid of all the real nurses, don't you? And the doctors too."

Henri looked down at her, his expression unreadable. He shrugged. "Shall we take a stroll?" He held his arm out and waited for her to move into the archway. She shouldered past him. They walked in silence down the corridor and out of a door leading into the courtyard. She didn't look at Henri but from the corner of her eye, she could tell he was swaggering along as if he hadn't a care in the world. The wind gusted, buffeting them as they stepped onto the portico. Adelaide wrapped her arms around her to stay warm. She gazed at the intricate topiary in the center of the courtyard rather than face him. "What do you want, Henri?"

He turned towards her, not sounding like his usual cocky self. "You know why I'm here. I want to know where my son is."

"You don't need to know where he is. He's safe."

"How do you know that? Have you been to see him? Or are you too busy flirting with the hospital director to visit him?"

Adelaide whirled on him, eyes blazing. "How dare you? What are you insinuating?"

Henri smiled, a smug twist of the lips. "Touched a nerve, did I? Why haven't you been to see our son? How old is he? Three months? Four? An infant. Do you think he remembers you at all?"

She ignored his question, holding onto her self-control. Her tone was calm, despite the storm raging inside her. "I can't just leave my job to go jaunting into the countryside. I don't have the money and they don't give me much time off."

He cocked his head to one side, studying her. She glared back. Henri shook his head, sadness dragging his face into a frown. "Visiting your infant son isn't exactly a jaunt. You just care more about this place than you do him."

Adelaide moved away from Henri and took a step down into the courtyard. "I'm doing important work here. I can't just leave. His foster mother takes better care of him then I could."

"Important work? You call scrubbing bedpans important?"

Adelaide paced along the stone step, rubbing her hands together to stay warm. "No, that's not what I meant. That's just the work that I get paid for." She stopped pacing. She'd said too much.

He pounced on her words. "What other work are you doing?" He gasped, horror filling his eyes. "Science. You're working here as a Scientist, aren't you? Where are your automatons stashed?"

She wrapped her arms around her waist. Her fingers were blue with cold. She shook her head. "No, don't be ridiculous, I can't practice Science legally anymore." Her words rang false, even to her own ears.

Henri stalked over to her, menacing and cold. "You're lying. You're secretly creating automatons and Watcher Spheres somewhere in the hospital. They haven't caught you yet, Adelaide Coumain, but with a quiet word, you'll go to prison. Where you sent me."

Adelaide shook her head wildly. "No, please. I'm not making automatons or Watchers, I swear. Please don't turn me in. I truly am doing important work here."

His face didn't change. "Sounds like lies from a desperate woman to me. You'll say anything to keep me from turning you in."

Adelaide reached out and put a hand on Henri's forearm. She looked up into his eyes. "It's the veterans. The Augmented ones. They come in and their Augmentations aren't working. They're in pain and frustrated. I try to repair them." She dropped her hand and stepped back. "I know it's against the law, but I hate seeing them in pain."

Henri considered her face, as if assessing her sincerity. "Empathy. I would not have expected that from you, Adelaide."

"I'm not cold. I have feelings too." She hated admitting such things to Henri, preferring to be seen as stoic.

He frowned, looking puzzled and a little surprised. "I suppose you must. But then how could you send our child away?"

She sighed and looked away. "I had to. Do you think it was easy for me to send my baby away? He was so tiny, just newborn." She stopped and took a deep breath. "I need to support myself so I have to work. How could I take care of a baby too? The nuns arranged the foster mother. They have a fund to help indigent mothers. Like me."

She looked back. Henri stood watching her, a muscle in his jaw twitching. "And so here you are, illegally practicing Science while supporting yourself as an orderly. What happens to our child when you are inevitably caught? You'll be imprisoned and when they find out who you are, probably executed."

Adelaide swayed on her feet. She'd never considered what would happen to the baby if she was in prison. How long would the foster parents keep little Henri? What would be his fate if she was executed? She stifled a moan. "Are you going to turn me in so you can get hold of the child?"

Henri reared back, shock on his features. "That's a horrible thing to say. You think so little of me? No, I'm not going to turn you in. I'm not that vengeful, as much as I try." He smiled, a glimmer of the old Henri charm showing, then he dropped his smile. "But you're living a dangerous life here and eventually someone will find out what you're doing."

She straightened her back. "It'll be fine. I'm careful. And maybe someday, the king will see that he needs people to take care of his Augmented veterans."

Henri gave her a sad smile. "I wouldn't count on it. You need to plan for our son's fate, Adelaide. Give him to me to raise. He'll be safe then."

"And give up my hopes? No, Henri, I will not. I will be able to have him with me soon."

Henri let out a growl of disgust and without another word to her, turned and walked away. Adelaide watched him tromp through the winding paths of the courtyard to the foyer and out of sight. She hugged herself tightly, her sobs locked inside her. She knew she trod a dangerous path but what else could she do? Give up all hope for the Augmented soldiers?

ഌ Φ ☙

The cold finally drove Adelaide back inside. The hospital interior was marginally warmer, its soaring ceilings making it impossible to heat well. She entered the veterans' ward to Nurse Emard's rebuking look.

Now to explain Henri's presence. What lies do I tell her this time?

Nurse Emard didn't get up from her desk. She called to Adelaide from across the ward. "Coumain, the porter was looking for you. Seems the foster parents brought your baby in for his checkup but he's ill."

Adelaide gasped. Her baby was ill? "Where is he?"

The nun-nurse had a gleeful look in her eyes, although she didn't smile. She must be delighting in Adelaide's panic. "Children's ward. Upstairs. You've got duties so don't be long."

Without responding, Adelaide pivoted and ran down the hallway to the stairwell. Her boots clattered as she raced up the stairs. She dodged nuns and orderlies, paying no attention to any of them. She reached the second floor and looked down the long central corridor. Where was the children's ward? She didn't remember seeing it during her nocturnal exploration. She flagged down a passing orderly. "Pardon, but can you direct me to the children's ward?"

The orderly looked her up and down. "You a new orderly in the ward?"

Adelaide smoothed the apron over her uniform dress. "No, I work in the veterans' ward. I was told that my child is here."

The orderly sniffed and pointed to the other side of the hospital. "Children are off the other corridor, about halfway down."

Adelaide thanked them and dashed off. She was out of breath and her side was cramping by the time she reached the other central corridor. There were more visitors on that side, their worried faces marking them as parents of the patients. What did her child's foster mother look like? Adelaide had only seen the woman once and her eyes had been for the baby, trying to memorize his features before he was taken away. She slowed to a walk. The cries of children ill or in pain reached her ears. She was in the right place. Adelaide took a steadying breath. It wouldn't do to rush into the ward like a madwoman. She needed to be calm. Adelaide scanned the faces of the worried parents hovering at the entrance to the ward. None of them looked familiar. Nuns bustled from bed to bed. The beds were smaller than in the Veterans' Ward and there were more of them packed into the long room. The familiar reek of urine reached her nose. The nuns up here were no better at cleaning than the ones in the adult wards. She wrinkled her nose and walked into the ward, hoping her uniform would allow her to pass unnoticed for a bit. Adelaide looked around and spotted a cluster of cribs at the end of the room, below a large window. The nuns had grouped the babies together. That made her search easier. She made her way through the bustle to the cribs. Some of the babies whimpered. She peered into each crib, hoping she'd recognize her child. Was that him? A nun turned from tending a patient and addressed Adelaide. "Is there a problem?"

Adelaide stammered, feeling the blood rush to her face. "I'm looking for a patient. An infant. His name is Henri Coumain."

The nun pursed her lips. "He's over there. That child is very ill. Why do you need to find him?"

Adelaide's flush deepened. "I'm his mother."

The nun drew back. "His mother? But ... his parents are with him now."

"They are his foster parents. I am his natural mother."

The nun huffed. "How irregular. Well. Go on, he's over there."

The foster parents looked up as Adelaide approached. Henri's foster mother had a look of concern. What was her name? Joubert? "Madame Coumain. The nuns told us to come here for a checkup but on the way, Baby started to look ill. He hasn't been nursing but he didn't look ill until we were on our way here."

Adelaide peered over the crib side at her son, her heart leaping at the sight of him. Of course she knew him. His dark curls were just as she remembered, although they were damp and plastered to his scalp. He was flushed and appeared to be gasping for breath. "How long has he refused to nurse?"

The foster mother shrugged. "A couple of days."

"He hasn't been able to nurse for two days?" Adelaide reached into the crib and laid a gentle hand on his forehead. He was too warm. He breathed with a whistling wheezing sound. She laid a finger on his mouth, opening it, and tried to examine his throat. He jerked away from her but Adelaide thought she spotted a white patch on the back of his throat. Adelaide closed her eyes for a moment then straightened. "He has diphtheria." The foster mother looked blankly back at Adelaide. "Putrid throat."

"Ah no, the poor child. He won't survive that." Madame Joubert sighed.

Adelaide stared down at her baby. How could this be happening? He was supposed to be safe in the countryside, away from the miasmas of the city. "There must be something we can do, some sort of treatment." She looked around the ward at the nuns.

If only they hadn't dismissed the doctors. They could have administered treatment. The Germans were using quick silver with some success. Perhaps the nuns have medicine.

She hailed a passing nun. "Sister, can you help us here? My baby has diphtheria ... putrid throat. You must have something you can do. He's having difficulty breathing."

The nun-nurse looked back at Adelaide then over at the child gasping for air in his crib. "I'll ask the head nurse. We are overtaxed today. Yours isn't the only child ill with croup."

Adelaide nodded. "Fine. I'll go with you." The nun-nurse didn't look pleased but said nothing. The head nurse sat at the nurses' station with piles of paperwork spread before her on the desk. Did the head nurses do anything but paperwork?

She looked up at their approach, a harassed expression on her face. The noise in the ward was enough to give anyone a headache. "Yes, sister, what do you need?"

The nun-nurse gestured towards Adelaide. Adelaide stepped forward and leaned on the desk towards the head nurse. "My child is very ill. I was requesting the aid of your nun-nurse here but she told me that I needed to ask you for help. Haven't you got medicine?"

The head nurse looked over the top of her spectacles at Adelaide. "Medicine? No. It will be as the Holy Spirit wills."

Adelaide's heart raced with panic. "But can't you do something? Please don't let my baby die."

The head nun-nurse sighed and looked at her subordinate. "Sister, perhaps you could gather a few of the sisters to pray for the child?"

The nun-nurse nodded and trotted off to gather a group of her fellow nuns. Adelaide whispered thanks and went back to the crib. She met the foster parents as they were walking out. She widened her eyes at their departure and caught the woman's arm. "Where are you going?"

Madame Joubert shrugged. "Nothing we can do here. We're going to find some luncheon." She smiled and they moved past Adelaide.

Eat? How can they eat?

She watched them go. They must be used to losing babies to illness, especially when the babies weren't their own. She glanced over and saw four nuns gathered around Henri's crib. They swayed like cobras in front of a snake charmer and chanted in an incomprehensible language. It didn't sound like Latin. Who were these nuns? Adelaide hovered behind one of them. The baby lay still, gasping for breath. With a start, Adelaide remembered the veteran who could walk again after they prayed over him. What were they going to do to baby Henri? She pushed between two of the chanting nuns. "No, wait, don't hurt him."

They ignored her and continued to pray. The chant coalesced into an eerie humming that crescendoed then stopped. Adelaide swayed on her feet. The nuns moved away without a word. Adelaide stepped closer to the crib and leaned over. She touched the baby's chest. He opened his eyes and wailed. The back of his throat looked clear where before, she thought she'd seen a thick mucus coating. She let out a shuddering breath she didn't realize she was holding. What had happened? Had the nuns healed him? Adelaide picked up the wailing infant. She held him against her and patted his back. "You're probably hungry, little one, but you'll have to wait until Madame Joubert returns." She paced up and down the ward, trying to soothe him. His cries softened to whimpers, then he fell asleep on her shoulder. The weight of his little body felt good in her arms.

However did I let him go? And how will I let him go again?

Adelaide breathed in the aroma of warm baby and dropped a soft kiss on his curly hair. In her pacing, she'd reached the entrance of the ward and with a sinking heart, saw Henri standing there, his face stricken. "Is that him? Is that my son?"

She nodded and halted a few feet in front of him. "He's been very ill. Best not to come too near."

Henri ignored her and approached, standing too close to Adelaide. He brushed a hand across the baby's sleeping head. "He's beautiful, Adelaide. How can you send him away?"

Adelaide swallowed a sob and turned away, shielding the baby from him. "We've had this discussion, Henri. It's best for him to be with a foster mother right now. I have no milk for him and she does."

Henri drew his eyebrows together in consternation. "There must be wet-nurses in Paris. If you let me take him, I could find one."

"Let you take him? What a preposterous notion."

His tone grew angry. "I can provide a home and a mother for him who doesn't feel the need to minister to others. My wife can take care of him."

A wife? Henri was married? Adelaide thought back to when she'd seen him at the Café de Flore. That lovely woman with him must be his wife. She felt a pang of jealousy but quickly suppressed it. "Have you discussed this with your wife? Are you sure she'd be willing to raise your bastard son?"

Henri opened his mouth, then closed it. He scowled at her. "He would be better off with me, his father, than with strangers who only take care of him for the money."

Nurse Emard appeared from behind a cluster of parents. "This is your child's father, Coumain? I thought he was dead."

Adelaide blanched. Where had she come from? The woman was like a phantom, apparating out of nowhere. Adelaide tilted her chin. "Yes, this is Henri's father. As you can see, he is not dead."

Nurse Emard smiled like a reptile, her eyes cold. "Not dead? A miracle. Now that your husband's found you, you'll be leaving, non?"

Adelaide glared at Henri then back at Nurse Emard. "He's not my husband."

Nurse Emard hissed and her lips curled back. "That means your child is a bastard. And you a fallen woman. I knew as much with your carrying on with the patients. I'm not putting up with this anymore." She wheeled away and stalked off.

Adelaide sagged, the sleeping child in her arms suddenly feeling like a sandbag in her arms. "Now look what you've done. Every time you show up, you ruin my life. You're like a tornado. Would you get out of here?"

Henri's shoulders sagged. "I'll go but this conversation isn't over. I want my son."

Adelaide sneered. "You'd better check with your wife, don't you think?"

He winced but didn't answer. He turned and walked away. Adelaide strode back to Henri's crib and laid him down. She looked at him for a long moment then left the ward. She needed to find out what was going on downstairs with Nurse Emard and she desperately wanted Mireille's advice.

༺ Φ ༻

Adelaide reached Mireille's office but the door was shut. She knocked but there was no answer. She joggled the handle. The door was locked.

Maybe she's in the courtyard.

She lingered a moment longer then headed across the main corridor and through the archway to the courtyard. Adelaide stood on the portico overlooking the gardens. Nuns were milling about at the entrance to the chapel at one end of the gardens, their grey robes flapping in the wind like gulls over the ocean. She squinted into the distance, looking for Mireille. Adelaide spotted the figure of a woman sitting on a stone bench, her vivid burgundy dress standing out among the dull greens and browns of the winter garden. She smiled with relief and made her way down the stone steps into the garden, meandering through the maze of paths towards Mireille. The wind gusted, pushing her skirts against her legs and chilling her. How could Mireille sit outside in this weather?

Mireille looked up from a small leather book as Adelaide approached, a welcoming smile on her face. "Good afternoon. What brings you outside in this weather, ma chère?"

Adelaide felt warm despite the cold air. With a smile playing about her lips, she responded, "I could ask you the same."

Mireille marked her place and tucked her book into her skirt pocket. "I needed a little fresh air. An escape from all the furor inside. You've upset Nurse Emard even more than usual, you know. She has finally discovered that your child is illegitimate and that makes you the worst kind of sinner in her eyes."

Adelaide crossed her arms to try to stay warm. "She got to you already? She must have flown. I suppose it was only a matter of time before she found out that I wasn't a widow. Now what? Am I to be dismissed?"

Mireille snorted and flapped her hand. "Nonsense. No, I have to figure out how to separate you two while placating Nurse Emard. She's bound to make a fuss with the Archbishop over it."

Adelaide bowed her head. "Thank you, Mireille. Your friendship is more valuable than I can say."

Mireille patted the bench next to her. "Come and sit down with me. Is something else bothering you? You didn't come out here to complain about Nurse Emard, did you?"

Adelaide sank down onto the bench next to Mireille, careful not to crush her intricately pleated skirt. "No, I didn't. I wanted to speak to you about something else." Mireille nodded her head, waiting. Adelaide took a breath then let it out. "My baby is here. His foster parents brought him for his checkup but he is very ill."

Mireille gasped and placed her hand on top of Adelaide's. "Oh, Adelaide, I'm so sorry. Is he going to recover?" Her dark eyes were full of concern.

"Yes. I insisted that the nuns do something. They refused to give him medicine but they did pray over him. It seemed to help. I don't understand what happened. Maybe it was a coincidence. But he was breathing easier when I left."

Mireille bit her lip. "I don't know what they do. It's a mystery to me as well. I suppose we don't need to know. It worked this time. That's what matters."

Adelaide sat thinking about what she'd seen. It was against all she had been taught as a Scientist. All that is real can be seen and explained. What was the explanation for these mysterious healings? "I'm still not comfortable with it. It doesn't make sense. I like things to make sense. But that's not why I came to talk to you."

Mireille squeezed her hand. Adelaide's cold fingers warmed under Mireille's touch. She seemed to thaw whenever Mireille was around. Mireille smiled at her. "Tell me what's on your mind."

Adelaide pushed a lock of hair off her face and tucked it under her cap. "It's my son. Seeing him again. I can't bear to lose him. I don't want to send him away again."

Mireille shook her head. "The reasons you sent him away haven't changed. You have nowhere else to go and he can't be here with you. Especially now that Nurse Emard knows that he's illegitimate. She'd make your life pure hell. And mine."

"There must be a way. Holding him ... it felt so right. It breaks my heart to think of him leaving, going back with that woman to the countryside. She doesn't love him, Mireille."

Mireille looked sad. "It's hard for foster mothers. Either the child doesn't survive or the natural mother takes the child once they're weaned. If they were to give their hearts to each child they foster, they'd be heartbroken all the time. It's better for her to be somewhat distant from him."

"But if he's not loved, won't he know?"

Mireille stroked Adelaide's hand. "She takes good care of him, no? Did he look well-fed? Despite being ill?"

Adelaide thought of her son's plump little body, so heavy in her arms. The foster mother was nursing him and giving him all the nourishment he needed. "Yes, even though she said he hadn't nursed for a couple of days."

Mireille sat back, triumphant. "You see. She's doing what she needs to do for him. She's not unkind, you know. She won't be cruel to him. She just won't give her whole heart to him."

Adelaide stared away, contemplating the statue of a mother and child. "So she'll give him back to me when he's weaned?"

"You know she will. That's the agreement. And in the meantime, we have to find some way for you to earn enough money to afford your own apartment for yourself and your child."

Somehow, the thought of leaving the hospital didn't sound as appealing to Adelaide as it once had, It wasn't that she'd miss the food or the dormitory full of snoring women and lumpy beds. It was Mireille. She didn't want to leave Mireille.

"Thank you for talking this over with me. You're always so calming."

Mireille put her arm around Adelaide's waist and pulled her closer. "It's my pleasure. Thank you for trusting me."

Adelaide looked at her with surprise. Trust? Mireille was right. Somehow, Adelaide had started trusting her. She wasn't sure how she felt about that but she wanted to continue exploring the feeling. With a sigh, she relaxed against Mireille's side.

"I wish there was some way I could stay here with you as well as have my son."

Mireille stroked wisps of hair back from Adelaide's forehead. "Yes, I would like that too. We'll figure out something."

Twenty-eight

Nurse Emard hadn't spoken to Adelaide for three days, not once since the day she'd discovered that Adelaide had a child born out of wedlock. Every time Adelaide was in Emard's presence, the nun looked right through Adelaide, her mouth flat and thin with disapproval. Adelaide shivered at the coldness of the woman's demeanor.

To escape the chilly atmosphere of the ward, Adelaide decided that the patients needed their sheets changed. She strode to the linen room to retrieve fresh sheets. She hefted an armload of the rough linens and teetered back down the corridor to the veterans' ward. Other orderlies passed her and ducked their heads, not meeting her eyes. Nuns breezed by, their stony glares fixed on a point behind her. Nurse Emard must have told everyone of Adelaide's status as a fallen woman.

So childish. I'm not the first woman to have a child outside the confines of marriage. Does that make me such a pariah?

She reached the door of her locked workroom. Adelaide had a project she was working on to help the veteran with the ruined Augmentation. She just needed to find a little time to sneak in to the workroom. Perhaps when the nuns took their midday meal and went to chapel. Nurse Emard would be gone for at least an hour.

Adelaide reached the arched entrance to the ward and stepped in. Nurse Emard was not in sight. Adelaide put the pile of sheets down and peeked into the bathroom. The nun wasn't around. Adelaide squinted up at the light coming in through the high windows, bright triangles painted across the high ceiling and walls. Was it already midday? The clouds made it hard to tell. She shrugged and moved into the bathroom, darting a look behind her. No Nurse Emard meant that she could properly flush the toilets. She turned on the water and flushed everything down. Adelaide sniffed the air. Better. She peeked back into the ward. Still no Nurse Emard. She looked longingly at the entrance to the secret passage to the storage room. Nurse Emard had been constantly present in the past week leaving Adelaide with no opportunity to work on her repairs. Deciding to take the risk, Adelaide slipped into the hidden entrance and pulled it closed behind her. The darkness surprised her. She had forgotten to bring a lantern in her haste. Adelaide found her way along the passage with her hands on both walls, moving with care. The panel in the wall of the storage room slid open partway then got caught. She had to force it open with a well-placed boot.

She stepped into the dim storage room, dodging the crates of supplies and broken cots.

Now where did I leave that lantern?

Adelaide peered into the dimness, trying to find the light. She remembered leaving it on a shelf but which one? Huffing to herself with frustration, she picked her way around the room until she found the lantern. She lit it and with a happy sigh, sat down at her makeshift workbench and picked up the mechanism she was working on. She lost track of time as she tinkered. Loud voices and tromping boots in the hallway outside startled her out of her reverie. She got to her feet, heart skipping a beat.

Someone tried the handle of the door to the storage room, rattling it with force. Adelaide stared at the locked door with wide eyes, willing whoever it was to go away. They pounded on the door—or was that a boot kick? The thumping increased, getting louder and more intense. Adelaide backed up and came up short next to a broken cot, on its side against the wall. The door began to splinter under the assault and the hinges shrieked as the screws popped out. Adelaide turned and scampered towards the entrance to the secret passageway. She tripped on a crate, banging her shin, and gasped at the pain. The door burst open and light from the hall streamed in, illuminating her like a cockroach in a dark room. A harsh voice called out, "There she is! Stop! Police!"

Adelaide reached the opening in the wall and climbed in, shaking with fear and pain. She tried to close the panel but it was stuck. She gave up and moved into the passage but the man who had been at the door was fast. He reached in and grabbed her arm. She screamed and struggled but he held fast and dragged her out of her hiding place. He took hold of both of her arms, pulled them behind her back, and with a click, bound her with iron wrist cuffs. She gasped at his roughness, her shoulders protesting being stretched so far.

A woman police officer stepped through the broken door into the room and fixed her with a steely glare. "Adelaide Coumain? You are arrested in the name of the king for crimes against the state." She surveyed the room and gestured to one of the police standing behind her. "Go through this room and confiscate any contraband. These tools. Whatever that mechanism is. All of it."

Adelaide sagged against the policeman holding her arms behind her. Her work. Her work was going to be destroyed again. The pain in her shin and her wrenched shoulders were nothing compared to this pain.

The policewoman approached Adelaide. "You do know the penalty for illegal practice of Science, madame? The king has made it abundantly clear that he will not tolerate this impurity. At best, you will be imprisoned for the rest of your life. But if things go badly for you, you'll be executed. The Bastille awaits you, madame."

She turned and walked away, followed by Adelaide and the policeman pushing her along. Orderlies gaped as she passed by. Her hair had fallen into her face during the struggle and she tried to shield her burning cheeks with it. Muttering filled the corridor as the police led her out. Where was Mireille? What was going to happen to her? The fear threatened to consume her. Her stomach wound itself into cramps. The police marched her out into the street and pushed her in to a waiting closed carriage. Adelaide bit the inside of her cheek, willing herself not to break down in front of them. The carriage lurched into movement, throwing her against the side. It was really happening. She was being taken to the Bastille. She lowered her head and wept.

Twenty-nine

The heavy iron gate clanged shut in Adelaide's face. She flinched. She was living her nightmare, locked in a cell in the Bastille. The smell of mildew choked her. She turned and examined her surroundings. The cell was small and dank, fitted with just a cot. No window. The only light in the room came from the barred opening to the cell. She was underground. There was no daylight, just the flickering glow of lanterns hung on the walls outside the cell. Rustling noises near the cot let Adelaide know that she wasn't alone. Vermin infested the prison. She shuddered.

Rats. I hate rats.

She leaned against the rough brick wall, uncaring when the dampness seeped through her dress. Her shoulders ached from the policeman's rough treatment.

What now? How long will I have to wait until my fate is decided?

She gnawed on her bottom lip. Did Mireille know she was here yet? Would she be able to help get her out? Adelaide sagged. No. She had been caught with scientific instruments. That was a high crime. The authorities weren't going to let her out of prison at the behest of a hospital director, no matter how well-connected. Her only hope was to receive a stay of execution. But was that even possible? Was she doomed to be executed? Executed. She could very well never see her son again. What would happen to her little Henri, still recuperating at the hospital? With Adelaide unable to defy him, Henri could take the child. Adelaide's mouth dropped open. Had that been Henri's plan all along? He must have reported her to the authorities so he could take the child.

Her despair burned up in the heat of her rage. She slammed her hand against the brick wall, sending insects scurrying into cracks in the masonry. This was Henri's revenge. Now that she'd been arrested, he would take her child and see her executed.

Just as fast as her anger had erupted, it dissipated. Had it been worth it? Defying the king's orders and helping the Augmented veterans had seemed like a good plan of action after the destruction of her Automated Dauphin. Or had her vanity blinded her to the consequences of her actions? She thought of her tiny son, warm and helpless in her arms. Despite Henri's warnings, she had not considered the child when she decided to continue her work secretly. In retrospect, her arrest had been inevitable. Could she not have done something of value that wasn't forbidden? The king probably didn't know the state of his veterans with their failing Augmentations. If she hadn't been so intent on defying his new laws, could she have asked for an audience for permission to help the veterans? It was too late now. She was imprisoned. She heaved a sigh. Her legs trembled with fatigue but she wasn't willing to sit on the cot. Adelaide pushed off the wall and paced the tiny cell. Ten steps in each direction. The scuttling silenced as she approached the cot then began again when she walked towards the door. Adelaide shuddered. How would she be able to sleep knowing a rat had lodged itself under her bed? A rat. Her worries had compressed to this.

Heavy footsteps outside her cell caught her attention. She scurried to the door and peered out of the grate. Someone carrying a lantern stood there, looking in at her. "Welcome to the Bastille, Number 8 de la Liberté. You must have done something quite horrible to be placed in the cachots. Another Scientist, perhaps?" The person spoke in an alto tone, and in the dim light, Adelaide couldn't tell if the speaker was a man or a woman. They came closer and Adelaide heard the distinctive click of an Augmented knee joint. Interesting. The Augmented joints had been reserved for the nobility. What was a noble doing down here?

Her voice croaked, hoarse from dehydration, when she tried to respond. "Who are you?" She cleared her throat. "I'm very thirsty. May I have a drink?"

"I'm the warder of this tower. Did the guards leave you with nothing to eat or drink?"

Adelaide took hold of the bars and looked through them at the warder. "No, nothing. Your knee. Does it bother you?"

The warder snickered. "Scientist. I knew it. They always put you people down here. Trying to kill you with the damp, I expect. Hasn't worked with Number 7 though. They transferred him been down here when the new king was crowned and he's still alive. Probably won't last the winter though. It gets bitterly cold down here."

Adelaide bowed her head against the grate. She already felt frozen through to her bones. Then what the warder said penetrated her thoughts. There was there another Scientist down here with her. Who could it be? Hamidou. Had he been caught tinkering with the Weather Machine in the park? No, the warder said he'd been imprisoned for a long time.

"You're not very chatty, are you, Number 8? Still in shock, I expect. Just wanted to welcome you." They snickered again. "I'll let you settle in. The guards will be down with your supper shortly." They turned and limped away, their knee clicking with every other step. Adelaide listened with a doctor's ear.

I can help them with that knee. Perhaps if I can get it to function properly, I'll be able to negotiate with them for help.

The thought was a small comfort. She resumed pacing, still unwilling to sit.

ଽ Φ ଔ

Adelaide waited for what seemed like hours before the prison guard approached and thrust a bowl of stew through the bars of her cell without a word. Standing, she swallowed the tepid muck and grimaced at the grease floating on top. This food was easily as bad as the gruel at the hospital. She wondered how Nurse Emard was getting along with just one orderly. How shocked she would be to discover Adelaide's fate. She glanced over at the cot and sighed. She would have to sit on it and go to sleep at some point. Not yet. The grease coated the inside of her mouth and she swallowed, grimacing. The gas lights on the wall flickered and she watched the flames dance.

I wonder if Mireille has found out what happened to me yet? Was Henri in her office gloating and demanding the baby once they took me away?

Adelaide sniffed back tears and shuffled over to the cot. She sank down onto it, not caring anymore about her rodent companion. The rat didn't make any noise. Maybe it had gone to another cell. Adelaide could only hope. She dropped the bowl and spoon onto the floor with a clatter and let her head sink into her hands. It was killing her not knowing what was going on at the hospital. She got back to her feet and paced again. Reaching the gate, she stopped and peered out into the dim hallway. She could see the grated door of the opposite cell. Who was imprisoned in there? It could be any of thousands of Scientists but who had been imprisoned since before the new king took power? She shrugged. Only one way to find out. "Hello, over there? Are you awake?"

Rustling and thumping in the other cell was the only response. Apparently, her fellow prisoner was not feeling social. She waited, then tried again. "My name is Adelaide. All I know of you is a number. You must have a real name."

A pale face appeared behind the grate of the opposite cell. "I heard the warder say you were a Scientist. And your name is Adelaide. Could it be? Has the great Adelaide Coumain been captured and imprisoned?"

Adelaide swayed on her feet, giddiness sweeping over her. She clutched the rusty iron bars. She knew that voice. Piorry. Her mentor who had tried to steal credit for her greatest invention. "Yes, it's me, Adelaide. I'm surprised to hear your voice, Monsieur Piorry." She kept her voice steady to hide her shock.

He barked a harsh laugh. "Surprised? You were the person who had me thrown into the Bastille, mademoiselle."

Adelaide took a calming breath. She wouldn't let him know that it shook her to discover him here. Her voice was cool and brisk. "If I recall, you tried to kill me. There was a very good reason for you to be imprisoned. I was merely expressing surprise that you would be housed in the same part of the Bastille."

"They moved me down here after His Majesty learned that a despicable Scientist was being housed in a comfortable suite of rooms upstairs. And now you're here too." He cackled. "I thought they would've executed a high-ranking Scientist like yourself, Royal Scientist-Doctor to the late King and Queen of France. However did you manage to escape them? It's been an age since the regime changed."

Adelaide stood there in silence. How much should she tell him? He had never been trustworthy. Best not to let him know of what had happened to her in the past year. "I guess I was just lucky."

He snorted. "Lucky. You've always been lucky. Ha, but now your luck has run out, hasn't it? You'll be tried then probably executed. No languishing in the dungeons of the Bastille for you. You won't be locked up alone like me. Alone, with nothing to do but dream of days of glory. Alone. Wishing to escape and recreate France. France, my beautiful France. Alone. Escape, escape. I must escape."

He subsided to incoherent mumbling. Had he gone a trifle mad locked up here?

"Escape, monsieur? Even if you were to escape, it would be impossible to bring any technology back to France without the King's support. It's all gone, monsieur. They destroyed all the Weather Machines, the Watcher Spheres, the steam omnibuses, everything. I couldn't even use the water taps at the hospital." She rested her forehead on the bars, remembering Nurse Emard's admonishments.

"They've banned running water? What savages we're ruled by. The ancient Romans had running water. Yes, the Romans. They lived a long time ago. Very long. Running water isn't a new invention. Everyone knows that. Romans had pipes. Pipes with running water. Lead pipes though. Made them all mad as badgers. We're mad as badgers too. All of us mad, even without the lead."

Mad as a badger? Yes, you are, old man. How different you are now.

Despite herself, she felt sad remembering how sharp Piorry had once been.

The old man's raspy voice grew more intense. "But you can do it, Adelaide, you must help bring it back. Repair the broken machines. Make France great again. You must escape this place. I'll help you. I'll distract the guard and then you can run. Leave your cell and run like the wind. You must do it. Only you can save France from these madmen. Adelaide? Are you listening?"

Leave a locked cell? He really had lost his mind. "No, I can't leave. I'm locked in here, just the same as you. It's over, monsieur. There's no escape for me and no regaining the France you built." A lead weight descended on her heart and she shuffled back to the cot. The rat licking her bowl scurried away but Adelaide was beyond caring. Piorry still called to her, admonishing her to escape and rebuilt his France. She blocked out his words and buried her face in her hands.

Thirty

Henri stopped to admire the Palace of Versailles glittering in the sunlight. The gold trim edging every cornice caught the light, making the walls seem to glow. He had never been a landscape painter, preferring to paint people, but the palace was a tempting subject. He continued to the Chapel Gate and hailed the guard yawning there. "Good morning! I'm here to see His Majesty."

The guard shrugged and leaned against the marble gate post. "Good morning, monsieur. I heard that the Court all went for a walk in the gardens. You'd be better off catching up with them out there." He waved in the direction of the South Parterre. Henri had seen that part of the gardens once. He'd peered over the hedges separating the public gardens from the Court's private one. He marveled that now he was admitted to that enclave. Henri Desjardins, painter of the common folk, allowed to wander at will in the King's private residence.

The gravel crunched under his feet as he traipsed along the long palace wall towards the gardens. He rounded the corner of the Orangerie and caught the murmur of voices and the tittering of nobles. He found them meandering among plants bereft of blooms or even leaves. How curious that the king had decided to walk out here in the cold. Perhaps he'd wanted some fresh air. Henri waved at one of the courtiers and smiled. It was the Duchesse de Fronsac, walking arm-in-arm with another lovely noblewoman. Their silk gowns glowed in the sunlight, trains caressing the gravel as the women promenaded.

"Monsieur Desjardins! What a delight to see you here. Come, join us." She held her free hand out to him.

The warmth he felt had little to do with the wan winter sunlight. The duchess's lovely smile entranced him as it had before but he was newly committed to Isabelle and would not stray. She had barely forgiven him for his affair with Adelaide. He reached the duchess's side and bowed over her hand. "Radiant, as always, madame." He caught the eye of the duchess's companion and grinned. "And madame, you too are a treat for the eyes. Or am I overly bold in addressing a lady who I have not been introduced to?"

The duchess laughed and slapped his arm with her fan. "Too bold? It's why I enjoy your presence. This is my dear friend, Madame de la Roche."

Henri kissed her hand. "Enchanted. Tell me, mesdames, why is the Court outside in this frigid, desolate garden?"

The duchesse de Fronsac lifted a delicate shoulder. "Who knows what goes on in the king's head? He declared that since the sun was shining, we were all to come outside and revere Nature. So here we are. Revering." She looked around the garden and giggled. Her friend joined in the laughter. Henri glanced around, looking for the king. As delightful as it was to flirt with two beautiful nobles, Isabelle would not be pleased if Henri failed again to receive his payment. Although if he came back with a commission, she would be mollified.

He eyed the women with a long scrutiny up and down. "You know, the image of you two, so lovely against the spare garden, would be a glorious painting."

The duchess quirked an eyebrow at him. "I'm not one to share attention." She shot a wry look at Madame de la Roche. "Especially with one so lovely as you, chérie."

Madame de la Roche giggled and tapped the duchess's arm with her fan. Henri looked closer at the pair. How old was this courtier? She had to be at least thirty but she acted like a girl. How typical of these nobles, not a care in the world. He grimaced. He'd once felt so carefree, before his world had fallen apart when he'd been imprisoned. And his so-called triumphant return to a restored France hadn't helped regain that freedom from worry. Now he felt the burden of his grandmother, freezing in her poor garret, his wife bearing their child, their future in this strange new France.

A burst of laughter from across the garden caught his attention. The king was standing in the center of a group of courtiers. Henri drifted closer and caught something about the wonders of Nature. He wasn't sure why that was so funny. The king threw an arm around his advisor, the comte de la Fontaine and declared something Henri couldn't make out, provoking giggles from the attending ladies. Henri drew closer. Perhaps it was the king's advisor who would know about his fee for the king's English portrait. The king's adviser looked paler than normal. He swayed in the king's embrace.

The king furled his brow. "My dear friend, are you still feeling poorly? You've gone so pale."

The comte shrugged. "Please do not concern yourself, sire. It's a passing spell. I'll be well in a moment."

Henri could tell that the comte was gasping for every breath although he was trying to hide it. The other courtiers chatted, seemingly unconcerned but the king leaned closer, whispering in the comte's ear. The comte smiled and glanced sideways at the king. They seemed oblivious to the crowd surrounding them.

Henri huffed out an impatient breath. He needed to get closer to the comte but with the king hovering near him, the attendants buzzed like a bee swarm around them. Henri suppressed a growl. No one here paid him much attention except for the flirtatious duchess and she had not picked up on his hint about a commission. He couldn't go back to Paris without securing income. He couldn't bear Isabelle's disappointment and with Gleyre's house sold, they needed the income for new lodgings.

A man in livery shoved his way past Henri and the gathered courtiers, excusing himself as he made his way to the king's side. "Your Majesty, news from the Bastille!"

Irritation on the faces of the nobles turned to avid curiosity. The king dropped his arm from around the comte's shoulders and fixed the messenger with a stern look. "You are interrupting my enjoyment of the glories of Nature."

The messenger flushed and sketched a hasty bow. "I beg your pardon, Your Majesty. The warden of the Bastille said they were certain that you would wish to hear this news immediately." He bowed again and waited for the king's response.

The king regarded him, his mouth pinched with impatience then sighed. "Oh very well. What does the warden feel is so important that they needed to send a special courier?"

The messenger straightened from his obeisance. "They wish to report that the notorious Scientist Adelaide Coumain was captured a few days ago and is currently imprisoned in the Bastille."

Henri gasped. Adelaide imprisoned? How had the police discovered her whereabouts? He watched the king for a reaction. King Henri stretched his mouth into a wide, triumphant grin. "Excellent. Fontaine, remind me, why was this particular Scientist important?"

The comte curled his lip with disdain, his color no better. His lips had taken on a bluish cast. "She was the Scientist responsible for keeping those two relics alive for far too long. Valmont had only attended them for a few months before they expired. Although his execution served as a warning to the other Scientists in France."

The king nodded. "Ah yes, mon cher. We had to rid ourself of the prominent Scientists before they could cause any mischief. But this Coumain woman. I remember now. She has been dismissed from her position at Court, disgraced. Perhaps she can be redeemed?"

The comte sniffed. "You can't trust that, sire. She was a high-ranking Scientist, was she not? And what was she doing that brought her to the attention of the police?" He stared at the messenger for an answer.

The messenger bowed again, quivering with excitement. "The warden said that she had been discovered at the Hôtel-Dieu, repairing the mechanisms on veterans there."

The comte shuddered. "Those mechanical men that the Scientists created? Turning people into freaks. Horrific. And she was doing what? Repairing the … mechanisms?" His tone dripped with disgust.

The king patted the comte's arm, but he was looking at the gardens behind the messenger, his expression distant. "Terrible. But don't upset yourself, my dear comte."

The comte smiled at the king and covered his hand with his own. Henri stepped forward, startling the courtiers who had not noticed his presence, rapt as they were with the drama unfolding. "I pray your indulgence, Your Majesty? This woman who's been arrested? I know of her. She is good and kind. She sees the pain your loyal, brave soldiers suffer and wishes only to help them."

The king raised his eyebrows. "Desjardins? The painter? What are you doing here?"

The king seemed to have forgotten their earlier meeting. Henri bowed then met the king's glare. "Your Majesty. I am at your service. I've newly arrived from England, following you in your triumph."

The king twitched his mouth into a half-smile. "Ah yes, you were a faithful servant when we were in exile. And now you are here to witness my triumph here at Versailles. But why are you defending this Scientist? How do you know her?"

Henri hesitated. How much should he tell the king? He didn't want to seem like a Science-lover. "Sire, I encountered her at the Hôtel-Dieu recently. She told me she was assisting one of the brave veterans of the war. I was astonished to hear of a Scientist engaged in forbidden activities but she explained why she was disobeying your orders. It was her compassion, you see? She just couldn't bear their pain. One young man was close to taking his own life to escape the suffering, and she helped him."

The king pursed his lips, his brow creasing in thought. He darted a look at the comte de la Fontaine whose face hardened. "These men are abominations, sire. Better for them to end their lives than linger as subhuman."

The king shrugged. He sighed and resumed his study of the gardens. "You are right, of course, my dear comte."

Henri suppressed a gasp. He swallowed. "But Your Majesty..."

The king held up a hand, not looking at Henri. "Silence. This woman has disobeyed my edicts as well as being well-known as a Scientist. I will be the judge at her trial immediately. Once I hear the evidence against her. I will not be merciful."

The comte's face tightened into an ugly smile. "No mercy, sire. This scourge of Science must be stamped out. Only then can France be pure and its people one with the Holy Spirit." He turned to the messenger. "Send word to the warden of the Bastille to fetch the criminal here. The king will see her tried today. Her execution will be an example to any other Scientists daring to disobey the king."

The messenger nodded, and with a bow, sprinted back to the palace. Henri gaped at the king. He really intended to execute Adelaide. The group of courtiers, led by the king, sauntered away. Henri stood watching as the king pointed out a flock of egrets flying overhead. Henri's plea for Adelaide's life had been brushed off as meaningless. Henri's shoulders slumped at the thought. He'd had a contentious relationship with her but she didn't deserve to die. And what would become of baby Henri? He would happily raise his son but his lack of funds and Isabelle's refusal to even consider it made that impossible, Henri clenched his hands into fists. And the man he had followed in England, the passionate, sincere believer in a return to the natural way of life? He was gone, replaced by this pompous king. The idealism of the Naturalist movement had been a sham, hiding the King's desire for power. He had no compassion for his own people. Henri trailed after the court, hoping still to speak with someone about his commission. Perhaps he'd have more success with that. Had he become nothing more than a sycophant?

Thirty-one

The click-click of the warder's malfunctioning knee joint echoed the drip-drip of water falling from the ceiling of Adelaide's cell. She lifted her head from the grimy, cold cot. Light from a lantern wavered on the wall opposite the grate, moving closer. She rose, her joints creaking. She winced at the stiffness in her back. Was it already time for the midday slop? She couldn't tell anymore. But why was the warder delivering her meal? Maybe it was another Scientist prisoner. Adelaide shuffled to the grate and peered out.

"Is that you, Warder?"

The warder sighed and limped into sight. "Yes, it is I." Their face was a frowning mask of shadows in the lantern light.

Adelaide grasped the rusted bars. "Have you news for me, Warder? Or are you bringing me what passes for food down here with your own hands?"

They laughed, a raspy sound lacking any humor. "I've heard nothing. And I don't have your meal. It's only mid-morning, prisoner 8."

Adelaide waited for an explanation. She'd learned some patience down here in the dungeons of the Bastille. There was precious little to do and she spent all of her time with her own thoughts. Piorry muttered to himself but hadn't engaged her in conversation since the first day.

The warder approached the grate and leaned close to Adelaide. The scent of lavender wafted from them to tickle Adelaide's nose.

How delightful it would be to be clean and lavender-scented.

The warder whispered, "You mentioned that you knew something of these accursed artificial knees, prisoner 8."

Adelaide quirked an eyebrow. Was the warder asking for her help? Her tone came out bitter and hard. "Warder, don't you remember that such knowledge is forbidden in these times? This accursed knee of yours? Yes, I know something about artificial knees. I was asked many times for aid when they malfunctioned. Once I was lauded for my knowledge and skills. Now I am imprisoned and sure to be executed for the same,"

They exhaled a pained breath. "Yes, I know, Leaving those of us who have been Augmented to suffer without assistance. I apologize. I should not have mentioned it." They took a step back and winced.

"It pains you, Warder?" Adelaide cursed herself for the unbidden compassion in her voice. She couldn't seem to help herself.

They nodded. "At first, my knee was just stiff but now, my leg cramps when I walk."

"The joint is frozen. It's a common flaw in that Augmentation. Did your scientist-doctor not tell you how to unlock it?"

The warder scowled at Adelaide, their dark eyebrows meeting. "Unlock it? You mean I can fix it myself? Do I need a tool?"

"I could help you but what about all the others?" She shook her head. "How I wish I could convince the king that some Scientists can be beneficial, if only to service the already Augmented people."

The warder burst out in an angry tirade. "The others? I don't care about the others. I'm tired of this damned knee and want you to tell me how to fix it."

Adelaide crossed her arms and regarded the fuming warder with a calm look. "You need my help. Let's negotiate. You get me an audience with the king and I'll show you how you can fix your knee when it locks up."

They growled and turned away, the lantern swinging. The light flashed into her face and she squinted. The warder hunched their shoulders but didn't leave. Adelaide waited, rubbing her arms to stave off the cold draft coming down the hallway. The hospital's rough wool uniform dress was itchy but didn't do enough to keep her warm in this drafty dungeon. The only sounds were water dripping from the ceiling and the warder's harsh breath. Adelaide shifted her feet, the scrape of thin leather against the stone louder than she expected.

The warder looked at her over their shoulder. "I have no influence with the king. He banished me from Versailles along with all the other Augmented courtiers. I can't help you, madame." They limped towards the stairwell. Adelaide lowered her chin to her chest and stifled the urge to sob.

Footsteps clattering down the stairwell caught her attention. She strained to see who was entering the dungeon in such great haste. A cultured voice called out. "Warder, I have a summons for one of your prisoners. The king requires the presence of Adelaide Coumain at Court immediately."

Adelaide shuddered, her belly clenching. So it was time. She hadn't needed to beg for an audience. The king must have decided to hold her trial himself but would he allow her to speak? Or would this be her end?

Thirty-two

Henri traipsed along the packed dirt path around the Water Parterre, following the court into the Apollo's Bath Grotto. It felt like he'd been following the court around all day although it was only an hour or two since his arrival. The verdant bowl, surrounded with evergreen trees, hadn't been warmed by sunlight and the chill penetrated Henri's coat as he entered. The soft grass underfoot was damp and his shoes squelched in a muddy patch. A couple of ladies grimaced as their slippers too sank into the wet lawn. The king, arm-in-arm with the comte de la Fontaine led his courtiers to the rough-hewn fountain of Apollo. He gently lowered the comte to a stone bench and placed his hand on his companion's shoulder. Henri could see the king's tender expression even from a distance. The monarch's reluctance to take a bride suddenly made sense to Henri.

A delicate touch on his arm startled him out of his scrutiny and he turned. The duchess de le Fronsac stood at his side, her mischievous smile lighting up her dark eyes. "I see you've noticed where the king's affections lie? I don't think he'll be siring a Dauphin for France, despite the hopes of the Senate."

Henri nodded in agreement, glancing from the king back to the duchess. "Won't they try to force him to marry? To carry on the line?"

The duchess shrugged, the lace at her decolletage moving in an interesting way. Henri willed himself not to look although her beauty was hard to ignore. When he dragged his gaze back up to her face, her eyes were dancing with amusement as she watched his struggle. "The king's younger brother already has a brood. If the crown passes to him, who's to complain? Let the king love where he may. Besides, no-one can get him to do anything he doesn't want to do."

Henri's shoulders slumped. "I know. He gets his mind fixed and that's it."

A wrinkle appeared between the duchess's eyebrows and the smile left her face. "He wasn't sympathetic about your Scientist, was he?"

"She's not my Scientist." He looked down at the duchess with a glower.

"Of course not. So why would you plead her case?" Her dark eyes bored into him.

Henri squirmed under the noblewoman's scrutiny. "She does good things for people who don't deserve to suffer." Henri lowered his voice. "I've never liked Augmentations but what's done is done and those soldiers should be cared for. Not left in pain and incapacitated."

The duchess surveyed the courtiers gossiping in little clumps and the king, still deep in conversation with the comte. She turned back to Henri and murmured her response. "Do you know, the soldiers aren't the only Augmented people in France. Many of the courtiers received Augmentations to repair faulty joints. Even hearts, in one case. Poor child, may she rest in peace. Once the king was crowned, he banished the surviving Augmented courtiers. The comte de la Fontaine told him they were impure."

Henri held himself still, hoping to hide his reaction to the duchess's remark about the child with the Augmented heart. She had to be talking about Marie-Ange. Had they known each other? Did the duchess know the circumstances of her death? Would that tragedy ever lift from him? He mumbled an incoherent response and looked away from the duchess.

A woman strode into the grotto, the tails of her burgundy coat fluttering behind her. Henri admired her form until he recognized her. It was Dr. Dutrochet, the director of the Hôtel-Dieu, What on Earth was she doing here? Could it have something to do with Adelaide? The two of them had seemed particularly close when he spoke to them at the hospital. Dr. Dutrochet had her gaze fixed on the king and made her way to his side, oblivious to Henri.

"Well, now isn't that interesting? Mireille Dutrochet here? It's the first time she's deigned to join us." The duchess murmured almost to herself. She drifted towards the ever-present clump of courtiers hovering around the king. Henri followed. The duchess thought the appearance of Dr. Dutrochet here was unusual? Henri 's curiosity grew stronger.

Dr. Dutrochet elbowed her way to the king and sank into a graceful curtsy. The king raised his eyebrows at her presence. "Mireille. It's been an age since you graced us with your presence. Welcome to Versailles at last, ma chère. What brings you here? All is well with your family, we hope?"

Dr. Dutrochet dipped her head, a tiny smile on her mouth. "Thank you for your concern, sire. We are all well. I am afraid I am here to beg a boon."

The king glanced down at the comte then back at her. "Has it to do with operations at the hospital? You know we promised you full autonomy, as long as the Sisters were allowed to follow their calling."

She shook her head, her dark curls bouncing against her cheeks. "Not exactly, sire. We are expanding our offerings to the veteran soldiers by opening a convalescent home just for them. And I had hoped to have an expert in treating their particular issues could be put in charge there."

The king's gaze turned icy. "What issues do you mean, ma chère?"

Dr. Dutrochet shivered under his regard and ducked her head. "Sadly, many of them are having difficulties with the Augmentations the previous regime had been so fond of. But I have found someone who can assist them. At your behest, of course."

Henri winced at her words and held a breath, waiting for the king's response.

The king squared his shoulders and glared down his Bourbon nose at her. "Mireille, you can't possibly mean for me to allow Science be practiced?"

The comte climbed to his feet and stood next to the king. "Dr. Dutrochet, have you lost your mind? How could you possibly conceive of this scheme?" He wheezed as he spoke and his face drained of all color. He swayed and fell against the king, then slid to the ground in a faint.

The king cried out and sank to his knees beside the comte. "Charles!" He looked up at Dr. Dutrochet, a beseeching look on his face. "Please help, Mireille. What's wrong with him."

The comte lay still, his skin grey. Dr. Dutrochet lowered herself to kneel by his head and laid her head against his chest. She sat back on her heels with a look of dismay. "No pulse."

The king's face whitened. "No pulse? Is he dead? No, no, Charles!" He grasped the comte's shoulders and shook him. The comte's head lolled backwards. The king groaned in pain. Mireille pushed him aside and lowered the comte back to the ground.

She held her hand in front of his mouth and confusion creased her forehead. "He's still breathing. Quickly, someone get me some smelling salts." A lady passed her a tiny vial and Dr. Dutrochet waved it under his nose.

The comte coughed and opened his eyes. "Please help me up." His pallor was unchanged and his breathing harsh.

The king gasped and helped the comte sit up. "Slowly, go slowly. You fainted." He supported the comte as he rose to his feet then helped him to the stone bench.

Once the comte was settled, the king turned to Mireille. "What's wrong with him? These dizzy spells are increasing. Please, Mireille. You must help him." His face was still pale with fear.

Mireille sat next to the comte and brought out a listening tube from a pocket in her skirt. She pressed it against the comte's chest, listened, then shook her head, her eyebrows drawn together. Henri offered her a hand and she rose to her feet, throwing him a quick smile of thanks.

"The comte has no heartbeat, no pulse, and yet he lives. His ailment is a mystery to me. I have an inkling of what is wrong but I can't tell you for certain. This person I spoke of earlier ... she would know what is wrong with the comte."

The king sat next to the comte and placed a protective arm around the man's shoulders. He scowled at Mireille. "You're being deliberately obtuse, Mireille. Can you help him or not?"

Mireille shook her head, frowning sadly. "I'm not a scientist-doctor, sire. I don't know how to treat a patient with an artificial heart."

The assembled court gasped as one. Henri's mouth dropped open with astonishment. The king drew back from the comte and studied him with an accusing glare. "Charles? What is she talking about?"

The comte pulled away from the king's embrace and lowered his head into his hands. "I'm so sorry. I was ill just before you came home, before the old queen expired. They said that my only hope was to have an operation to replace my own heart with an artificial one. I couldn't tell you. I'm one of the Augmented people like the ones you banished from Court."

The king knitted his eyebrows together in confusion. "But you were the one who insisted that I send the Augmented courtiers and palace guards away. I don't understand. What was your motive?"

The comte didn't lift his face from his hands. "I thought if I was fervent about purity and nature, that you wouldn't guess that I was one of the tainted ones. You must despise me now that you know." He raised his tear-streaked face.

Henri shook his head in disgust. Versailles was full of lies. Lies hidden behind masks of sanctimonious purity. There was no purity within the palace's walls even after the great revolution.

The king rubbed his hand across the comte's back. "No, I could never despise you. You've done so much for me, been my faithful companion, my trusted advisor through my ascent to the throne, my dearest ... friend."

The comte sat without speaking. A small smile tugged the corners of his mouth. The king smiled in return and squeezed the comte's hand. He addressed Mireille. "If you can't help the comte with his heart, we must find someone who can. Who is this person you hinted at? I'm guessing she's a Scientist? I will for the moment forgive you knowing of a Scientist without turning her in."

Mireille nodded. "I thank you, sire. I apologize for keeping her presence from you. She is indeed a scientist-doctor and I came to beg for her release. She's currently in the Bastille, arrested a few days ago for the high crime of practicing Science."

"You mean Adelaide Coumain? But how do you know her?"

"She's the inventor of the Archimedean Heart, sire, the heart that doesn't beat. There were only two ever constructed. The comte de la Fontaine must have been a recipient. I read Madame Coumain's scientific papers on the subject. Before you returned to France, of course."

The king lowered his head and rubbed at his eyes. "Science. I thought it would be so easy to simply outlaw it. But it's entwined all through my country, isn't it? Even my closest friend is beholden to it." He gazed at the comte. "You look terrible, cheri."

The comte shrugged. "And I feel worse. I don't know how much longer I have. The heart must be failing."

Mireille, her face drawn with worry, stepped closer to the king. "Will you have Madame Coumain attend the comte, sire? Before it is too late for the comte."

The king looked up at the trees surrounding them, his face wistful. "They're bringing her here for her trial today. I will decide then. Come, let us go back inside. The comte needs to rest."

He got to his feet and held out a hand for the comte. Dr. Dutrochet curtsied and backed away. The king processed back to the palace, trailing courtiers, Dr. Dutrochet, and Henri. Henri was due home but he needed to see how this ended. Would Adelaide be spared?

Thirty-three

The Palace of Versailles looked just as it had the last time Adelaide had been there. This time, the beauty of the building failed to stir her. She had left after being removed from her position and now, at the nadir of her fall from grace, she was heading back for her final fate. The soldiers escorting her hurried her along and she tripped on the paving stones leading into the palace doors. Curious servants and courtiers watched her as she passed by, her grubby dress and the hair falling down her back marking her as an interloper, the guards showing her as a prisoner. The familiar marble floor echoed under her feet and the statues looked down at her with pity on their frozen faces. The soldiers led her to the courtiers' wing, not to the King's audience chambers. Adelaide frowned, looking around her.

This isn't part of the public area. Why are they bringing me here? The king is obliged to give me a fair trial. He can't be intending to try me in secret.

She started to speak but her guard shushed her. He took a firm grip on her elbow and guided her in through a painted wooden door. The room beyond was definitely not a reception room. They entered one of the grand bedchambers of the Palace. A canopied bed dominated the room, surrounded by a crowd of richly dressed courtiers. With a start, Adelaide spotted Mireille and Henri in their midst.

What's going on? Why are they here?

Henri was talking to a lovely dark-haired noblewoman. Adelaide squinted. The woman looked familiar but Adelaide didn't remember her name. Then Mireille turned and their eyes locked. Adelaide's heart beat harder, and she opened her mouth, desperate to speak to Mireille, to demand an explanation for her presence here, but the guards drew her closer to the bed.

The senior guard cleared his throat. "Your Majesty, the prisoner Coumain is here."

A short man with a decidedly Bourbon nose turned from the bed. He must be the king. He glanced at her shabby outfit and grimaced. A guard nudged the back of Adelaide's knee, forcing her into an ungraceful curtsy. She bit down on her protest and steadied herself, waiting to be told to rise. She kept her eyes down, and the king's feet, clad in well-polished shoes, came into view.

"Recover yourself, madame." His voice held a hint of concern, some tension in his smooth refined tones. Adelaide straightened and looked into the worried eyes of the king. Why would her appearance worry him? He had all the power here.

"You are the inventor of the so-called Archimedean Heart, are you not?"

She gaped. How did he know about an obscure piece of technology like the Archimedean Heart? "Your Majesty?"

He waved an impatient hand at her. "Come now, madame. There is no need for you to be coy. We know all about your prior service to the mechanicals who ruled France for so long. We have been informed by Madame Director Dutrochet that you also invented an artificial heart."

Adelaide's gaze flew to Mireille standing in the crowd of courtiers. Had she been the informant after all? Were those weeks of supposed friendship a sham? Adelaide's heart turned to stone. Mireille had betrayed her. She was at the king's side because she was his lackey,

Adelaide inclined her head to the king in agreement. "It is true. I invented an artificial heart dubbed the Archimedean Heart." She gulped down the bile rising in her throat. The king must be building his case against her in preparation for ordering her execution but why here, in this bedchamber?

The king exhaled a sigh, rubbing his hands together. Relief crossed his face. "Excellent. We require your ... scientific ... expertise." He twisted his mouth at the word scientific.

Again, Adelaide was bereft of words and could only repeat herself, "Your Majesty?"

The king stepped to one side and gestured to the bed behind him. A man lay there, conscious but only barely. He was panting for breath, his face ashy, his lips blue.

"The comte de la Fontaine is unwell. Director Dutrochet tells me that he has this abomination called an Archimedean Heart installed in his chest but it is not functioning properly. She bade me to summon you here to help him. She said you were the only person who could save the comte's life." His tone lowered. "Please, madame. Can you save him?" The king's mask slipped for a moment, showing Adelaide the naked despair underneath.

Adelaide wrinkled her forehead. "But how could this be? I only installed one of those hearts and that patient is ... deceased." She closed her eyes for a second, Marie-Ange's face flashing across her mind. Adelaide recovered herself and approached the bed. She peered down at the comte but he was unfamiliar. "This man was not one of my patients. How could he have an Archimedean Heart?"

Mireille's soft, too familiar voice reached Adelaide's ears. "I examined him myself, Adelaide. He has no pulse and yet he lives. It can only be your invention in his chest moving his blood."

Adelaide stiffened but didn't turn to look at Mireille. The comte gasped for breath and Adelaide leaned closer. "Monsieur, is it true? Do you have an artificial heart? When was the surgery? Who was your surgeon?"

The comte wheezed, his voice faint. He flicked his gaze to the king standing beside him. "It's true. I have an artificial heart. My own had been failing for years. I would have died without a replacement."

The king patted his hand. "It's of no concern, mon cher. Go on."

"The doctor, Valmont, examined me and told me that I needed a new heart. He said there was an artificial heart available since the old queen couldn't use it. That was shortly before she died."

Adelaide's lips twisted. She should have taken the heart with her when she'd been dismissed. She straightened and cast an icy scowl at Mireille, then addressed the king. "Why should I help this man? Science has been outlawed and I am a criminal."

The king's face reddened and he looked down at the comte.

Before he could respond, Mireille stepped into Adelaide's line of vision. "Adelaide. I told the king that you can save his life with your skills. But why do you stare so coldly at me?" Her lovely face was creased with worry.

Adelaide stole a glance at the king, then back at Mireille. "How else should I regard you? You betrayed me, Madame

Director. You told the king that I invented the Archimedean Heart. Was that before or after you reported my illegal scientific activities to the Police Secrète?"

Mireille gasped and stepped back as if struck. "Betrayed you? I told the king that you invented the heart within his lover's chest so that he would bring you here to save the comte. That they would see the value of Science. I was not the one who reported you to the police. How could you think that of me?"

Adelaide bit the inside of her lip. "You didn't report me? Who did? Was it Henri after all?"

Mireille shook her head. "It was that harridan Emard. I told you she hated you. She must have snooped around after seeing you go into the storage room too many times. I told you to be careful, Adelaide."

Adelaide released her breath. Mireille hadn't betrayed her after all. She shook her head. "Emard was going to figure it out eventually. She watched me like a hawk, desperate to find something to fault me for. She did and now she has won, whatever the king decides to do with me."

Mireille took Adelaide's hand. She lowered her voice so the distraught king wouldn't catch her words. "Save his lover and he may be convinced to be merciful. Please try, Adelaide. I don't want to lose you."

Adelaide clenched her teeth to hold back the sob threatening to escape. Mireille had always been trustworthy. She hadn't betrayed her. Adelaide shook her head. "What's the point? I'm no mechanic, I'm an inventor. I am no good at repairing these mechanisms."

"You want to still be a Scientist? Still do good for France? You need to adapt, Adelaide." Mireille's dark eyes didn't let her go.

Adelaide sighed, her shoulders slumping. "Science is all I'm good at."

"Then do it. Save the comte with Science."

Adelaide moved closer to the bed and addressed the comte. "I'll need to listen to your heart. Has anyone got a listening tube?" She didn't face the audience, didn't want to see those curious faces, avidly watching her for a mistake. Someone pushed a listening tube into her hand without a word. Mireille's perfume tickled her nose. Adelaide bit her lip then leaned over the comte. She listened to the workings of the mechanical heart in his chest. It ran smoothly, no clicks or halts in the whirring of its workings but the movement was slow. Adelaide fixed the comte with a stare. "There's nothing wrong with your heart, monsieur, save that it's moving too slowly. You aren't winding it properly so your blood is sluggish, unable to move around your body."

The comte wrinkled his forehead. "'The heart is working? I'm not dying?"

Adelaide snorted. "Dying? Of sloth, perhaps. You will die if you continue to lie about and not move. Did Valmont not instruct you on the proper care of this heart? You must walk for fifteen minutes every two hours while awake and use your rocker bed at least six hours every night." She looked around the bedchamber. "Where is your rocker bed?"

The comte glanced away and released a wheezy sigh. "I thought his instructions merely suggestions. And I got rid of that bed. The king abhors technology. We're trying to return France to a more natural state and must set an example."

Adelaide rolled her eyes. "You foolish man. You're barely hanging on. You won't survive much longer without that bed. And regular exercise."

The king crouched down next to the comte's bed and grasped the comte's hand in both of his. "We can make exceptions when someone's life is at stake. Charles, I can't lose you. Let us not be merciless in our vision of purity."

He gazed at the comte and they exchanged tender smiles.

Adelaide broke into their silent exchange, "Does that merciful exception only apply to courtiers in your favor, Your Majesty?" Her tone was defiant. A collective gasp echoed in the room.

The king scowled over his shoulder at Adelaide, his face thunderous. "What are you saying, madame?"

She lifted her chin. "Veterans of France's wars are suffering from your ban on technology and scientific pursuits. They bravely submitted to Augmentation in order to be strong soldiers for France's glory, and now they are bearing pain from the neglect of their Augmentations."

The king narrowed his eyes at her. "Ah yes, the veterans. You were arrested for repairing those corruptions, despite my clear prohibition of the use of Science. We are trying to purify this country, rid ourselves of the scourge of technology."

"Sire, I'm not suggesting that we create new Augmentations and other technologies. These men are suffering for their patriotism. Are they not worthy of your mercy?"

The king growled. "I didn't ask them to hack off perfectly healthy limbs in order to become corrupt machines."

Adelaide's shoulders slumped. It was no use arguing. The king's views were clear. His sole exception to any use of Science was for the man in front of her. "I see. There is a limit to your mercy. Now what is my fate? I've helped your noble exception. Am I to be executed for saving his life or will your mercy see that I am imprisoned in the Bastille for the rest of my days?"

The king didn't answer. He tugged the comte to a seated position. "Stand up, mon ami. Let's take a stroll and see if this ... Scientist ... has indeed repaired your disorder."

The comte got to his feet, the king steading him. They linked arms and meandered through the crowded room, the king keeping a tight grip on him, Adelaide watched them as they moved about, greeting the courtiers with a nod and a smile. After a few turns around the room, the blueish cast to the comte's lips began to fade. As he drew near her, Adelaide could see that he was breathing more naturally. "Monsieur le comte, pause a moment if you would so that I may listen to your heart." She extended the listening tube to his chest and listened. She nodded, a small smile tight across her face. "The mechanism is speeding up. Good. Your heart is responding to your movement, Keep walking."

The comte sighed his relief and strolled away on the king's arm. Adelaide met Mireille's gaze. "There, I've done as you asked. The king is probably going to send me back to the Bastille now that I've helped his special friend."

Mireille placed her hand on Adelaide's arm, the contrast between Adelaide's grubby sleeve and Mireille's well-manicured hand stark. "Don't be too sure. I have an idea. Follow me and be respectful to him." She raised her voice. "Your Majesty? A word?"

She sauntered towards the king, her smile bathing him in warmth. Adelaide followed. He returned Mireille's smile, relief relaxing his face.

"Mireille, ma chère. Doesn't the comte look better already? How clever you are, knowing exactly what he needed."

"Thank you, Sire. Do you feel better, monsieur? Your color has improved."

The comte took her hands and shook them. "I do, thanks to your medical knowledge and His Majesty's timely summons of the Scientist."

Mireille shook her head. "Without Madame Coumain's brilliant mind, both of those things would have been in vain. She is the one to be thanked for your recovery, monsieur."

The king cleared his throat. "Ah yes of course. We are most appreciative to Madame Coumain. Despite her blunt manner."

Adelaide stepped around Mireille and curtsied low. "I thank you, Your Majesty. Please accept my apology for the lack of courtesy. I fear I have been overwrought in past days and neglected to grant you the respect your position deserves." She swallowed down the bile threatening to choke her. The king needed to be flattered if he was going to pardon her. Adelaide didn't want to die.

The comte de la Fontaine placed his hand on the king's forearm. "Perhaps you could pardon the good doctor, Sire? Since she saved my life?"

The king wrinkled his forehead, staring at the comte. "But I thought you said Scientists should all be wiped from the face of France? Only then can we be pure."

The comte hung his head. "Sire, I fear I have been too fervent in this matter and have advised you rashly. Perhaps some exceptions can be made. In the name of mercy."

Adelaide hid a smile at the echo of her words.

The king frowned and turned, taking the comte's hands in his. "Why have you changed your mind, mon ami?"

The comte looked into the king's eyes and sighed. "I thought I had to be absolute about this belief. I am Augmented but kept it from you. I hid my lack of purity behind a mask of perfection. I felt so guilty about my deception but it seemed like the only way. Will you forgive me?"

The king's face lit up in a smile. "I would forgive you anything. This artificial heart keeps you alive. Can technology be so very evil? Without it, I wouldn't have you." He turned back to Adelaide. "I will pardon you, madame, despite your crimes against the state."

Adelaide swept down into another curtsy, murmuring her thanks. Relief made her knees shake.

Mireille smiled winningly at the king. "If I may suggest, Your Majesty? Madame Coumain is a talented doctor and I could use her skills in our new convalescent home."

The king nodded, his hands still clasping the comte's. "You know you don't need to ask me about staffing issues, Mireille."

"This is a special facility, Sire. It's for the Augmented veterans. They need a great deal of specialized care that the Sisters can't give them."

The king grimaced. "Ah yes, you asked before. I take it that you intend for Madame Coumain to care for their ... mechanisms?"

Mireille nodded, her hands clasped at her waist. "Yes, Sire. There would be no new mechanisms added, just care of the existing ones. It would save them so much pain to have Madame Coumain's attention."

The king looked at the comte who smiled his approval. "Very well. Madame Coumain, you may repair our veterans who come to the veterans' convalescent hospital for treatment but there will be no new inventions, understood? And please, be discreet. I don't want to hear about this from the nuns."

Adelaide's heart soared and she grinned. "Your Majesty! I thank you. Your mercy is magnificent." She glanced at the comte. "But what about the courtiers who are Augmented? May I aid them if they are in need?"

The king waved his hand at her and sauntered away, tugging the comte along. "As you wish. But I don't want to hear about it."

She curtsied at his retreating back then turned to Mireille, clasping her hands. "Oh Mireille, thank you! Without your interceding, he would never have suggested it. I can't wait to get to work."

Mireille beamed and drew Adelaide's arm through hers. "Let's go straight there. I think the artists have moved along. But we'll need to get you cleaned up first. That dress is too awful. And your hair is a fright."

Adelaide laughed, the first time she'd laughed in what felt like years. If Mireille had any say, Adelaide was about to become a fashion plate. They strolled out of the bedchamber and into the marble corridor They stopped in the bureaucrats' wing for Adelaide's written pardon. Henri sauntered into the of-fice and stopped short when he saw Adelaide. He smiled at her with uncertainty in his eyes.

Adelaide crossed her arms and sighed. "Are you following me, Henri?"

He shook his head and tried unsuccessfully to keep his smile in place. "No, of course not. I'm just here to collect my commission. For the painting I did. But I am glad to see you here. I'm so glad. So glad that you were pardoned."

She almost smiled at his stuttering, so unlike his usual smoothness. "As am I." She turned back to the clerk who handed her the pardon. Adelaide thanked them and linked arms with Mireille, preparing to step past Henri. He moved closer, a hand held up.

"Will you be staying in Paris with little Henri? Could I visit him?"

Adelaide smirked at him. "In all likelihood. We can discuss that later, monsieur. Let us get set-tled first."

The two women swept past Henri and continued out of the Palace. Mireille squeezed Adelaide's arm. "We can set you up with your own suite of rooms in the Gleyre house so you won't need to find accommodations for you and the baby. And you'll be close to the hospital."

"Not too close. I'd hate to encounter Nurse Emard again."

Mireille waved a hand in dismissal. "She's gone. Retreated back to her nunnery. She said that Paris is too full of sin for her to bear anymore."

Adelaide grinned. "I can come and visit you without worrying then."

Mireille nodded. "Indeed. You'll be autonomous, you know. Your own woman, beholden only to the board. Equal to my position."

Adelaide tilted her head, "That will be lovely. Equal to your position? Mireille, what are you hinting at?"

Mireille drew Adelaide's arm closer. "I won't be your superior any longer. We can see each other socially."

Adelaide's heart sped up. Seeing Mireille without sneaking around sounded exciting. Her life was becoming a real life, not just a dreary existence. "That would be ... very nice."

She walked into the courtyard, the high walls of Versailles rising around her, sparkling in the setting sun. She turned and once more, the beauty of the palace filled her eyes.

FINIS

About the author

BJ Sikes is a 5'6" ape descendant who is inordinately fond of a good strong cup of tea, Doc Marten boots, and fancy dress. She lives with one large cat, two sweet teenagers, a multitude of chickens, and one editor-author.

For more stories in the world of the Roboticist of Versailles, head over to my blog at [https:\\bjsikesblog.wordpress.com](https:\\bjsikesblog.wordpress.com)

Acknowledgements

I can never thank Aaron, my delightful editor, enough for his encouragement, insight, creativity, keen ear for the right phrase, and great hugs. He makes a pretty good cup of tea too. Is it any wonder I married him?

My dearest friend Dover Whitecliff is an embodiment of the word supportive. She always cheers me on as I write, providing the sunlight to my clouds. She never fails to stay positive even when I am glum.

My darling daughters Margaret and Charlotte inspire me every day with their passion and creativity.

Many thanks to Sharon Cathcart for providing feedback on Paris and the French language. If I still got something wrong, it wasn't her fault.

I can't forget my loyal Clockwork Alchemy fans, Sandra and Gene Forrer, and Lora and Greg Price, who have been asking for this book since they read *The Archimedean Heart*. Your enthusiasm kept me going. I hope it was worth the wait. <grin>

And once more, my deepest gratitude to Emperor Shen Nung for discovering tea in 2,737 B.C.

www.ingramcontent.com/pod-product-compliance
Lightning Source LLC
LaVergne TN
LVHW052318290426
837647LV00015B/869